Selected Stories

SRLT

Northwestern University Press
Studies in Russian Literature and Theory

SELECTED STORIES

Alexander Veltman

NORTHWESTERN UNIVERSITY PRESS / EVANSTON, ILLINOIS

Northwestern University Press
www.nupress.northwestern.edu

Printed in the United States of America

10 9 8 7 6 5 4 3 2 1

ISBN 978-0-8101-1526-2 (cloth)
ISBN 978-0-8101-4932-8 (paper)

Cataloging-in-Publication Data are available from the Library of Congress.

Contents

Introduction

AMONG THE LESSER-KNOWN WRITERS of nineteenth-century Russia, Alexander Fomich Veltman (1800–1870) presents an unusual case. His career has been compared to the flight of a meteor,[1] suddenly appearing and flashing brilliantly, and then, just as suddenly, burning itself out. Actually, the evolution of his literary career was less dramatic: following his initial successes in the 1830s, Veltman continued to write and publish until his death in 1870—despite the less favorable reception of his works in his later career. Although today he is invariably included in that nondescript category of "minor writers," he did have a significant role to play in the development of Russian literature. His most enthusiastic advocate, the Soviet critic V. F. Pereverzev, goes so far as to claim that without Veltman there would have been no Dostoevsky.[2] The stories presented here are offered as an introductory sampling taken from the very large output of a writer whose works otherwise would be completely unknown to the non-Russian reader. Veltman's stories contributed to that large fund of cultural raw material from which the great writers of the day fashioned their art.

It is remarkable that although Veltman was largely self-educated, his output includes some fourteen novels, fifteen prose tales, and numerous other pieces in prose, verse, and dramatic form. In spite of his humble origin—his father had reached no higher in the tsarist bureaucracy than titular councilor, the rank held by Gogol's poor clerk in "The Overcoat"—he managed to achieve notable success in three different careers: first as an army staff officer, retiring in 1831 after fourteen years of service with the rank of lieutenant colonel; then, during the thirties and forties, as a Moscow man of letters; and, finally, during his last years, as the director of the Kremlin's Museum of Armaments *(Oruzheinaia palata)*, a job with the rank of actual civil councilor. During this last period he devoted himself to the study of antiquities, particularly the early history of the Slavs, producing several publications on the subject. It should be mentioned that these latter works were largely dismissed by serious historians so that, perhaps contrary to his own inclinations, it was his literary work and not his scholarly efforts that gained him a measure of fame.[3] His early works were welcomed by both Pushkin and the great critic Belinsky;[4] the major literary journals of the 1830s and 1840s sought his contributions, and both Dostoevsky[5] and Tolstoy expressed favorable opinions about his works, the latter going so far as to say that he was sometimes "better than Gogol."[6]

Veltman was born in St. Petersburg on 8 July 1800, the first of four children of Foma Fomich Veltman and Maria Petrovna Kolpanicheva. All available Russian sources indicate that Veltman was descended from Swedish nobility,[7] but there is evidence to suggest that his immediate ethnic background was German. His father, according to an *attestat* dated 6 July 1816,[8] entered the Russian service "from the Russian nobility (the word *Russian* was a later correction)" in 1786 in Reval (now Tallin), where, at that time, German was the predominant cultural ethos.[9] Among Veltman's papers are several letters written by his father to his mother and to other relatives in Reval, and they are all written in German.[10] The letters written by F. F. Veltman to his son offer the most convincing proof of his German background: their spelling practically duplicates that form of "phonetic" transcription of Russian used by Russian authors to convey a German accent (usually for humorous purposes).[11] F. F. Veltman first served in the Russian military in a number of minor posts, and later in various civil service assignments, the last one being with the police.[12] His attainment of the rank of titular councilor technically conferred on the family hereditary nobility, but, like many of the literary figures of his time, Veltman's class status could best be defined as that of the *raznochinets.*[13]

Veltman's education began at home. In his unpublished "Tale about Myself," the only extant source we have about these early years, Veltman states,

> [M]y first teacher and mentor was my dear mother. From the age of five she began to teach me to read and write, sometimes winning over my laziness with promised rewards for good work. I also had Uncle Boris [not a relative, but Veltman's father's orderly] who was both an excellent shoemaker and a wonderful teller of tales. It was impossible for him to stitch and sew shoes and at the same time watch over a mischievous child; therefore, while sitting at his last, he would cleverly bind me to himself by means of a long folktale, never for once imagining that, with time, I too would become a teller of tales.[14]

Note that Veltman calls himself a teller of tales *(skazochnik);* the influence of Russian folklore can clearly be seen in both the form and content of many of Veltman's works.

Veltman's formal education began at the age of eight at a private school *(pansion)* for Lutherans where he was accepted apparently by mistake, being taken for a Lutheran, and probably for a German,[15] because of his last name. In 1811 he entered the famous school for the nobility *(Blagorodnyi pansion)* attached to Moscow University, but his studies there were interrupted by the arrival of Napoleon's legions in 1812. The cataclysmic events of that time no doubt produced an unforgettable impression on the twelve-year-old Alexander. The figure of Napoleon—invariably presented in a negative light—will subsequently make his appearance in several of Veltman's literary works. Along with most of the population, the Veltmans had to flee the city of Moscow, finding refuge in Kostroma.

The Veltmans returned to Moscow soon after the French retreated, and by 1814 Veltman had resumed his formal education, this time at a *pansion* run by the Terlikov brothers. A real opportunity appeared when General Nikolay Nikolaevich Muravyev decided to establish a school in his home in Moscow to train staff officers for the Russian army.[16] The school, called the *Korpus kolonnovozhatykh,* accepted its first students in 1815 and was soon granted official status, so that its graduates were granted commissions in the Russian army. In July 1816, at the age of sixteen, after passing the entrance examination, Veltman was accepted into the *Korpus.* Since the *Korpus* was established to produce staff officers, the curriculum emphasized such subjects as mathematics, cartography, surveying, and military engineering; the summers were spent at a military camp established on one of the general's estates. Veltman seems to have thoroughly enjoyed his time at the *Korpus,* and he recalls those days with particular fondness in his "Tale about Myself." On 26 November 1817, having passed the final examinations at the *Korpus,* Veltman was commissioned as an ensign *(praporshchik)* in the Russian army. Thus, at the age of seventeen, he had completed a formal education that included, at most, a total of eight years of instruction. Nevertheless, in later years he was to publish works on such diverse subjects as the beliefs of Buddhism, the campaigns of Attila the Hun, and the origins of the Indo-European peoples, as well as attempting translations from Sanskrit and Persian. If nothing else, Veltman was not reticent when it came to publication: while still a student at the *Korpus* he wrote an arithmetic textbook that was published in 1817.[17]

Shortly after his graduation, Veltman was posted to the headquarters of the Second Army, then located in the southern Ukraine at Tulchin. His first assignment was to work on a topographical survey of Bessarabia (present-day Moldova) which had become part of the Russian Empire under the provisions of the Treaty of Bucharest in 1812. He was to spend the next twelve years in this area; thus it is not surprising that the region figures prominently in his literary works. During this period he also found time to pursue his "scholarly" interests, publishing a book in 1828 on the history of Bessarabia.[18]

From his earliest days, Veltman had been trying his pen in the various literary genres. Among his papers is a hand-written collection of his poems, preserved from his school days, entitled "A Collection of the Original Compositions of Alexander Veltman."[19] Soon after arriving in Bessarabia, Veltman began to acquire a certain popularity among his fellow officers through his humorous verse; for some of them he was even known as the "Kishenev poet." This literary recognition was to be of short duration; it could not compete with the celebrity of a nationally recognized literary figure: in the fall of 1820 Alexander Sergeyevich Pushkin arrived in Kishinev. Although he was just twenty-one years old, Pushkin was already establishing himself as Russia's foremost poet, and, as a result of his political verses, had sufficiently aroused the wrath of the authorities to be exiled to Bessarabia. When Veltman first heard that Pushkin was to arrive, he frankly admitted that the news produced in him "a feeling of jealousy toward the muse"[20] and that subsequently he felt awkward in the presence of the great poet. As Veltman put it,

> When meeting Pushkin in society and among friends, I was completely unable to approach him; for others he could seem an equal, but to me he seemed unapproachable. I even tried to avoid him, and as far as I can now understand the mysterious, incomprehensible feeling which I had then, I was afraid that someone in the group might say to him in my presence, "Pushkin, this fellow of ours also writes poetry."[21]

Contrary to Veltman's initial fears, he and Pushkin eventually became quite friendly and had animated discussions on literary matters. As I. P. Liprandi, one of the many memoirists who wrote about Pushkin's stay in Bessarabia, tells it,

> [Veltman] . . . was one of the very few who could provide Pushkin with spiritual nourishment and therefore the discussions with him were of another type. He did not unconditionally approve each line of verse pronounced by Pushkin, but rather was able to and did comment on and analyze the verses and this did not displease Alexander Sergeyevich, in spite of his unlimited vanity.[22]

It was not long before the opportunity arose for Veltman to read some of his poetry to the master. As Veltman recalls it,

> Soon Pushkin, having found out that I too wrote verses and was working on a Moldavian folktale in verse entitled "Janko chaban" [Janko the shepherd], came to see me and asked me to read him something from "Janko." Three cantos of this clumsy poem-bouffe were already written; blushing from head to toe, I could not refuse the poet and I began to read. Pushkin laughed heartily at several places describing how my Janko, a giant and a fool bursting with health, grew so fast that soon there was not enough room in the hut for his father and mother, and the child, having broken through the wall with his arm, crawled out of the hut as if out of an egg.[23]

Some excerpts from this poem later appear in Veltman's first significant literary work, his burlesque travel account, *The Wanderer,* published in 1831–32.

It also turns out that we have Pushkin's recorded opinion of this work, found in a letter to Elizaveta Mikhailovna Khitrovo, who had apparently asked Pushkin to get her a copy of Veltman's work:

> Voici, Madame, le *Strannik* [The wanderer] que vous m'avez demandé. Il y a du vrai talent dans ce bavardage un peu maniéré. Ce qu'il y a de plus singulier, c'est que l'auteur a déjà 35 ans [Veltman was actually thirty-one at the time] et que s'est son premier ouvrage.[24]
>
> [Here, Madame, is *The Wanderer* that you have requested. There is real talent in this slightly affected idle chatter. What is more peculiar is the fact that the author is already thirty-five years old and that this is his first work.]

At about this same time Pushkin was planning to express his opinion of *The Wanderer* in print in his friend Baron Delvig's *Literaturnaia gazeta*, but, as he says, because of laziness he failed to carry out the task. Therefore, in a letter to P. V. Nashchokin, a mutual Moscow friend, he includes a word of apology apparently to be passed on to Veltman:

> I have just seen in *Literaturnaia gazeta* a review of Veltman, very unfavorable and unjust. May he not think that I had anything to do with it. The point is that I do share in the guilt: through laziness I failed to keep a promise. I did not do the review myself, but then there wasn't time.[25]

Veltman's stay in Bessarabia came at a time when the area was a hotbed of illegal political activity. The southern branch of the Decembrist movement, perhaps more radical than the northern, was made up chiefly of army officers attached to the Second Army. Several of the officers who were later arrested were Veltman's friends and some of them appealed to him for help many years later when they returned from exile in Siberia. The Soviet scholars who have attempted to reintroduce Veltman to the Russian reading public have emphasized his Decembrist sympathies; there may be some truth to this, but no one has been able to produce any documentary evidence to support this contention. As for Veltman's post-Decembrist literary works, a recurring theme that does stand out is his criticism of Western political ideas and influences—in other words, a pronounced antipathy for many of the ideas that were the basis of Decembrist ideology. In addition, it should be mentioned that in terms of his social and cultural background, Veltman had little in common with the officers who took part in the Decembrist movement, most of whom came from prominent, landowning families. Looking at Veltman's own life and career, it is clear that he was able to achieve considerable success by operating within the system. If indeed he had been presented with the opportunity to take part in a highly dangerous scheme to challenge imperial authority, he may well have chosen, unlike Pushkin's Herman—the poor army officer of German descent in the "Queen of Spades"— to stick to his three reliable cards: "calculation, moderation, and industriousness *(raschet, umerennost' i trudoliubie).*"[26]

Soon after taking part in the Russo-Turkish war of 1828–29, Veltman decided to leave the army to pursue a career in literature. On 22 January 1831 he was officially retired from the army with the rank of lieutenant colonel.[27]

Veltman began his literary career with a full head of steam. Even before leaving the army he had already published individual poems and excerpts from longer works in a number of literary journals, so that his name was not unknown to the literary establishment. Beginning with *The Wanderer* (1831–32), the works poured out in a torrent: *The Fugitive, a Tale in Verse* (1831), *The Forests of Murom, a Tale in Verse* (1831), *The Manuscript of Martin-Zadeka: The Year 3448,* in three volumes (1833), *Deathless Koshchei, a Bylina of Olden Times,* three parts (1833), *The Sleepwalker: An Incident,* two parts (1834), *Svyatoslavich Nursling of the Devil, a Wonder from the Time of the Red Sun Vladimir,* two parts (1835), and *The Ancestors of Kalimeros: Alexander Filippovich Makedonsky,* two parts (1836). He also published a collection of prose tales in 1836, two of which are translated here. In 1837 two more novels appeared: *Virginia or a Trip to Russia* and *The Heart and the Mind (Serdtse i dumka),* the work that made such a favorable impression on the young Dostoevsky. In 1840 he penned the last novel from this most prolific decade, *General Kalomeros.* Although it is difficult to succinctly characterize this rather large body of work, certain features predominate: episodic and often fantastic plots, sketchy characterization, and the pronounced presence of a highly eccentric and ironic narrator. Apparently Veltman's first readers were most struck by his originality. For example, Belinsky, in a review of *The Ancestors of Kalimeros,* remarks that Veltman's talent is "unique and original in the highest degree; he imitates no one and no one can imitate him. He has created for himself some sort of special world, attainable to no one else."[28]

In spite of this considerable initial output (which also included a number of prose tales appearing in various literary journals), Veltman was still in need of additional financial support. He had married in 1832 and was raising a daughter, born in 1837. In 1842 the ideal opportunity presented itself for a man of Veltman's interests: the post of assistant director of the Kremlin's Museum of Armaments. Veltman's application for the position was supported by some highly placed people, including the director himself, the popular historical novelist M. N. Zagoskin. The application was approved and Veltman was appointed to the post, effective 13 March 1842, with the rank of court councilor, the civil service equivalent of his military rank of lieutenant colonel.[29] From this point on Veltman's life was an unqualified success: he received a good salary and a government apartment, he was able to pursue his antiquarian interests, and he still had time for literary work.

Clearly the most important literary work of this "later" period was the cycle of novels that appeared under the general title *Adventures Drawn from the Sea of Life*. The cycle consists of four novels that were published during the years 1848 to 1862, and a fifth, "The Foundling," that survives in manuscript form.[30] In these novels we see Veltman's unique response to the more realistic direction that Russian literature began to take in the 1840s. His chief concession to the new tendency was not a change in style but an attempt to place his works in a contemporary social context. But the problem was, as the critic L. N. Maikov then observed, that he "presented extremely unnatural, improbable events as though they were completely possible in contemporary Russian reality."[31] However, in defense of Veltman, it could be mentioned that not everyone saw it this way. In 1849 the future literary critic A. N. Pleshcheyev wrote a very enthusiastic letter about Veltman to F. M. Dostoevsky (at the time both men were members of the Petrashevsky circle):

> A few days ago I read Veltman's novel *Adventures from the Sea of Life* [Pleshcheyev is referring to *Salomeya*, the first novel in the series] and I find that it is a first-rate work. It's been a long time since I read such a forceful, biting satire on our society. Education, Moscow family life, and, finally, army officers in the person of the hero are thoroughly scourged. Under some of the scenes one could boldly write the signature of Gogol. There is so much humor and typicality in them. And, along with this, it's tremendously engrossing.[32]

In a discussion of Veltman as a nineteenth-century literary figure, one should make note of his journalistic activities. In 1848 he was invited by his friend M. P. Pogodin to join him in editing *The Muscovite*, a "thick" journal founded by Pogodin in 1841 and now in serious financial difficulty. Veltman accepted and the pages of *The Muscovite* from January 1849 through March 1850 bear his considerable imprint in the form of the numerous articles and reviews written by him as well as through his rather arbitrary editorial treatment of the contributions to the magazine written by others. Friction soon developed between Veltman and Pogodin, and this eventually led to Veltman's resignation.

Veltman's first wife died in 1847, and he remarried in 1850. His second wife, Elena Ivanovna Kube, was also a successful writer, publishing first under her maiden name and then using Veltman's name after her marriage. When M. N. Zagoskin died in 1852, Veltman was appointed to succeed him as director of the Museum of Armaments. With the promotion came a large government apartment near the Arbat where the Veltmans entertained their guests on Thursday evenings. This was a time of great prosperity and contentment for the Veltmans; several memoirists have described the pleasant evenings they spent with their genial host and hostess.[33] Veltman's wife died in 1868 and he died two years later in 1870.

The stories presented here were selected to give the non-Russian reader a brief but representative sampling of Veltman's considerable literary output. The first story, "Erotida" (1835), is Veltman's contribution to a popular genre of that time, the society tale, and it may evoke Pushkin's "Queen of Spades" which preceded it by a few years. Veltman's peculiar treatment of the genre includes his predilection for linguistic puns and a bizarre resolution of the plot. This early story reveals a recurring problem in Veltman's fiction: the humorous, satirical parts succeed better than the attempts to convey drama or serious emotions.

The second story, "Roland the Furious" (1835), is a satire on provincial life that has much in common with Gogol's famous play, "The Inspector General," which was first performed in 1836. The basic plot line—provincial officials mistaking a traveler for a high-ranking government official—was of course exploited to maximum effect in Gogol's play; it would be difficult to prove that Veltman's story influenced Gogol since at the time many anecdotes were in circulation regarding such occurrences in real life. The names Veltman and Gogol have been linked together on several occasions, perhaps the most interesting one, mentioned above, attributed to Tolstoy.

The next story, "Travel Impressions and, among Other Things, a Pot of Geraniums" (1840), clearly belongs to the "travel notes" genre that was quite popular in the 1830s and 1840s. Along with its satiric, humorous tone, it contains fascinating details about traveling by coach in those days, as well as what may be the first description of railroad travel in Russian literature.

In "A Traveler from the Provinces; or, A Commotion in the Capital" (1841), Veltman produces a satirical commentary on the contemporary literary scene. His traveler, a would-be poet from the provinces, achieves literary celebrity almost overnight and then, just as quickly, is forgotten. The work ridicules the Moscow literary salons for their habit of immediately bestowing the title of genius on each new literary pretender who for some reason manages to capture the public fancy. In his story Veltman seems to have in mind a particular poet, V. G. Benediktov (1807–1873), whose literary career paralleled the events of the story but in a less exaggerated form. One of the traveler's poems is clearly a parody of a poem by Benediktov.[34]

The last story, "It's Not a House, but a Plaything!" (1850), well illustrates Veltman's predilection for employing elements from Russian folklore in his stories, a feature that figures prominently in several other works. In this case, however, his narrator is not a *skazochnik* (teller of tales), but a man of letters who has great empathy for the traditions and beliefs of the people. The plot revolves around the fantastic conflict that arises when two houses, each having its own *domovoi* (house spirit), are joined together under one roof. The story also has a literary connection: Pushkin's Moscow friend, P. V. Nashchokin, who was something of an eccentric, for his own amusement had an elaborate dollhouse constructed and furnished, and it is this dollhouse that is the "plaything" of the story.

Throughout the translation I have used what I would call a "popular" system for transliterating Russian: all adjectival endings are reduced to *y*, softening vowels are expressed by an additional *y (ya, ye, yo, yu)*, except for *i*, and, where they exist, accepted renderings of Russian names are used, for example, Dostoevsky. In the notes, however, wherever specific bibliographic information is given, I have used the Library of Congress system of transliteration (omitting only the diacritical marks) so that, for example, Alexander Veltman becomes Aleksandr Vel'tman.

Erotida

IT WAS, IT SEEMS, during August of last year—yes, that's right. The guests had come to celebrate the name day of the lady of the house. It was a family of modest means; they did not go in for extravagance. The dinner was both tasty and lively. The host drank to the health of his guests, and they to the health of their young hostess and to "the Poet"; that's how his good friends referred to their host who—let it not be said in his presence—could compose verses, such as "On Delia's Pimple," and stories for the journals.

After dinner, as was customary, the ladies went into the drawing room, and the men gathered in the host's study to burn tobacco.

These *postprandials* with a convivial group discussion are like a living journal. During such a time all the sections of a journal—the scientific and literary contributions, the criticism, the miscellany—can be produced impromptu.[1]

In one corner, with a cigar clenched in his teeth, sits a voluminous article on agricultural machines and management entitled "On the Uses of the Beet and the Potato." In another corner, stretched out on a couch, Philosophy holds forth on the difference between *philosophie* and *philozophie,* while Philology is explaining that the word *philology* comes from *filos*—friend—and *logos*—word; that the French word *filou*—rogue, cheat—also has its root in the word *filos,* but that it has acquired an opposite meaning from the time when people started to use the word *friend* as the most effective means of deception; and that from the word *logo*—I speak—comes the Russian verb *lgu*—I lie—in as much as *I speak* and *I lie* are to some degree synonymous.

Pale Poetry, inhaling Ukrainian tobacco, drifts about the room like Aeolus, murmuring couplets to himself.

"Erotida" first appeared in the journal *Moskovskii nabliudatel'* 1 (1835): 330–81. This translation is based on the text appearing in Aleksandr Vel'tman, *Povesti i rasskazy* (Moscow: Izdatel'stvo "Sovetskaia Rossiia," 1979).

History, with his hands in his pockets, expounds his views on the chaos of time and of nations; Mechanics—about the difference between centrifugal and centripetal forces; Metamechanics—about the laws of spiritual movement in nature; Geology—on the thickening of the earth's crust; Botany—about the public and private life of plants.

But the separate conversations finally come together as Miscellany where general attention is directed toward rumors, bits of news, repartee, and town gossip. Only Criticism sits sulking, listening and watching—all eyes and ears—seeing everything and despising everything.

The postprandial passes imperceptibly. Life's purpose is fulfilled: the food gets well digested; the soul is at peace and forgets about watching the clock.

The postprandial at the poet's also began this way. First came the philosophical article "What is Woman?"; then came Mechanics: "Concerning the Forces Acting on the Heart"; this was followed by Astronomy: "On the Constellations of Love"; then Agronomy: "On the Cultivation of the Feminine Heart and the Reasons for a Poor Harvest of Family Happiness." After this there began a critical analysis of women in all respects, and after that, miscellany, stories, anecdotes . . .

"I'm not much of a storyteller," said the host, "but I can read to you a true account about the extremes to which a woman may go for the sake of love."

"Excellent!" exclaimed several of the guests, although the majority of them frowned at the word *read*. The poet took no notice of this but took a notebook out of his desk, had a glass of water placed before him, and began to read the following.

PART ONE
THE BRIGADIER. IN OUR GOOD OLD DAYS.
SUITORS. THE LANCER. AN OBSERVER OF THE SOCIAL GRACES.

I

About twenty-five years ago Brigadier Khoikhorov (his ancestor had been brought here from the Caucasus) was living out his retirement on the estate that had been granted to him in return for his services to the crown. He was one of those people who praise only their own past, love old customs as if they were old wine, see nothing good in the present, and think that everything around them is losing its vigor, its beauty, is decaying and sinking into ruin.

Reminiscing about the past does have a certain charm, but among the old-timers of our era there is a special passion, or perhaps even a bias, for the times of Catherine II.[2] Whenever they begin to speak of *their* past, their cheeks become flushed and their eyes flash.

As they would have it: "Now everything has become abbreviated: the clothing, the intelligence, even the lives of people. Where can you now find people like those of our time? Rumyantsev, Potemkin, Orlov, Suvorov, Sheremetyev . . . They were true grand seigniors of glory, honor, and wealth! If, for example, Peter Borisovich or Nikolay Petrovich should decide to have a party and to receive their guests at Ostankino or Kuskovo,[3] the entire household staff would be arrayed in French formal dress embroidered with gold! Forty thousand people would line the road from the Moscow toll gate right to the entrance of the estate: peasants, merchants, major and minor officials in blue coats of pleated velvet, their wives and daughters in brocade dresses trimmed with pearls and wearing golden veils! And the master himself would drive by in a gilded carriage with gilded trappings, while runners ran on before him and giant footmen rode behind. After him would come Moscow high society. At Kuskovo a hundred cooks would already be at work. The meal itself would last five hours; they would keep on bringing in golden dishes—there was no end to them! Having dined, the honored guests would sit down to play *préférence, la mouche, panfil, tercet, bassette, mariage, hombre* . . . The ladies would stroll in the garden, where the trees would be hung from top to bottom with pineapples, oranges, and peaches . . . On the pond from a gilded boat came the sound of horn music—as if it were the last coming. Then would come a brilliant theatrical performance . . . Oh, the mastery of the actors and all of them homegrown! As for stagecraft, there were all kinds of machines—things moved by themselves! Then would come the ball: the *polonaise,* the *pergudin,* the *monimaska,* the *minuet.* And what gowns! God is my witness! Nothing but the glitter of gold—what fell on the floor would have been enough to keep an ordinary person for life—the floor sweepers would have a rich harvest afterward! It even happened that the empress herself would be impressed: 'Well, Nikolay Petrovich,' she would say, 'Aren't you the rich and generous one! You have thrown some party! How are we to compete with you?'"

So it was that even Brigadier Khoikhorov had witnessed the passage of both heavenly and earthly comets and was not overawed by the stars.

Having outlived his wife, he was left alone with his only daughter *Erotida* (he loved enigmatic Greek names and he had found this one either in the *Hypotyposis* or in the *Complete Church Calendar*); he took an immediate fancy to the name Erotida—"one whose love is revealed in her face."

He took upon himself the task of educating his daughter. "I will not turn her over," he had said to his late wife, "either to *Madame* or to *Monsieur.*"

"But look, my dear husband," his wife used to say, "the only thing you know is your army regulations!" But with the death of his wife all objections ceased, and the brigadier dressed the child in a riding outfit, bought her a wooden horse, and gave her toy soldiers, a musket, and a drum to play.

"Erotida is going to be my brave little girl!" he thought. "Now, Erotenka, forward march!" And Erotenka slung her drum over her shoulder, took up her musket, and began to march around the room. Her father was enchanted.

When Erotida had reached the age of twelve and the wooden horse had become too small for her, the brigadier taught her how to ride and took her with him on the hunt. The other aspects of her education, i.e., reading, writing, and religious instruction, he turned over to his village priest, Father Lazar, a kindly old man who loved to listen to the brigadier's stories about his military exploits.

As the brigadier grew older, so did his wooden house, along with all its outbuildings. The walls and roofs became blackened and overgrown with moss and high grass. But who doesn't understand the notion of love for one's accustomed surroundings? Who hasn't felt a certain regret when one's old furniture is replaced by new?

Although the walls had to be propped up in places, the brigadier would not even think of repairing the house.

"But look, your excellency," Father Lazar used to say, "your house has already been standing for some forty-odd years during my time, and it was built even before the arrival of my predecessor—one would think you would consider some repairs, if only for reasons of safety."

"And, brother," the brigadier would usually answer, "it will stand long enough for me; what do I need with a new house? Today's architects—the devil take them—will build you a house without heat or comfort, and, if you don't look out, it will collapse and crush you to death. You don't have to look far for an example . . . Remember what happened to our neighbor, what's-his-name? Well, the devil with him too—it's not worth recalling."

"Kasyan, Kasyan . . . God help my memory!"

"What Kasyan are you talking about, brother? I don't know any Kasyan, but I was a close friend of his father. The son is a wastrel, he's arrogant, he puts on French ways; he had himself a house built in Moscow and let it out to lodgers. Comes the first snow and the rafters gave way, the ceiling caved in—brother, it nearly killed a whole family."

"I heard about it, your excellency, I heard . . . Grigory Mikhailovich's house."

"It's about time you got your wits about you, Father Lazar. You will soon be forgetting what pigs' offspring are called."

"Sorry, your excellency."

"Well, there you are brother, now go and see about Erotida's lessons."

"I was about to . . . I wanted to make a small request . . . your excellency."

"What, again about your sowing some grain? No, Father Lazar, I'm not about to let you have any seed grain."

This was the way the brigadier treated everybody; somewhat unceremoniously, but always honestly. He never used the polite form of the pronoun *you;* he didn't consider it necessary to observe the niceties of grammar just out of politeness. But though he was rough in his speech, he was generous in his deeds. The priest knew very well that on the next day he would be sent a load of rye, millet, barley, and oats from the master's barns. The neighbors all loved him and came to see him a few times a year: on holidays and on important family occasions.

It was only the younger generation that tended to avoid him. His first question was always: "And you, brother, are of what age? It's about time you served your country! Twenty years old and still tied to your mother's apron strings! Shame on you! Join up and don't show yourself around here before you've attained captain's rank; then you can think about requesting retirement."

So it was that the brigadier's circle of friends was limited to *living legends of bygone days.*[4]

The men wore powdered wigs with greased pigtails and little pouches tied at the ends that resembled flyswatters; long coats of satin or velvet sewn with gold thread with buttons made of porcelain, steel, or cloth trimmed with sequins; medallions; velveteen shoes.

The older women wore huge satin *caliches*[5] that were supported by wire frames and had lace trimming around the face, elaborate *polonaises*[6] with slits in the sides through which the panels of their satin underskirts were drawn so that they hung down like silk window draperies of two different colors; they did not wear whalebone stays but instead had padded side pockets.

The women of middle age, that is, those over fifty, wore Suvorov caps or a coiffure of abundant curls crowned with a *chiffonet* of Indian silk that was fastened by a black *bordon*[7] decorated with pearls which was passed through the hair arrangement. They wore flowing *mantillas* with hoods, and on their feet were white shoes decorated with sequins and steel beads that had three-inch heels and pointed toes resembling the nose of a sturgeon.

The younger women, that is, those who were not yet fifty, were adorned with a coiffure of powdered hair, whipped up into something resembling swan's down and having several feathers of various colors covering one side of the head; their dress did not lag behind the fashion: very full skirts and an extremely high waistline, the neck covered by a nearly transparent muslin kerchief, the plump arms bare to the shoulder with their lower portions in long kid gloves; on their feet they wore shoes of red morocco.

They all made a fuss over the fourteen-year-old Erotida, called her a little darling, treated her like a baby, barely refraining from picking her up in their arms.

II

Such was the brigadier, his entire clan, and all the surrounding neighbors; but his daughter, Erotida, was an amazing girl. In spite of the fact that her parental training was preparing her for service in the dragoons, she somehow, God only knows from where, acquired all the feminine graces. In spite of the fact that her father taught her to march at a parade-ground pace, she failed to adhere to the regulation thirty-inch step; you could not call her dainty appendages feet, for, even at the age of fourteen, when placing one of them into a tiny slipper—as if into a little cradle—one could have sung "Rockabye baby, in the treetops." Erotida's eyes were blacker than anything in the world, and her eyelashes were like those to which Firdousi compared the lances of his hero Giv in Peshen's tower.[8] Her hair, which came down to her shoulders in ringlets, was of the most exquisite chestnut color, favored by all throughout the centuries—except for that time when red or ginger was in fashion. Her carriage was majestic, her waist slim, her bosom full, her neck white, and her blush crimson.

She was an absolute angel in whom there was not yet a sign of her being spoiled; she was still not contaminated by the misfortunes of life, not corrupted by the bad habits of those surrounding her. She was a child-maiden, not yet bound to the earth, either by fear or expectations.

Do not cast before her the seeds of flattery, do not try to entice this bird of heaven! Do not try to compel her to love, do not demand pledges of fidelity, do not oppress her with your desires! Let us contemplate this divine miracle to the fullest extent, let us bow down and pray before her! When the process of decay begins, when even she is touched by the cold hand of time—then you may have her for yourself!

Erotida attained her fifteenth year. A neighboring friend of the brigadier, rich, unmarried, a retired second major whose chest was adorned with the gold cross of the Ochakov campaign, a man who had been suffering from the gout for thirty years before Erotida's birth, made the following proposal to his friend:

"Look, brother, you know that I have led a decent life, am not in debt, have a pretty good income, and, thank God, am still vigorous. You and I, brother, are old and true friends—why not become relatives? There surely is an occasion—your Erotida—she's a bride, brother—"

"And, brother," the brigadier answered him, "Erotida already has one decrepit father; why hang another one around her neck?"

These words truly offended the second major; he no longer came to see his friend.

Thus it was that Erotida escaped her first suitor.

A second appeared. He handed the brigadier a letter from his aunt, an old friend of the brigadier's late wife.

"I am glad to make your acquaintance," said the brigadier after he had read the letter in which there was a brief reference to Erotida's future followed by a long recommendation concerning the bearer of the letter.

"Glad to make your acquaintance!" repeated the brigadier. "And where, my lad, is it your pleasure to serve?"

"I served as a corporal in the First Musketeer Regiment but had to retire because of domestic circumstances; and now sir, after my parents, I am completely in charge of the estate and I would be very happy to—"

"You are still too young, my lad, too young; one must serve, yes serve."

"My health will not permit it, sir."

"Well that's another matter; indeed, I know from my own experience that service demands health and strength just as marriage does. Well, what's to be done? You must get well, my lad, get well; we have an excellent doctor in this district—"

"But—"

"Yes, yes, improve your health and go back into service; for after all, brother, what kind of a rank is that—a corporal in the reserve? And if military service is too strenuous, then find yourself a place in the civil service—copying documents is not such hard labor."

The brigadier's words were not what the guest wanted to hear; he turned his head toward the window.

"What a beautiful place this is!"

"Not bad, not at all bad."

The cuckoo stuck its head out of the clock and cuckooed once.

The guest got up from his chair. "It's already one o'clock and I'll have to drive ten miles before dinner."

"Farewell, my lad, farewell; glad to make your acquaintance!"

Thus it was that Erotida escaped her second suitor.

They did not have to wait long for the third. The brigadier's cousin arrived; she was a woman who was always involved in all sorts of errands and commissions.

"Well, brother, I am lucky to have gotten here in one piece! What an impossible road! My carriage was nearly shaken to pieces. Listen, sit a little closer—it's about time your Erotida got married. Have you ever seen at my house—do you know Ignaty Ivanovich?"

"How could I not know that chancellery rat? I wouldn't let him marry my house cat."

"How can you slander people when you hardly know them! It's unforgivable! My dear sir, I do not receive unworthy people in my house!"

"Is that true? Well, then don't be angry, sister. I was going by what I have heard, and, as the proverb says, 'Don't believe everything you hear.'"

"Well, there you are, sir—he is a most honorable man!"

"Tell me, is he still a department head?"

"A department head, and such a favorite of the governor general! He's very highly regarded; he will go far!"

"Hmm . . . I have a little problem . . . Remember that lawsuit over the boundary strip?"

"What? Do you mean to tell me that that down-at-the-heels neighbor of yours is going to win the case?"

"Yes, so it seems; it's the land that I hate to lose."

"Well, brother, I will help you get to know Ignaty Ivanovich better. He will do anything for me; surely your case is not as difficult as the Rytvins'?"

"So?"

"They won."

"I am not familiar with the Rytvin case, but I don't have the legal title to this land; my opponent has all the documents; no matter how hard I fight, I'll still have to pay out a couple of thousand—"

"Nonsense! Both the land and the money will go into Erotida's dowry."

"That wouldn't be bad—it's about time Erotida got married. Tell me, sister, what kind of a man is this Ignaty Ivanovich?"

"You won't find a better match. His career is going well, he is still young, and he has some property."

"Is he a man of honor?"

"He is a most noble, most honorable man—you have my word on that."

"But look, sister, didn't you just now promise me that he would help me to rob a poor man!"

The old woman got very angry and left.

Thus it was that Erotida escaped her third suitor.

III

The brigadier continued to repel the advances suitors made on his daughter; as for Erotida herself, she wasn't even thinking about them, for one must first have at least a theoretical conception of love; but she was completely enveloped in the previous century, and at that time people did not speak in the presence of maidens about things they were not supposed to know.

Erotida enjoyed her military drills and her father's stories about his campaigns and about how the Turks used to cut off the heads of commissary agents during the last war against the Ottoman Empire.

She almost never appeared in anything but her riding costume, which consisted of a *pierrot* of military cut, a beige taffeta vest, and a soft hat decorated with ribbons.

Erotida's heart was free, her soul was pure, her sky was blue, her path in life was strewn with flowers, but in her character there was something bold, decisive.

And so, Erotida knew nothing of love; but the time would come when the coconut would burst open loudly.

One platoon of a lancer regiment was assigned quarters in the village belonging to the brigadier. The platoon commander, Lieutenant G., a handsome young fellow and a scapegrace, on entering the village had already found out from his "hostages" what sort of man the landowner was, what kind of a mood he was in, what the daughter was like, how old she was, what his name was, what her name was, and so on. As a student of military strategy, he had thoroughly learned that a military man must show foresight in everything, must be able to take advantage of the slightest opportunity, must be able to estimate the target range, must be decisive, and, when entering an area, must conduct a reconnaissance to determine the customs and state of mind of the inhabitants.

Erect, hands on his hips, astride his gray horse with its neck highly arched, its tail held out straight, he rode by the windows of the brigadier's house.

Everything in the house that could be counted among the living either poured out into the yard or occupied all the windows; the brigadier himself took a seat by the window and admired the formation of brave, well-fed lancers, while Erotida stared only at their leader.

As he rode by the windows the lieutenant made a polite little bow and raised his hand to his shako, while at the same stealing a quick glance at Erotida.

The brigadier took all this as a token of respect for his rank, but the bold Erotida, frightened by something for the first time in her life, started back from the window.

The lieutenant, no worse than an experienced farmer, recognized that this was good, yet unplowed soil from which each glance, each word, would yield a hundredfold. The lieutenant had social graces: he would never pass up the opportunity to pay his respects to parents, to compliment daughters. And so, in full uniform, he called on the brigadier, honored him by addressing him as "your excellency," and asked what orders he would like to give with regard to the quartering and provisioning of the troops.

The brigadier could not resist such expressions of courtesy, such respect for his merits. He sat the lieutenant down and for three hours straight spoke enthusiastically about his accomplishments in the service, how he had "displayed bravery and skill and served with great distinction in various actions against the enemy," how correct he had been with regard to all the circumstances and occasions of the service, how methodical he had been when reporting to his superiors about the status of the equipment, that is, the "official inventory," of the regiment assigned to him, about the supplies and the personnel, how he had commanded a combined detachment in the Turkish war, and so on.

Lieutenant G. listened patiently to the old man, very patiently—he couldn't have been more patient—and who doesn't appreciate a patient listener?

They were talking about Prince Potemkin, and for a contemporary of Catherine II, an eyewitness to the fabulous events of the last century, there was plenty to talk about. It was an endless story in which the brigadier had played various roles: private, corporal, sergeant, ensign, lieutenant, captain, second major, and so on.

The story was not yet finished when a servant, wearing a gray caftan that reached his heels, entered the room and announced dinner was served.

The lieutenant knew how to behave. He rose, clicked his heels, and prepared to take his leave, but the brigadier prevailed on him to stay for dinner. They entered the dining room where Erotida had also appeared. The brigadier did not stand on ceremony but the lieutenant clicked his heels, and Erotida, blushing, bowed to the guest.

The brigadier sat down at his accustomed place at the head of the table; he seated the guest on his right and Erotida on his left. The remaining places were occupied by various voiceless residents of the house.

The brigadier continued his story; the lieutenant listened attentively, but his gaze . . .

Oh, the eyes can be a terrible thing! Especially when, going beyond their usual functions of looking and seeing, they take a notion to speak. Brevity, clarity, conviction, strength, thought, spirit . . . and to whom are they speaking? To the heart, to that sensitive, timid admirer of eyes, cheeks, lips, breasts . . . to that poor prisoner of the gloomy depths, to that heart which is ready to burst out of its breast, either from joy or grief, ready to jump into the outstretched hand of any deceiver, any coquette five feet, two inches, whose gaze is sharper than a ray of sunlight!

How many times Erotida attempted to hold the lieutenant's gaze; she would lift her glance, the lieutenant would immediately catch it, and then would answer it with such a look that Erotida would become angry inside; why must she sit opposite the windows and opposite the lieutenant? She was also angry because her face kept taking on a red glow that nothing could extinguish.

But dinner ended, as did the story; liqueurs were carried around, coffee served, and they got up from the table. The lieutenant, taking his leave, clicked his heels: a bow to the father, a glance at the daughter.

"Good-bye, good-bye, Lieutenant. You are welcome at any time," said the brigadier, as he put on his nightcap—a sign that his honor, or in cases of special respect, his excellency, liked to take a nap right after dinner.

But the lieutenant knew the customs; without a specific invitation he would not show up at the house. Demands of the service, however, required that he gallop past the brigadier's house several times a day.

Erotida found herself work to do near the window; there arose in her a desire to do women's handiwork, and she began to knit something—probably a gift for Papa on his name day.

The lieutenant would ride by, bowing to her so adroitly, so appealingly. Would Erotida be so impolite as not to answer the bow?

The brigadier's name day arrived. The lieutenant was invited to dinner. He came in so respectfully, so cleverly congratulated his excellency on the occasion—and of course he also had to congratulate the daughter, propriety demanded that.

The *robe ronde* and the miniature cap atop a huge coiffure built on felt strips and held in place by foot-long hairpins might have daunted even the most intrepid Don Juan, but Lieutenant G. got the chance to say a few words to Erotida.

What he said, and how she answered, is difficult, impossible, to repeat. In spoken Russian language, words describing the temptations of feelings still do not exist; except, of course, that most universal expression, "I love you"; the lips remain silent, stupid, and thankful, thankful that the eyes speak for them.

The lieutenant made only one clever, deliberate remark:

"I've heard that you like to go horseback riding."

"I really love to ride," Erotida answered him.

"If I could be so fortunate . . . (an expression one can't manage without), if I could accompany you on your rides . . ."

"Erotida! Erotida!" came a voice from the drawing room. And Erotida did not get the chance to reply, "I would enjoy that very much."

The name day went by; several days went by during which, however, the brigadier did not miss the lieutenant, even though he had no one to listen to his stories of "events of bygone days, legends of olden times." "No," thought he, being no fool himself, "I know these young gallants . . . next thing they will be raising the stakes!"

And the brigadier continued to live as usual, going riding with his daughter, but without any company.

He continued to manage his affairs, and the lieutenant went about his duties. Only Erotida could not concentrate on anything.

One day by chance Lieutenant G. met the old cavalryman and the beautiful amazon[9] out riding. After bowing toward them, he was about to resume a position of coming to attention—eyes right!—when the brigadier honored him with a question:

"Where are you headed, Lieutenant?"

"Nowhere in particular, I was just out riding."

"Oh, what sort of a ride is that with no place to go? I recommend that you take a look at my sugar mill; it's interesting to see how they soak the beets. Here, take this path."

"Very interesting!" answered the lieutenant, and, having cast a regretful glance at Erotida, he took his leave of them.

"You old rogue!" thought the lieutenant as he made his way along the path. "You just wait, the joke will be on you!"

Two days later the lieutenant called on the brigadier before dinner to go fox hunting—the quarry was an old, wily fox.

"You will see what hounds I have!" said the brigadier. He was a passionate hunter.

"What do you think, Lieutenant, why not match your best dog against my Sunshine?"

"A pleasure! Shall we bet on it? Even money?"

"Agreed!"

The preparations did not take long. Horses were saddled up for Erotida and the brigadier. The lieutenant's orderly lent a hand; he had become well acquainted with all the servants and he was brushing and patting Erotida's horse.

They saddled up and headed out into the field. Grooms, carrying the quarry in a cage, were sent out ahead. The dogs were straining at their leashes.

The brigadier and the lieutenant began talking about hunting. Erotida rode along at her father's side; her horse was prancing as if proud of its rider . . . But suddenly it laid back its ears, swished its tail, and began to go at a faltering, uneven pace.

Our amazon was an excellent rider; she was pleased by the horse's playfulness and tugged at the reins . . . sh, sh! . . . But her horse suddenly twisted, reared up, flung itself forward like an arrow, and took off at full speed. Erotida's efforts to restrain the horse were in vain.

By the time the brigadier managed to cry out, Erotida was far ahead. The lieutenant managed to catch up to her, grab the horse by the bridle and jump to the ground . . . The horse broke away, but Erotida was already in his arms.

"Oh, what happiness!" he shouted, covering her hand with kisses. "I have gotten the chance to save you from danger! I would have died myself, I could not have endured it if the slightest harm had come to you!" All this was said involuntarily, and because of that, it was excusable.

"Were you frightened, Erotida?"

Erotida wanted to answer that it was nothing, but some inner, feminine feeling told her that she should seem slightly dizzy, confused.

Gasping from fear, her father rode up.

"Are you all right, Erotida?"

Erotida, leaning on the lieutenant, was slow to answer.

"Thank you, thank you, Lieutenant . . . I don't know what got into that stupid horse; he seemed so gentle."

"Probably something frightened him," answered the lieutenant.

Some of the brigadier's men, having noticed from a distance that something had happened to the young mistress, also galloped up. A carriage was sent for; they carried Erotida home in a thoughtful mood. The fright had had a strong effect on her.

The rescuer was entitled to pay a visit to the rescuee and inquire about her health.

But what a change could be seen in the glance of the rescuee after an incident like that! She now looked at her deliverer without timidity, without fear—and out of their glances an unseen spider (probably that same spider, who, according to the Negroes, wove the creation) spun a web that ensnared the illusive heart.

And now the time had come, and for the first time the tongue began to speak freely:

"Oh, Erotida, I could not have gone on without you! That accident showed me that my happiness is found in you!"

Then, after a short pause:

"Erotida! Erotida! Just one word!" But Erotida remains silent, her hand already being covered with kisses . . . she is already in the arms of . . .

But this is a dream, a bold flight of fancy. Her parent was taking his usual after-dinner nap. On awakening, he began to think about his daughter's welfare . . . She was already at his side, her cheeks burning, her heart fluttering like a dove that wanted to fly out of her body.

PART TWO
CARLSBAD. GAMBLING. TOO LATE. A NEW ARRIVAL. AGAIN GAMBLING. LOST!

I

In the year 1814, when all of Europe was celebrating the casting off of their shoulders the burden of the little corporal, many Russian officers in Paris—the wounded, the sick, and those whose health was otherwise impaired—were given leave to take the waters or go anywhere else they might desire.

Captain G. of the lancer regiment was also eager to take the cure. With his uniform decorated with awards for his service in the defeat of the common enemy, he wanted to enjoy some free time and try his luck at the gaming table.

He had heard a lot about Carlsbad,[10] and he had long dreamed of going there. There the waters flow over gold, and the banks of the Tepl and Eger are covered with wild flowers; there both the waters and love are at a temperature of 165 degrees; there one may imbibe, in addition to the waters, the fragrant breath of those suffering from melancholy, insomnia, lack of appetite, and all manner of complaints that require for their treatment diversion and *der Sprudel* at 165 degrees, and love—love, that healing ailment that is the cure for all ailments, that opium that stimulates the activity of the senses, that light in the midst of darkness, that blissful suffering.

Perhaps for Captain G. the waters at Wiesbaden or Pyrmont or even at Teplice would have been more beneficial, but Captain G. preferred Carlsbad—Carlsbad which could more accurately be called "Aphroditenbad" because its waters were a Pool of Siluam for the fair sex and because Venus herself, in the case of illness, would have chosen no other waters to restore her health.

And so Captain G. set out for Carlsbad.

He had already crossed the Austrian border, had already cursed the bridges, both large and small, for whose upkeep he was obliged to pay, cursed the *geld* and the *trinkgeld* and the *deutsche Sprache* which he did not understand.

And here he is riding into Carlsbad . . . and now he hears *"Halt!"* and *"Erlauben Sie!"* The man at the gate slowly takes up his horn, sounds a welcome to the visitor, and then demands money from him for the *Trompeterstückchen.* The captain pays him, but he is still detained by a dozen questions, a dozen offers and recommendations, both spoken and printed, on behalf of all the hotels and *tables d'hôte* of Carlsbad: Where would he like to stay? For how long? Daily, weekly, or monthly rates? Where will he be taking the waters?

The captain got fed up with the demands.

"I don't care; take me wherever you wish," he said.

"But that's impossible," they answered. "We have expensive hotels and we have cheap hotels; *Gott weiss* what you might like, there are many from which to choose: there is *Der Böhmische Saal* and *Die Roten Ochsen;* one may stay under the Golden Shield, or under the sign of the Deer; perhaps you like to play billiards . . ."

The captain chose the Golden Shield. He took a room for a month, but new emissaries appeared with new proposals: How did he wish to take the waters? Did he want his name included in the *Badelist* for a fee of thirty kreuzers? Did he want to have his own copy of the *Badelist?*

That evening outside his door they played *Nachtmusik* and demanded money.

The next morning the innkeeper appeared and proposed the taking of Carlsbad salts as a necessary means of purgation before taking the waters.

Finally they ran out of offers; Captain G. had become one of the patients of Carlsbad. His shoulder had been creased by a bullet and he had his arm in a sling—and how this intrigued all those earthly creatures in silk epaulettes trimmed with lace fringe, armed with golden daggers, and wearing watches attached to their belts—those earthly creatures bedecked with earrings—earrings! A sign of slavery according to the foolish traditions of the East.

Captain G. was already strolling the path under the chestnut trees. Instead of a sword, he had a gold lorgnette in his hand; instead of his uniform, he wore a frock coat; but his wide, striped trousers, his high-heeled boots with spurs, revealed he was a soldier—and what a soldier! He had a bandaged arm, a curled mustache, wavy light-brown hair, high shoulders modishly slumped, a *pour le mérite* around his neck, and the number twenty-five entered into the age block in his service record. All these qualities were capable of acquiring for him both love and friendship.

After several days the Carlsbad waters produced their effect: the captain had become acquainted with everyone, his room was usually full of young convalescing officers, and with his wounded arm he could already deal the cards and reckon up his winnings and losses.

Time flew, the corks flew; youth bubbled, as did the champagne. Oh maidens, maidens! Oh women, women! Look at these young men, look at these 52 cards, a number that for the ancients signified the number of weeks in a year, while 364, the point total of all the cards, was for them the number of days in a year. Look how each of them keeps betting on his queen and with what hopes he doubles the stakes on her, while both in his heart and on the table there is a *transport!*[11] But now he reviles his queen *ander Stück Manier,* tears her to pieces, throws her under the table, gets up and goes out to torment the first *Susanchen* he meets. Her cries of *Lassen Sie mich, herr Oberster!* will be in vain.

One evening in the main hall of the Golden Shield, where, for those on a strict diet, they prepare two hundred special dishes; where they serve, in addition to sweet, salt, sour, and bitter water, Melniker, Ungar, Rhenish, and Champagne; where for exercise there are billiards, cards, dice, roulette, backgammon, even checkers; where for diversion of the ear there are both blind and sighted musicians, an orchestra and an *orchestrino,* Captain G., surrounded by players, was dealing Stuss. He was having no luck, was being taken to the cleaners. Silently he wiped the perspiration from his brow, picked up a new deck (having torn the old one to pieces), while the glass of *Karolina* stood near him, untouched.

Someone broke the bank. Captain G. took out his purse and dumped its contents on the table; there were a hundred gold pieces: this was all he could risk.

He had already cut the deck; players were fiddling with their cards, trying to decide which one to put their money on.

"I'll bet the pot!" a voice rang out from the corner of the table. The captain started, looked up at the new player. It was a young man, his face showing no fear; thick, black sideburns and long mustachios made him seem even paler than he was. He was wearing a cossack coat and riding breeches with wide red stripes.

Throwing his purse on the table, he repeated, "I'm betting against the pot! Everything goes on the queen!"

Captain G. glanced at him and then looked around.

"You may remove the first card," he finally said with some agitation after he had placed the deck on the table.

The young man removed the card.

The captain took the deck, and, holding it face up, dealt the cards, one to the right and one to the left.

"The queen loses!" shouted several players at once.[12]

"Enough!" said Captain G. after finishing the deal and raking in his winnings.

"What a hotheaded young innocent," he thought. "I would like to get to know him better."

"You chose the wrong time to play for such high stakes."

"Yes," answered the young man. "I'm just not lucky."

"Unlucky at cards, lucky in love!"

"I don't believe that . . . Perhaps that's been your experience."

"I'm not lucky at cards."

"But in love?"

"In love? Well, in love it's hard to win if you don't risk your whole heart."

The young man did not answer.

"Have I met you somewhere before, or perhaps you have relatives?" continued Captain G. "For there is something familiar about your face."

"Perhaps," said the young man, turning toward the window.

"Have you been here long?" continued the captain.

"I arrived yesterday."

"Are you on leave?"

"No, I have left the army; I served with the Mamonov Regiment."

"If you don't have many acquaintances here, I would consider it a pleasure if you would spend some time with me. Where are you staying?"

"At the Three Stars."

"That's a little closer to the waters . . . Are you headed that way now? I'm going out for a stroll, and we seem to be going the same way; meanwhile, since you are new here, I will point out the sights of Carlsbad. For example, here comes *schöne Kristinchen!*"

"Lassen Sie mich, Kapitan!" screamed the young Kristinchen, a chambermaid they met on the stairs who had to struggle to free herself from the captain's embrace.

The young man, still inexperienced, blushed like a maiden and lowered his eyes; it seemed this was his first lesson in a branch of knowledge that was new to him.

The captain took him by the hand, and they went out onto the boulevard.

"Do you speak German?"

"Not a word."

"What a pity! A Russian officer who knows German can have a great time here. It seems to me that women everywhere have some sort of special weakness for Russians . . . And, of course, here at the waters flirting is required; it stimulates the blood . . . Today, it seems, all the stars are in the firmament . . . Take a look! Those are the patients! I wonder how many champagne glasses have been emptied to their health . . . To who else's health do they themselves drink the waters? Ah, there she is! How do you like that dear little face under the blue hat? Charming!"

"Not bad."

"Is that all? You must already be in love. Your indifference hurts me. But then after all I am glad that you won't be one of my rivals. I usually take care of them *à coup sûr.*"

The women came closer. The captain cast a meaningful glance at the girl in the blue hat; she responded with a glance even more meaningful. The young man noticed.

"Perfection!" exclaimed the captain when the women had passed by. "And it's even better that it's not she, but her mother who is swilling down the 165-degree *sprudel,* because, in my opinion, there is nothing worse than an *overcured* woman. How much better is a blossom yet untouched by chronic melancholy, a blossom still not infused with medicinal health. What's the point of converting a rose into a lily!"

"And if love takes a hand in this conversion?"

"It doesn't matter! Oh, but you are a dreamer, you have been bewitched by sighs. That's shameful! Of course for a woman, an ultra-sensitive being, it's another matter, but for a young man to waste away from love . . . By the way, let's stop off at the post office; I am expecting some letters from the regiment . . . Then we can go back on the boulevard and to my place for Russian tea if you like."

They went up to the window where letters were given out. The captain gave his name and was given a letter.

"Bah!" he exclaimed as he unsealed the letter, "I recognize the handwriting! Long-overdue sweet news dated 12 June 1812! Oh this is curious! Let's go down this path and sit down. In fact, you look tired; I can see it in your face."

They went down the path and sat down.

Captain G. quickly read through the letter and laughed out loud.

"Well, look, you be the judge. It was back at the beginning of 1811 and my platoon was quartered in a village belonging to a retired brigadier, a character of the old school who had a daughter. I was younger then, wilder, and I fell in love with the daughter. There was no lack of response on her part. The old man would not have even considered me a suitable match for his daughter because I had nothing to my name but my honor. I thought about eloping, but I couldn't decide—how can a girl marry without her papa's consent! But meanwhile youth was not thinking about the consequences. Upon leaving I swore by all that was holy that my love for her was infinite and eternal; I swore I would write to her, that I would serve until I had attained the rank of brigadier, and then I would formally request her hand. Before the war began I did write to her, but once the war was on there was no time for love. We advanced into Germany, into France; there were pretty women everywhere, each one more beautiful than the other, each one more ardent; conquest followed conquest—everyone was ready to lay down their arms before the victors. And so three years have passed and now here is a letter from my dear Erotida; it has finally found me so far from home—but it's too late! She says she is free, that her father has died, that she is waiting to give me her hand. Too late! No, after three years I am not going to waste the travel expense money. Too much water has flowed under the bridge since then, and girls don't like having to wait for suitors; besides, one must admit, she doesn't know how to write: 'My deer preshus frend, I am free . . . Papa . . . Akh! I kant say it, my hart overflows . . .' Some style! She has put in enough Akh's and Okh's! I can't stand this sentimentality. Now when it comes to style . . ."

Here the captain took a notebook out of his pocket and pulled a letter out of it.

"Read this."

"Excuse me, I don't understand French."

"Well, I'll read it myself and translate for you: *Monsieur, je tiens trop à votre estime*, i.e., Dear sir, I remain very much to your respect, *pour n'avoir pas montré à ma mère dans une circonstance aussi importante pour la reputation d'une jeune personne, la lettre que vous venez de me fair l'honneur de m'écrire*, i.e., that I didn't show my mother, in such an important instance for the reputation of a young person, the letter which you did me the honor of writing, *Oserai—je vous avouer, monsieur, que je ne laissais pas redouter son sentiment sur vos propositions*, i.e., Do I dare admit that I was afraid of her feelings toward your propositions, *Et n'est-ce pas assez vous fair entendre que mon coeur partage tous vos projets,—Adeline*, i.e., And is it not enough to enable you to understand through this that my heart partakes of all your projects!"[13]

"There you have true female courage and complete trust! Such a heart deserves to be liberated from parental embrace."

"Yes, that's true," answered the young man with indignation. "Your enterprise has a legitimate basis . . . A bird in the hand is worth two in the bush . . . However, I have to be going. I have to drop by the office to get a ticket for the waters . . . Excuse me . . ."

Captain G. continued down the boulevard and plunged into the crowd, and the young man turned to the side. He did see, however, how the captain approached the woman in the blue hat, how he parted from her, and how the ladies crossed over to Neu Weise Street and entered a house on the corner.

The young man went up to the entrance and asked the doorman who was staying in that house.

"*Pani Ksiezna* L. . . . from Poland," the doorman answered.

"Is she here with her daughter Adelina?"

"That's right."

The young man headed back to his hotel—under the sign of the Three Stars.

"I will save her! I will save her!" he pronounced several times almost out loud.

II

Evening came. The captain was shuffling the cards while waiting for his guest. But the young man did not appear. Meanwhile a group of young men had assembled. At first the conversation was about women, then about cards; they laughed about the young man who had lost the hundred gold pieces—surely all he had—and the young man was forgotten.

On the next day, as was the custom, the captain and all his young acquaintances headed for the boulevard after lunch; on the boulevard there was a new arrival who was attracting the crowd's attention.

Everyone who considered himself *ein flinker, gewandter Bursch* was trying to get close to her; they were all appraising her—with and without lorgnettes—squaring and hunching their shoulders, squinting and opening their eyes wide, and, shifting from one leg to the other, whispering to themselves: *ah, c'est une divinité!*

The general commotion caught the captain's attention. With the gesture of a connoisseur he aimed his lorgnette and exclaimed: "God, what a beauty!"

He took a second look. His vanity expressed itself in the words of a gambler: yes, here he would be playing for the kind of stakes that made all others insignificant.

It was being said that she came from Russia and owned several thousand serfs. Accompanying her was neither mother nor father nor grandmother nor husband, only an old German doctor. Consequently, she had to be a young widow trying to recover from her loss.

The beauty of all the female patients at Carlsbad faded before her like the moon before sunrise.

The captain looked at her again and sought her gaze, caught it, and noted there was something in it that . . . and abruptly forgot his young Polish Adelina. Adelina was too fair-haired, too short, too shallow: she did not have that proud nobility, that sense of one's own worth; she lacked that fire in her eyes, that something that made for a glorious conquest, that flattered all the senses.

"A miraculous being!" the young men who had gathered at the captain's were shouting. "She has probably come here to ease her grief . . . Gentlemen, let us not abandon her to her widowhood!"

The captain remained silent, but in his heart he was ready to defend her honor, ready to challenge anyone who took it into his head to vie openly for the conquest of her heart.

The captain was losing steadily; it was her fault, for he was distracted. No woman had ever inspired in him such passion; for the first time he was experiencing absentmindedness and insomnia. He seemed to see her everywhere . . . but then he had to laugh at himself; he was sure of himself as a universal conqueror; he knew how to capture glances, how to make women blush—that's the way he was made. Passion could impart to him even more decisiveness, and this made him proceed straight to his goal without looking back.

"Whoever you may be," he thought, like Telemachus, "goddess or mere mortal, you will be mine!" and he began to pursue her in the *Sprudel* gallery and on the path under the chestnut trees like someone who already had the right to defend the young beauty from the lorgnettes and the crowd of admirers.

Several days passed and Captain G. found an opportunity to speak with her while taking the waters. He rejoiced on noticing that a spark of love for him had already been enkindled in her heart. There was no way to conceal from him that pensiveness, those glances, those modestly suppressed sighs.

But could this be kept hidden from the hundred-eyed Argus of envy? Would hundred-mouthed gossip keep this a secret?

Would a woman defend the honor of another woman? Defend her from slander? Or would she be the first to abandon her sister to disgrace?

The first time Captain G. went up to Madam Emilia Horeff (that was her name according to the *Badelist*) and began to chat with her and the doctor accompanying her, everyone who walked in the gallery, either voluntarily or because the exercise had been prescribed, everyone understood, everyone unraveled the mystery, smiled, whispered, began to talk about a rapid conquest, and then—about feminine virtue, modesty, decency . . .

Evil rumors were already blackening the reputation of the beautiful visitor to Carlsbad, while she, like the sun, remained above the clouds that were obscuring her light.

Only Captain G. was in a position to know and experience the uncompromising strictness of her behavior, the absolute purity of her soul which remained immune to temptation. In his conversations with her his arrogance lost its edge; he was becoming a daydreamer. He talked to her about Russia, awakened in her a desire to see the surroundings of Carlsbad: the little Versailles, the ancient castle of Stein-Elnbogen, where there is a stone that fell from the sky, and Hirschensprung, where there is an enchanting spot called "heaven on earth."

"Oh, how blessed," he said, "is the man who may experience heaven on earth, who may meet an angel-woman and dare to pronounce the words, 'I love you,' and these words find their echo in her heart!"

"Bliss on earth," she answered thoughtfully, "does it really resemble a gloomy niche in the rocks bearing the name 'heaven on earth'? Perhaps the person who gave it that name was himself tortured by repentance for a moment of hope and joy experienced on that very spot! Do the words 'I love you' have only one meaning? Don't they sometimes mean 'I am playing with you'?"

"To play with a sacred feeling!" Captain G. objected, "Oh, no! . . . I have not yet experienced it, have not yet pronounced those words, have not taken possession of anyone's heart, but I defend the meaning of those words."

Captain G. continued to describe love, fidelity, and earthly bliss in bright colors, and, apparently without noticing it, pursued Emilia to the very doorstep of the house she had taken opposite the Golden Lion.

At the entrance he made all manner of excuses for having been so carried away by the interesting conversation.

"Who doesn't get carried away with words? . . . But often such lack of restraint is dangerous . . . Thank you."

Captain G. was about to take his leave, but the beautiful patient of Carlsbad stopped him with the words:

"You have stimulated my curiosity to see 'heaven on earth.' If you would like to take me there I will be waiting for you at the morning stroll, at ten o'clock."

As if anticipating the captain's acceptance of the invitation, she ran into the vestibule without waiting for an answer, while the captain, rejoicing in his heart, went to the boulevard, walked all around Carlsbad, and returned to his room after midnight to avoid his inquisitive comrades. He wanted to see nothing, hear nothing, and know nothing except ten o'clock in the morning.

After a tortuous, sleepless night, morning came; but until ten o'clock there still remained 10,800 seconds.

Finally Captain G. was flying to Emilia on the wings of love. He found her in the drawing room; before her on a table lay a gold ring. Apparently she was thinking about the ring and was startled by the captain's entrance; her face betrayed her confusion.

"Excuse me for coming in unannounced; your doctor said you were in . . . But have I been the cause of some distress, some recollection . . . concerning the ring?"

"No, the ring was not the cause of my sadness . . . There are no pleasant memories associated with it . . . It's not a token of love! I value it about as much as you value that ring you have on your finger, and to prove it I am willing to exchange rings with you."

"Oh," said the captain, coloring slightly, "I could not give up a token of love, but I do have the right to exchange a ring of my mother's . . . I would be glad to exchange it for yours."

"I won't go back on my word. You may take this ring which is of no value to me . . . It's yours!"

"You are bestowing happiness upon me!" exclaimed the captain as they exchanged rings. He wanted to say something else in his enthusiasm, but Emilia interrupted with a question:

"It says here 'Erotida, 1811.' Surely that must be your mother's name?"

"Her name." The captain answered in an unsteady voice. "You have bestowed happiness upon me!" he continued as he put the ring on his finger and kissed it.

But Emilia was not paying any attention to him. She got up and left the room.

"What can this mean?" thought the captain. "Oh, I understand—an outburst of love and the shyness of a woman overcome . . ."

Instead of Emilia a maid came out and announced that her mistress was not feeling well and begged his indulgence for postponing the trip out of town.

"Aren't you the sly one!" thought the captain as he was going out, while looking at the ring Emilia had given him. A name had been inscribed in it but had been scratched out. "Perhaps it's the name of . . . but it doesn't matter! The past doesn't concern me! The golden keys to the city have already been delivered to the conqueror and soon it will be ours!"

The captain went home. For him diversion was essential; his gaze was bright; he was generous at the common dinner table, ready to pour champagne on the head of anyone who refused to drink. After dinner he laid out gold pieces on the table and shuffled the cards. The players fiddled with their cards, the gold pieces were put in the pot, and the game proceeded as usual.

"I'll bet the pot!" was heard from the corner of the table.

The captain looked up. It was his young acquaintance.

"Ah, my respects! Better not to bet it all, but what's to be done, I owe you a chance to recoup."

"Everything on the queen!" said the young man.

The captain began to deal . . .

"The queen loses!" was heard from all the players.

"I have no luck at cards!"

"Surely you are too lucky in love," said the captain as he counted the gold pieces.

"You're right. Would you like to play for a gold ring? I see that you too have one on your hand—my ring against yours."

"I cannot bet my ring," answered the captain. "But if you wish, I'll bet five gold pieces against yours."

"Perhaps you will place a higher value on *this* ring."

The young man took the ring from his finger and threw it toward the captain.

The captain picked it up and looked at the inscription: 'Erotida, 1811.' Angrily he jumped up from his seat, grabbed the young man by the arm, led him away from the table, and said in a choking voice:

"Where, my dear sir, did you get this ring?"

"My dear sir, I am not obliged to answer your question."

"You must answer or I will force you, sir, at a distance of four paces!"

"It would be a pleasure. I accept your challenge."

"Tomorrow, then, at six o'clock in the morning!"

"Not tomorrow, but this very day! It's still light out; right away! I shall be at the place called 'heaven on earth'!"

"Very good, sir! I am sure you will not be as lucky at this rendezvous with me! But the seconds?"

"Not necessary . . . Why do we need witnesses? Love does not tolerate them, and hatred must not love! Good-bye; I'll be there in half an hour."

The young man left.

"Why all the histrionics?" thought the captain.

At the appointed time he had his horse saddled, took his Kuchenreuter pistols, and rode to Hirschensprung. The young man was already there.

"At how many paces—including the barrier?"

"You challenged me to answer you at a distance of four paces and I accept, but to the death; I will accept no other terms."

The young man's determination thoroughly shook the captain.

"Good enough!" he answered. "Load the pistols!"

They loaded the pistols, paced off the distance.

"I say again, sir," said the captain, "if you will answer the question I put to you, the matter will be ended without bloodshed."

"Your answer, sir, is in the barrel of this pistol; you may repeat your question by shooting!"

The captain cocked his pistol, and the young man did the same. He advanced right up to the barrier and deliberately took aim at the captain.

The captain did not wait; he squeezed the trigger and a bullet struck the young man in the chest. He dropped his pistol and fell to the ground, his hand clutching his wound.

"I've killed him!" the captain involuntarily cried out, running toward him.

The young man raised himself up, tore off a false mustache, and said in a fading voice:

"Leave me . . . your assistance is of no help, neither for your rival, nor for mine . . ."

"Emilia!" cried the captain as he fell to his knees.

"No, not Emilia . . . but your long-forgotten . . . Erotida . . . Farewell . . ."

"Erotida!" The captain could hardly speak. The barely audible "farewell" was heard again. The last rays of sunlight disappeared behind the mountain, as though night was hastening to draw a black veil over Erotida's lifeless body.

° ° °

"Can you imagine," Captain G. told me in 1818 in M . . . , "that I was so blind I didn't recognize Erotida in Emilia, nor did I recognize Emilia in that desperate young officer of the Mamonov regiment."

"What did you do with the unfortunate one's body?"

"With my own hands I consigned it to the waves of the river Eger! I returned to Carlsbad. The very next day I heard the latest news: everyone was saying that the beautiful Emilia had completely disappeared along with a certain young man, my rival, who had become frightened by the challenge to a duel . . . For a long time Adelina was angry with me, but eventually we made peace; she parted from her mother. At the first church on the Russian border I knelt next to her at the altar; the priest placed the candles in our hands and performed a requiem service instead of a nuptial one . . . Now I don't know how things are going for her in Mogilev on the Dniepr."

"That's how Captain G. ended the story from which I have fashioned either a true account or a fanciful tale—I'm not sure which."

"An excellent story, excellent!" said the listeners.

"Yes," said one, "but the ending is a little obscure; besides, Erotida as herself is scarcely educated, yet she was brilliant in the role of Emilia and unbelievably courageous as the young officer."

"But what can upbringing, time, and love not make out of a woman!" answered the host-storyteller as he put his notebook back into the desk.

Roland the Furious

CHAPTER I

In one of the 50 provincial capitals and 555 district towns of the Russian Empire, in a wayside Jewish tavern, a man of about thirty, of imposing appearance with fiery black eyes and ruddy cheeks, was pacing the room from corner to corner. He was wearing a dark blue frock coat with three stars gleaming on his chest. Alarm and confusion were expressed in all his features.

The door leading to the innkeeper's bedroom was partly open. At a stove near the bed a young Jewess was cooking kugel for the Sabbath and preparing tea for the lodger. Several yidlings[1] in trousers, aprons, and caps crowded around her, mumbling in their native tongue. Suddenly there resounded a loud exclamation from the lodger. The yidlings rushed to the door and by turns peeked through the crack into the room occupied by the lodger.

"Angelica!" he pronounced in a desperate voice.

The yidlings scurried away from the door in terror.

"*Voss sakt er?*" mumbled one of them and again placed his eye to the crack.

"*Haim! Haim! Schlom!*"

Haim and Shlyomka also moved toward the door.

"Angelica!" repeated the distinguished lodger, pausing in the middle of the room. His eyes stared fixedly, his upraised hand trembled.

"Nature," he continued, "you are deaf to the outcries of the unfortunate! My tears have worn through savage stones, but they have not moved

This story first appeared in O. I. Senkovsky's journal, *Biblioteka dlia chteniia* 10 (1835): 208–43, under the title "Provincial Actors." Senkovsky, who was notorious for his arbitrary editorial practice, drastically revised the story, essentially neutralizing Veltman's highly eccentric style. When Veltman later republished the story in his collection *Povesti* (1836, 1837), he eliminated Senkovsky's "corrections" and restored the original title. Soviet editions have followed this last version; this translation is based on Aleksandr Vel'tman, *Povesti i rasskazy* (Moscow: Izdatel'stvo "Sovetskaia Rossiia," 1979).

you to return what is rightfully mine! . . . I will transform the universe into a barren waste so that in its limitless expanses Angelica may not hide herself from my gaze! . . . Angelica! Can there be a place in the wide world capable of concealing you?" After a few moments of silence, he struck himself on the chest and continued in an anguished voice:

"Almighty God! An endless struggle! . . . Or has there not been suffering enough? . . . What Fury has bathed her poisonous dagger in my blood? . . . In a vale of tranquillity, in her embrace, in a moment of bliss . . . he executed his own sentence! . . . Perhaps she preferred the tender name of shepherd to the stern title of warrior! Capricious divinity of love! Pour the poison into my wounds! . . . They feel it no longer! . . . Why do I delay! Go forth, seek her out, unhappy one!"

With these words he lunged to one side.

"Careful, sir!" the Jewess cried out in her lisping speech, after having evaded the grasp of the maddened lodger. In her hands was a tray which held a greasy teapot, hot water, milk, a saucer with four pieces of sugar, and some Jewish bread.

"Ah, Rifka! you shall not escape me now!" shouted the distinguished lodger, squeezing the Jewess in his embrace after she barely had time to place the tray on the table.

"*Voss macht er, Haim?*" whispered the yidling[2] peeking through the crack in the door.

"Shsh! Careful, sir!" cried the Jewess, while trying to defend herself from the kisses being rained upon her face; then she managed to break loose from the lodger's grasp and run out of the room.

As she was leaving the room, the stranger followed her with fiery eyes; then he poured himself a glass of tea, threw it down in one gulp, took a few strides about the room, stopped in the center, threw out his arms, and continued:

"Cursed one! and you did not hurl them into hell! . . . Yes, I shall destroy everything that bears upon itself the stamp of shameful love! . . . Perish, unholy shades, participants in infamous revelry and witnesses of my shame! . . . Oh, may my breath be like a wild whirlwind!"

Following these words the curses flowed in a torrent; Rifka ran out of the kitchen and, chasing the yidlings away from the door, placed her eyes and then her ear to the keyhole.

"Oh, Sun!" continued the stranger, "Hide thyself if thou shouldst ever approach on the golden path this vale of tears! Moon! Turn away thy heavenly light from this vile spot! Eternal night! Cast thy cloak over this infernal abode! Death-dealing air! Corrupt the flesh of the wanderer who approaches here! . . . Fierce tigers! Here is your lair!"

Just then the door squeaked and someone entered the room. The stranger continued, but in a much calmer voice:

"The sun is hastening to hide its face from this horror! Look! Don't you see that virtue is in rags and vice is arrayed in silk? Do you see the turtle-dove? The hawk circles above her . . . he seizes her, tears out her heart, still throbbing with love . . ."

"Ready, sir," said the person standing in the doorway. By his voice one could conclude this was the Jewish agent.

The wooden clock hanging on the wall cuckooed six times.

"It's time!" said the stranger. Throwing on his cloak, he left the room; the agent led him along the corridor with a candle. It was already dark outside; near the gate stood a small Polish carriage hitched to a single horse and driven by a Jew with huge curly side locks and wearing a shaggy cap.

"A tip for the agent, sir?"

"Go to the devil!" answered the stranger, jumping into the carriage.

The Jew sitting on the coach-box flailed at the emaciated ribs of his nag, and the agent with the candle went back inside; the hooves clattered on the hard ground and the carriage rattled off. Along both sides of the street the lights of the Jewish Sabbath twinkled. The carriage rolled on without incident; suddenly, as they were descending a hill, they met a column of wagons coming the other way. The Jew veered sharply to one side. From a nearby house a beam of light lit up the street.

"The ravine! . . ." screamed the stranger. His words were cut off. The carriage careened, the stars on his cloak flashed, a groan was heard, and then there was silence. All that could be heard were the oxen toiling up the hill, the whistles of the drivers, the cracking of whips, cries of "Giddap! Giddap!"

The column of wagons passed by. All was silent.

A pitiful moan was heard from below. But then once more the voice of the Jewish driver could be heard from below the hill; once more the crack of a whip was heard, hooves again clattered, and the carriage went rattling on.

Again a dull groan was heard near the lighted house by the bridge over the ravine.

CHAPTER II

On the day of the holy martyrs, Saints Minodora, Mitrodora, and Nymphodora, the guests were flocking to the mayor's house. On the occasion of the name day of his honored spouse, the mayor had invited all from far and wide to attend the feast.

In the homes of all the town's important personages, who knew the manners of high society no less well than Pavel Afanasievich Famusov,[3] the day was noted on the calendar: on a clean slip of paper opposite the tenth of September were the following words: Nymphodora Mikhailovna's name day.[4]

On that day, in solemn ceremony, the archpriest himself said the mass in the town cathedral, while the chairman and members of the council, judges, and other higher officials made the following entries in their official diaries: "Owing to the nonreception of the necessary information, defer the resolution of all cases until the next session." The postmaster and his assistant delegated the reception and dispatch of correspondence to the letter carrier on duty; the town doctor gave his medical assistant the instructions necessary for carrying out his duties; the constables placed their policing responsibilities on their subordinates, and all, in complete full-dress uniform, set out to pay their respects to Nymphodora Mikhailovna and her spouse, and from there to mass, and then back to the festive table of honor.

The three merchant guilds of the town also remembered the day: after dispatching their clerks early in the morning with sacks containing everything that was needed for the proper management of Nymphodora Mikhailovna's household, they themselves set out around noon to pay their respects to the lady being honored. On that day an excellent cook was released from the stockade where he had already spent almost five years in connection with a criminal case; he had not been sent to Siberia, either because the investigation based on his testimony was still in progress in fifteen provinces or because they still had not caught his accomplices who were scattered all over the Russian Empire or because of illness or other legitimate reasons.

The feast was magnificent.

What brush can depict that unanimous pleasure that filled all who were present at the table? Toasts to the health of Nymphodora Mikhailovna, her spouse, and her whole family were repeated with heartfelt feelings of loyalty, with dutiful feelings of respect for the honored chief of the town, and with wishes for every blessing and happiness: for a yearly income of 100,000 and for a hundred years of life plus twenty or at least fifteen. The letters of the honored lady's name, molded out of candy and draped with a sugary web, rose up from the center of the table; nearby were marzipans, plates of jam, cantaloupes, watermelons, pears, and apples. The firemen's choir sang "Many Years."

While Nymphodora Mikhailovna undertook to measure out the allotments of layer cake, the host broke the seal on a bottle of champagne; the cork hit the ceiling and fell to the floor from where it was retrieved by order of the judge, a connoisseur of wines, and passed from hand to hand as a marvel. Several voices reverently exclaimed, "V.C.P.[5] with a star!" And when the goblets were filled and passed around to the guests, all stood up and pronounced with one voice: "To your health!" Then came a volley of rapid-fire compliments to the wine: "Wonderful wine!" "Old wine!" "Very old wine!" "Perfect wine!" "Pure wine!" "The wine of tsars!" When dessert had been served, accompanied by ratafia, aromatic vodka, and cherry brandy, when the guests were full and flushed, the hostess rose from her place, the chairs rumbled back, and everyone kissed the hand of the hostess and went into the drawing room. The ladies sat on the sofa next to a round table on which stood another dessert: Vologda *pastila*,[6] nuts of various kinds, fruit, and jams. The men of higher rank sat along the sides of the room and occupied themselves picking their teeth and sniffing snuff; the others, people of lower rank, crowded around the fringes, whispering or admiring the room's rich decorations: Moscow wall paper depicting shepherdesses in farthingales and shepherds in breeches playing on pipes, furniture upholstered in green Morocco leather, and prints by Loginov in narrow gilt frames depicting the stories of Genevieve, Paul and Virginia, and the Prodigal Son, as well as the distorted features of tsars and generals with inscriptions and verses in their honor.

"Imagine!" said the postmaster, spearing a piece of pastila with his fork, "In France, in Paris, they have lunch on forks."[7]

"Is it possible? How can that be?" cried several voices.

"I can't say; I can only cite the evidence of Mr. Kotzebue's book of reminiscences of Paris. Mr. Kotzebue is trustworthy; he wouldn't lie."[8]

"But surely that's just an expression," said the mistress of the house gravely, "just the same kind of expression as when we say 'on pins and needles'?"

"It must be so!" affirmed the chairman of the council.

"A city has its customs, a village has its ways," said the archpriest as he stroked his beard.

"Truly!" said the seminary student, who taught in the town school.

"As Cicero says, '*communem consociationem colere, tueri, servare debemus,*' that is, we must serve custom—"

"Just so, sir!" the postmaster interrupted, "but in Mr. Kotzebue's chapter about rugs it says that the 'expounding Cicero himself understands little.'"

"How can you say that!" said the horrified teacher, "Cicero was a Roman orator!"

"Well, sir," answered the postmaster, "he could have done some traveling and visited Paris. I myself would be very interested in having a look at a city where even the tradesmen are knights and have coats of arms."

"How can that be?" exclaimed all.

"Just read Mr. Kotzebue on Paris," answered the postmaster with dignity. "Yes sir," he continued, "but what a depraved philosophy they have in France! Imagine: Napoleon Bonaparte himself quoted to Mr. Kotzebue Voltaire's rule that 'all people are good except those that are boring.' What do you think about that: all people are good except those that are boring!"[9]

"That's terrible!" cried the guests, "All people are good except the boring! Then it follows that the robber and the thief are good because they're not boring."

"Terrible!" everyone repeated but the general indignation was interrupted by the request that one of the young ladies play something on the clavichord.

"But really, I've forgotten how, Nymphodora Mikhailovna."

"Do us the honor, young lady, and entertain my guests," said the mayor's wife. All the guests likewise directed their humble entreaties toward the virtuosa.

"But really, I have forgotten everything!" she repeated.

"Now, now, Sophia! I don't like your putting on airs! One is not taught in order to forget," announced the girl's mother. And Sophia, pouting, sat down at the clavichord. The keys clattered and the strings thrummed; the pedal, which had been adjusted for marches and Turkish music, struck the sounding board like a kettledrum, and the clavichord began to jump about on its folding legs.

The guests, who had surrounded the virtuosa, were amazed at her skill, but the astonishment of many increased to an unbelievable degree when Sophia's right hand crossed over her left and began to play the bass notes.

"That's surely the French variation!" exclaimed the chairman.

"Exactly so," answered Sophia with self-satisfaction. "It's the French quadrille."

"I guessed it!" continued the chairman. "With them everything is backward. Well, why not? Play with the right hand instead of the left, and the left instead of the right."

"Sophia!" came the strict, parental voice of her mother. "How many times have I told you, just play the music and don't cross over with your hands! What stupid showing off! As if one couldn't play in a proper manner!"

Sophia abruptly got up from the clavichord and left the room. Her mother considered it impolite that she hadn't waited for the applause and the expressions of gratitude for her playing; she followed her daughter in order to reprove her and scold her in private, to teach her the manners of society.

Meanwhile, the men took their seats at several tables to play Boston, and the hostess sat down with her guests around the dessert.

The clock struck six. The card tables were marked up with the losses, and the blue cloth on the dessert table was littered with nutshells.

"Gentlemen!" announced the mayor. "It's time for the theater; we can recoup our losses later."

"It's time! It's time!" repeated the ladies. "Do you have the theater announcement? They say the actors are excellent."

"But of course, the impresario presented me with a list of the actors. They will be presenting excellent plays by my selection: *The Virtuous Criminal, or a Criminal for Love*, a drama in three acts, and *Roland the Furious*, a comedy in five acts."

"How interesting! It's time, it's time!" repeated the ladies, impatiently waiting at the door for their carriages.

The Boston players played out their hands, threw in their cards, reckoned their losses, grabbed their hats—in haste a big winner forgot to pay for his cards—and all, on foot or in carriages, headed for the theater.

CHAPTER III

The town in which the events described took place was situated on the bank of the glorious Dniepr[10] and was divided by a deep ravine. The main part of the town was on the high ground and featured a wide square bounded by Jewish taverns, the Polish church, the Orthodox cathedral, and a wooden theater with a shingled roof. Another part of the town was called "beyond the bridge" and contained no noteworthy buildings or decorations except for the public bathhouse, the brewery, and a rendering plant where they turned out the finest dog fur. The third part of the town, "under the hill," was settled by Israel and featured a wooden Jewish school, overgrown with moss and standing in impassable mud among some shacks. The whole town was famous for the beauty of its Jewish women: the Goldas, Rifkas, Rokhlas, Leikas, Ganzas, and Peisas, with their red turbans, their beauty spots, and their hair cascading to their shoulders, conquered regimental hearts.

To this same town came a traveling company of actors, and Mr. Impresario, having paid the penalty to the police for his intention to put on tragedies, comedies, operas, dramas, and melodramas, received permission, to the delight of the public, to make use of the theater that had passed into the town's hands from another troupe of actors who had been driven out of town for having dared to postpone a performance by one day because some members of the cast were ill.

This troupe of actors belonged to a time when the public no longer was summoned to the theater by the beating of snare drums and kettledrums; nor when actors did not dare step onto the stage without first informing the audience about the merits of the play and begging its indulgence; nor when the latter, without a preliminary excerpt or explanation of the play expressed in a prologue, would understand nothing; it did, however, belong to an epoch when vice and virtue would dare not be combined in one and the same character but would struggle separately, against each other, not within the human soul.

The fatal hour arrived: six hours after midday. The theater was lit up with lampions; four Jews with violin, cello, cymbals, and a triangle took their seats in front of the stage. The curtain, bearing the image of Apollo and the nine muses painted with yellow ochre and red lead, wavered in the agitated air. The cast was ready to begin except that the Marquis La Fast—"a criminal for love" as well as the main character—was missing. The King of France, in a black swallow-tailed coat with ribbons and stars and a taffeta mantle bedecked with sequins and tinsel, angrily paced the stage, gave instructions in the wings, repeated his lines from a small notebook, and continually asked everyone if Zaretsky had arrived.

Sophia, "the virtuous criminal," was also expressing concern.

The public was already filling the theater. The mayor and his family had arrived. The orchestra struck up a mazurka, but still there was no Marquis La Fast.

"The devil!" exclaimed the king in despair.

"Lord!" exclaimed Sophia.

"I'm going to get rid of him or I'm no impresario!" exclaimed the king.

"We'll see how you get rid of him! Then I'll leave, too!" exclaimed Sophia.

"What can I do? How can we manage without him?" exclaimed the king.

"They can wait; it's no great misfortune," said Sophia.

"What do you mean, wait?"

"Just that; even in the capitals they have to wait, not just in this provincial hole!"

They wait; but still no Marquis La Fast.

The Jews have already played all the polkas and mazurkas, so they begin again with the *Mazurechka panna.* The spectators, following the example of the mayor's wife, clap their hands and stamp their feet; the mayor sends a constable backstage with an order to begin.

"What the devil can we do?" cries the king once more. "No! He's out, out of the troupe!"

"We shall see!" says Sophia once more. "And I'll take off this costume immediately!"

"What can we do without him? We're finished! What can we tell the public? I won't even be able to find a place for myself in prison!"

The clapping and stamping becomes louder and louder; once more the constable appears and orders that the curtain be raised.

"The devil!" cries the king in despair. "Raise the curtain! Louis d'Or begin; cut out all the scenes with the Marquis La Fast! Begin with scene 3!"

The curtain rises.

The actor playing Louis D'Or runs onto the stage and cries out in a terrible voice: "What have I heard? What have I seen?"

The entire audience begins to applaud; the play goes on without its main hero, goes very well, takes on new meaning, appears to be the prototype of a new school of drama.

The public is pleased. They are enraptured with the acting of Sophia, "the virtuous criminal." They keep shouting "Bravo!" after each monologue, and poor Sophia has to keep reappearing to repeat monologues lasting several pages.

But still no Zaretsky; in the second play he is supposed to be Roland the Furious; they wait—he doesn't appear.

And again the king—who is now Charlemagne—encouraged by the success of the first play, likewise decides to begin *Roland the Furious* without Roland the Furious.

"But where is Roland the Furious?" the spectators begin to ask one another toward the middle of the play, and the mayor sends his messenger backstage to find out.

"Roland the Furious? In absentia," answers the impresario, removing his crown before the police official sent by the mayor.

"What do you mean—in absentia?"

"In absentia, sir, but he will arrive toward the end of the play."

And this answer satisfies the public; they are all awaiting the conclusion of the play with impatience. Sophia is now Angelica, Louis d'Or is a Chinese knight, a sorcerer and a shepherd appear . . . but no one gets any applause; all are awaiting Roland. Charlemagne hears the murmuring of the public. "I'm lost!" he says, throwing off the royal purple and the crown.

Suddenly a noise is heard outside.

"What's going on out there?" asks the mayor.

"Is the doctor here?" asks a voice from outside.

"What is going on out there?" repeats the mayor in a threatening tone.

And all the policemen who are in the theater rush out to discover the reason for the noise. The doctor's servant breaks through the crowd. They seize him by the collar.

"What are you up to, you rogue?"

"Some general is asking for my master, Osip Ivanovich; it's a general who is staying at the treasurer's house," answers the servant breathlessly.

At the same time the police clerk runs up to the mayor.

"Your Excellency!" he whispers, "It seems a new governor general has arrived!"

"Is it possible?" says the mayor in dismay. "What a calamity! How they deceived me! We expected him two weeks from now. Is it really the governor general?"

"Yes, Your Excellency: he has just arrived and demands the presence of the mayor; he seems to be suffering from the effects of the trip."

The mayor rushed out of the theater without saying a word. "The governor! The governor!" was being whispered throughout the theater. At the mention of that name, all the civil servants rose up from their seats and, oblivious to the play, began to bustle about and make their way between the chairs toward the exit.

"I beg your pardon, most honored ladies and gentlemen!" the impresario announced in a pitiful, pleading voice, after having run onto the stage looking desperate. "I beg your indulgence and your forgiveness! I am not to blame because my actor has disappeared."

In the general confusion that ensued as the audience prepared to leave no one paid attention to the words of the impresario, who thought the public had finally guessed there would be no Roland the Furious on stage.

In fact they took the impresario himself to be the Roland who was to appear at the end of the play, and going out of the theater, they applauded and shouted "Bravo!"

The impresario repeated his apology, and the curtain came down.

CHAPTER IV

"The governor general! The governor general!" resounded through the crowd leaving the theater. "The governor general!" echoed through the streets of the town. And the civil servants returned to their homes thinking "the governor general!" and around this thought a web of ideas involving accountability for errors and irregularities was being formed.

The town doctor was also in a state of terror. He never imagined that the governor general might have need of his services; after all he was not touring the provinces to look for medical attention but rather to seek out negligence in the performance of duty.

As a consequence of this thought, the town doctor hurried home to throw off his frock coat, don his uniform, and arm himself with his sword; at the same time he sent for his assistant, waited for him impatiently, cursed him for his slowness, ordered him to compile a list of patients at the town hospital, and, with trepidation, drove to the treasurer's house. As he entered the foyer, he wiped the perspiration from his face and asked the servant if his most high excellency was receiving.

He is led into the reception room. The treasurer and his wife and two daughters meet him, walking on tiptoe, and, in a whisper, they recount the terrible events: how his most high excellency was in a collision and how his most high excellency fell out of a carriage (fortunately near their house); they explain that his most high excellency is badly hurt and is lying unconscious on a couch in the sitting room, and they ask him to go in and examine his most high excellency's injuries.

"How can I do that!" says the doctor. "Enter without a specific order to that effect from his most high excellency! Wouldn't it be better to wait until he regains consciousness and calls for a doctor?"

"What do you mean, Osip Ivanovich? What are you saying? His most high excellency needs immediate medical attention because it happens that his entire head has been reduced to a bloody state from the impact of the fall."

The treasurer's words convinced the doctor to act. Adjusting his uniform and sword, and taking his three-cornered hat in his right hand, he entered the sitting room.

On the sofa lay a middle-aged man with a bloody face and a huge bluish bump on his forehead. He was wearing a frock coat on which three stars shone.

"Feel his most high excellency's pulse, Osip Ivanovich," said the treasurer softly.

The doctor felt his pulse and regained consciousness himself because his most high excellency truly was unconscious.

"What do you think?"

Osip Ivanovich shook his head.

"Shouldn't he be bled?"

"Yes, he should! His most high excellency is unconscious. It wouldn't be a bad idea to send for my assistant."

"You must help him, most honored Osip Ivanovich! Imagine, his most high excellency will consider you and I to be his saviors. If it wasn't for me, he surely would have died from loss of blood. Something like this would have to happen: I was leaving for the theater, and as I came out of the gates, I heard the sound of a carriage and in the distance a shout; from the ground below me I heard someone groaning. What can this mean, I think to myself. Stop! I climb down from my carriage, and what do you think? His most high excellency is lying in a ditch, badly hurt, as you see. The carriage must have tipped over and the horses bolted down the hill, surely right into the Dniepr—"

"It was unusually fortunate," added the treasurer's wife, "that the carriage tipped over when it did, otherwise his most high excellency would surely be in the river—"

"Please do something right away, Osip Ivanovich," the treasurer interrupted. "For saving his life he will place you under his protection."

"I will use all my skill. We will bleed him . . . Have you sent for my assistant?"

"We have! We have!" answered the treasurer's wife and two daughters.

The doctor approached the patient.

"His head is badly hurt! . . . I'm afraid the brain may be damaged," he added importantly.

The assistant arrived. They rolled up the patient's sleeve, stretched out his arm, and tied the sleeve above the elbow; the vein stood out, the lancet pricked, and blood spurted toward the ceiling.

"Oh, unhappy one!" the patient cried out jerking his arm away, "Let me embrace you! . . . We will battle against death!"

"Lord! He's dying!" all the women cried and ran out of the room.

"What? Is there no hope, Osip Ivanovich?"

"We shall see. Help me hold his most high excellency's arm," answered the doctor, and, with the help of the treasurer and the assistant, they stretched out the patient's arm and once more the lancet struck and out spurted a stream of blood.

"A mortal blow!" screamed the patient in his delirium. The doctor jumped back in fear.

"Lord, what have you done!" said the treasurer.

"Corruption has enveloped all my limbs!" the patient continued, stretching out the arm from which blood was streaming.

"All-devouring time will destroy all memory of me! The earth is opening its jaws! Wait! . . . We will destroy the earth with us! . . . It is trembling! . . . Away!"

A convulsive spasm shook the patient; his delirious speech continued for a long time, but his words were drowned out by the chattering of his teeth.

Finally he became silent and fell into complete unconsciousness.

"Is there any hope, Osip Ivanovich?" asked the treasurer.

"We will see what the night offers," answered the doctor.

All night the doctor and the treasurer dozed at the side of the patient. Toward morning he began to stir; a deep sigh escaped from his chest.

"Thank God! He's going to live!" cried the doctor.

"To live!" repeated the patient.

"He's coming to!" said the treasurer, crossing himself.

"My tsar speaks to me, my friend . . . I believe . . . I shall live . . ." said the patient, and he continued incoherently.

"Did you hear that? A friend of the tsar! His most high excellency has come directly from the capital!" whispered the treasurer into the doctor's ear.

Again the patient said something indistinct, and then continued:

"I know, Your Majesty . . . I consider all virtue to lie in that which makes people happy . . . but now . . . Oh, how unhappy I am!"

"Be calm, Your Most High Excellency; Osip Ivanovich will help you. Please do me the honor of considering my house your home—"

"Shsh!" the doctor interrupted. "Don't try to speak with his most high excellency now; he has not yet regained consciousness. Let him be; he seems to have fallen asleep. Meanwhile I'll go home to rest up a bit and prepare the required quinine mixture—oh that's the latest true remedy for all illnesses: it knocks down fevers of all kinds in the wink of an eye, and all illnesses are nothing else but fevers. You yourself can see an example in the case of his most high excellency. The injury itself is nothing but an external inflammation, but he was very badly shaken; we only have to stop this internal trembling and all will be well."

And the doctor left for home. But at the gates he ran into the mayor in his full-dress uniform, hastening to present himself to the governor general.

"Ah! Osip Ivanovich!"

"Where are you going?"

"To report to his most high excellency concerning the prosperity of the town."

"That's impossible!" cried the doctor, "He cannot receive anyone; he has only just now regained consciousness; he had a very bad accident. I have taken all the necessary measures."

"What kind of measures, my dear sir, were taken on your part? As mayor of this town, it is my duty to take all the measures and to be the first one to report to his most high excellency in order to receive instructions."

"As you wish, Mr. Mayor, but I will not be responsible if his most high excellency does not recover!" answered the doctor.

The mayor entered the foyer. The treasurer came out to him on tiptoe.

"Shsh! His most high excellency is asleep."

"I am amazed, Mr. Treasurer," said the mayor sternly, "at the manner in which you dared to offer your house to his most high excellency and to interfere with police functions!"

"But you see," answered the treasurer, "his most high excellency's horses bolted right before my eyes, and I picked him up in front of my house, badly hurt, unconscious—"

"All the worse for you! You had no right to pick up an unconscious man off the street, even less to carry him into your house without the knowledge of the police! It's my business to investigate who is lying in the street unconscious, and, if it's the governor general, to convey him to an appropriate lodging and not to a shack, sir! . . . This is intrigue, my dear sir! You are attempting to subvert authority, you are a troublemaker, sir, you are ignorant of protocol! The governor general is in your house and you dare to walk around in a bathrobe! I shall lodge an official complaint against you, sir! Hey, constable! Report to me immediately as soon as his most high excellency awakens!"

The mayor quickly strode out of the foyer and headed for the police station to get everything in order.

The treasurer was frightened by the mayor's words and began to regret getting involved in someone else's affairs.

The treasurer was a good man, a learned man; in matters of the law he was a real antiquarian and this caused trouble, leading him to quarrel with everyone.

He had read "The Russian Law," the "Charter of Holy Prince Vladimir," and Tsar Ivan Vasilyevich's code of laws, and he knew that the title of treasurer in ancient times was a distinguished one and that at one time the treasurer's chief duty was to maintain the tsar's clothing and safeguard it against witchcraft and sorcery.

He had quarreled with the mayor when he told him that in ancient times town governorships, that is, mayoral appointments, were granted out of royal favor in lieu of salaries and sustenance as a means of support, and that in the petitions for town governorships they used to write "I request that this be granted in order that I may feed myself," and that town governors were formerly "judged together with elders and *tselovalniks* (tavern keepers)."

This last point was taken by the mayor as a mortal insult. He considered it an accusation of insobriety, for the treasurer did not take the trouble to explain the older meaning of the word *tselovalnik* (tax collector).

The treasurer had quarreled with the *stryapchy* (solicitor) of the town council because, when describing to him the ancient office of *stryapchy*—to dress, wash, and comb the tsar and, because there were no pockets in those days, to carry the tsar's handkerchief—he had dared to add that the *stryapchy* was under the authority of the *klyuchnik* (housekeeper).

With his own superior the treasurer was on bad terms because he would not enter into the ledger as official expenses sums spent for unofficial purposes.

Therefore, seeing no advantage in being the fly in the ointment for his superiors and fellow civil servants, the treasurer wanted to petition his most high excellency for a transfer to another town.

CHAPTER V

Meanwhile, the convict performing the duties of police clerk was taken back to the stockade. The cabinets that contained, instead of the dossiers that were lying about on and under the tables, the remains of supper—a chunk of roast beef, crusts of bread, and a bottle of something or other—were cleaned out. The incompletely sobered up police force was turned out for duty. The chief clerk, his nose blue from several blows by his superior, sat down to prepare a report about the prosperity of the town and a list of convicts being held in the stockade. A squad of policemen ran through the town requisitioning workers and carts for cleaning the streets.

From the town council chamber and the other administrative offices all glassware and other paraphernalia not specifically required for the prosecution of civil, criminal, or administrative matters was removed. The judges began to review their past decisions, make backdated entries in their official diaries, and record abstracts in ledger books.

When news about the governor general's arrival reached Lieutenant Colonel Adam Ivanovich, the commander of the district garrison, his heart was gripped with terror.

The reporting soldier stood at respectful attention near the door, hands at his sides, and awaited the commander's orders.

"But didn't our general also accompany him?" the commander of the garrison asked finally.

"I cannot say, your honor, the police messenger didn't say; perhaps he came, perhaps he didn't."

"Have you been to Ivan Ivanovich's?"

"Yes, but his honor was not in his quarters."

"My God! Not in his quarters! What am I to do! . . . Run! Find him! Tell him the garrison commander requests his presence!" cried Adam Ivanovich while pacing the room.

"Yes, sir!"

And the soldier, placing his left hand on his short sword, did a left about-face, stamped his right foot, and was about to leave when the commander's wife, returning from a social call, collided with him in the doorway and stopped his left foot, which was raised to execute a quick march, with the following question:

"What are you doing here?"

"Reporting to his honor!" answered the soldier standing at attention.

"From whom?"

"From the police. His most high excellency has arrived—the governor."

"The governor! Oh my God! What can you be thinking about, Adam Ivanovich! Aren't you the commander? You're supposed to assemble the troops and present them for inspection!"

"But look, my dear, Ivan Ivanovich is on his way; instructions must go through the chain of command."

"Nothing ever gets done without Ivan Ivanovich!" screamed the commander's wife. "That's just the kind of do-nothing commander you are! Whatever a subordinate wants to do, he does! Ivan Ivanovich has you wrapped around his finger! Without asking Ivan Ivanovich, a soldier won't even carry the slops out of my kitchen, not to mention doing work around the place! Well, sir? . . . Why aren't you yourself running to Ivan Ivanovich? Shall I wait and see how you pull on your old worn-out uniform? In twenty years of service you haven't been able to save enough for decent clothing for either yourself or your wife!"

The commander's wife did not stop talking until the arrival of Ivan Ivanovich.

Ivan Ivanovich, a dashing lieutenant of about forty, in a faded green uniform trimmed with a pair of drooping epaulets with worn leather borders, entered the room. His huge sword knocked against his legs and bumped across the floor. The spine from what had been a black feather was sticking out of his three-cornered hat. His left eye squinted, the left side of his mouth twitched, his sideburns hung down like the shaggy ears of a hunting dog, and his forehead was wrinkled.

"What are your orders?" he pronounced, while inserting the index finger of his right hand between the third and fourth buttons of his tunic.

"Ah, my dear Ivan Ivanovich! You have heard that the governor general has arrived? We must take the necessary measures and issue orders to the troops."

"Of course, sir, since in the event of the arrival of his most high excellency, the troops may be assembled with full equipment and in prescribed order presented for an inspection which may take place. And also, in the event of the arrival of his most high excellency, an honor guard may be assigned to the house occupied by his most high excellency."

"Quite right, Ivan Ivanovich; therefore you will assign an honor guard."

"And would it not be appropriate to present a report about the well-being of the troops, the number of guard posts, and the number of those on the sick list?"

"Quite right, Ivan Ivanovich. Of course I am required to present a report on the well-being of the troops assigned to my command."

"By the way, Adam Ivanovich, you could report to his most high excellency that the mayor has dared to employ garrison troops without your authorization and has been imprisoning soldiers without your knowledge."

"Yes, yes, Ivan Ivanovich, that's true; on his most high excellency's next visit, I will report about all the abuses committed by the police, but this time we shall only submit a report about the well-being of the troops."

"As you wish, but I would have told the mayor to his face: 'How dare you do such things!' "

"I will tell him, I will! He won't dare!" said Adam Ivanovich pacing the room.

"So then, what's to be done? Do you order the troops to assemble tomorrow on the square?"

"Yes, yes, certainly, on the square with full equipment."

"I'm going to the quartermaster's barracks to order them to clean and polish things up a bit."

"Good, good, Ivan Ivanovich; tell them everything should be in regulation order and cleanliness."

The lieutenant departed and his honor the garrison commander, satisfied with his instructions, filled his heirloom meerschaum pipe with knaster and began to lay out a game of *grande patience.*

CHAPTER VI

Morning arrived. Lieutenant Ivan Ivanovich, wearing a tight cloth sash and with his sword unsheathed, walked around the troop formation straightening out the ranks and waiting for the garrison commander.

Accompanied by an orderly, Adam Ivanovich finally appeared; he was wearing huge boots with spurs, chamois breeches instead of white cloth ones, a pale green tunic with hollow glass buttons, and a yellow standing collar that over time had become a folded down one, a three-cornered hat pushed back on his head, and a light tricolored sash, apparently worn to hold up his stomach. Adam Ivanovich looked like Charles XII of Sweden.

"Greetings, men!" he cried out as he approached the formation.

"Your health, sir!" shouted the soldiers.

"Would you like to conduct a rehearsal of the troops?" said the lieutenant approaching him and saluting.

"A rehearsal, a rehearsal!" said the garrison commander importantly.

"Attention! . . . Look men, don't be nervous; do whatever Adam Ivanovich commands," said the lieutenant addressing the formation.

"You may give the commands, Ivan Ivanovich!"

"What do you wish?" answered the lieutenant while holding his salute.

"Give the commands . . . according to what is required."

"Yes, sir!" answered the lieutenant. "Look men, don't be nervous; carry out whatever I command," he shouted as he turned to the troops.

And the lieutenant assumed his position in front of the formation, put his sword in his scabbard, drew himself up, and opened his mouth.

"Ah-ten-n-n—"

"Adam Ivanovich! What are you doing?" interrupted the ringing voice of the mayor who was galloping about the town getting things in order and who had just stopped in front of the garrison commander. "Please! You have still not posted an honor guard for his most high excellency; you haven't even provided aides and orderlies!"

"I know my duties well!" angrily shouted Adam Ivanovich after the retreating mayor. "Ivan Ivanovich, be so good as to assign an honor guard, aides, and orderlies to his most high excellency."

"All right, men, who should be assigned to the honor guard? Step forward!" commanded the lieutenant.

And the soldiers began to argue among themselves about who should be in the honor guard.

"Wouldn't it be a good idea, Adam Ivanovich, to place two guard posts at the gates for his most high excellency?"

"Certainly, certainly! And don't forget to assign two footmen for his most high excellency's carriage."

"Yes, sir!" answered the lieutenant. Adam Ivanovich, accompanied by the orderlies, set off to report to his most high excellency.

Meanwhile the mayor, all the ranking and serving officials, and the merchants had rushed to the home of the treasurer and were now entering the small reception room on tiptoe. In uniform, with expressions of servile solemnity on their faces, they lined up at the doors of the room in order of seniority, their left hands placed on their swords, and with three fingers of their right hands holding their three-cornered hats in the prescribed manner.

Observing a respectful silence, they looked toward the open doors of the sitting room.

A reception room is like a sector of the solar system in which planets of various magnitude describe their orbits. Bright and swift Mercury moves from the cabinet chamber to the reception room and from the reception room to the cabinet chamber, revolving feverishly near the sun, glowing importantly with reflected light; high-ranking Jupiter, in an embroidered collar up to his ears and with his four satellites, stands with his feet apart and looks down on everyone; distinguished, bald Saturn, having acquired a bright halo through his long service, sits gravely and quietly in a corner of the room; cold Uranus with his blue nose, gloomy and morose, stands in the opposite corner—he is out of favor with the sun (no one looks at him, no one sees him except the observant astronomers and seven pitiful underlings); Mars in his red collar, his fingers inserted behind the button of his tunic, flushed and puffed up, stands with his neck stiffly extended and shifts his eyes from right to left, always ready to snap to attention before the bright eye of his chief. All the other planets and satellites of lesser magnitude, scattered about the room like fixed stars, stand in a respectful pose, looking toward the East and waiting for the sun. He is announced by Lucifer;[11] as he rises, the planets lose their significance, they are no longer visible. It appears there is no one in the room but the sun.

In the treasurer's reception room all this was simpler, more provincial.

But then suddenly the door leading to the sitting room opened; everyone shuddered, drew themselves up . . .

The treasurer came out.

"Shsh!" he said softly. "His most high excellency is not receiving now; he is sleeping."

They all approached the treasurer on tiptoe, surrounded him, and showered him with questions, but his superior, the mayor, having full right to demand his absolute attention, exercised that right by taking his subordinate by the hand and leading him to one side for interrogation.

"Oh, God!" cried a loud voice from the sitting room. The mayor jumped back from the treasurer, the scattered group of officials rearranged itself into ranks, and the treasurer rushed into the sitting room. Next to the bed stood the doctor with a spoonful of medicine that he was about to pour into the patient's mouth.

"She has nearly deprived me of reason and liberty; she is robbing me of the time that I am obliged to devote to the responsibilities placed on me by tsar and country!" said the patient, and he went on muttering unintelligibly. Suddenly he threw back his head, leaped up, and cried out: "What do I see? Is this the home of Sophia? Is this the temple where the divinity of my soul dwells?"

The doctor glanced at the treasurer; the treasurer flushed all over. "I don't understand," he thought, "when could his most high excellency have ever visited us and seen my daughter!"

The mayor, having heard the voice of his most high excellency, could no longer restrain himself. He was thinking: "I am the mayor of this town; it is my duty to report to the governor general—who does the treasurer think he is, going into the room of his most high excellency without being announced!" And he went into the sitting room.

The patient glanced in his direction and shouted, "How dare you!"

"Your Most High Excellency! . . . I am . . . the mayor . . . I have the honor to—"

"Who has dared to deprive me of the most important pleasure in life? Speak!" continued the patient in a threatening voice.

"I cannot say, Your Most High Excellency! . . . I was not informed of your arrival . . . I have lodgings ready for your most high excellency . . . I have been zealously carrying out my duties for six years—"

While the mayor spoke, the treasurer and doctor maintained a respectful pose, staring at the floor; the patient continued to mutter to himself, but suddenly interrupting the mayor, said aloud, "What are you trying to tell me?"

"I have the honor to submit a report concerning the performance of the duties entrusted to me—"

His words were interrupted by the garrison commander. Entering the room in his shako, he approached the sofa with measured tread, saluted, and pronounced loudly, "Your Most High Excellency, I have the honor—"

"Please leave me alone!" the patient cried out in a pleading voice.

Adam Ivanovich fell silent, stepped back, trembling.

"Can they all be against me? Can they all have conspired in my doom? Doom? No!" and with these words he cast a threatening glance at them, tore off his bandage, and launched into a torrent of incoherent words.

The mayor, Adam Ivanovich, the treasurer, and the doctor could not believe their eyes.

"What does this mean?" continued the patient, once again speaking coherently. "They are all following me around and they won't leave me alone for a minute!"

The mayor, Adam Ivanovich, the treasurer, and the doctor, obeying his most high excellency's wishes, left the room, while he continued to speak loudly and angrily.

"Let us go, gentlemen," said the mayor. "His most high excellency has been turned against us. It's all the shenanigans of Mr. Treasurer."

"There's nothing in what you say! Nothing!" repeated the treasurer as they were leaving.

CHAPTER VII

In the treasurer's bedroom a terrible quarrel was taking place between husband and wife.

"That's enough, my dear sir! You are thinking only of *your* daughter while you are ready to consign *mine* to the kitchen, to get her off your hands, to marry her off, even to a policeman. I heard him say the name Angelica with my own ears."

"But my dear, how can you say such a thing! You can ask Osip Ivanovich. I can still hear his most high excellency saying, 'This is the home of my Sophia, my dear Sophia!'"

"Oh, that's you all over! You'd give your last cent as a dowry for your dear Sophia! . . . No, my dear sir, this shall not be!"

"You're speaking like a true stepmother, the devil take you! As for me, it's all the same: Angelica is my daughter too; but then, who knows—"

The treasurer angrily left the room without finishing his sentence.

"Bald-headed devil! You doubt even your own self!" grumbled the treasurer's wife, and she called Angelica.

"Have you been prettying yourself up? That's right! Good; fix that kerchief so it falls down a little lower on the shoulders. Now leave me; tell them that you want to give his most high excellency his medicine."

Angelica was of the Vyatsk breed, pockmarked and portly; after receiving her mother's instructions, she went into the patient's room. He was lying in a state of oblivion, his eyes staring at the ceiling. Angelica tapped on the glass.

The patient looked around, sat up, and fixing his gaze upon her, said,

"I will go to her . . . but would that not arouse suspicion? . . . No! . . . May I ask, Miss, what is disturbing you?"

"Medicine for Your Most High Excellency—"

"But you have lodged a complaint against someone?"

Angelica flushed. "Lord!" she thought, "He must have heard me complaining about Sophia to Mama!"

"No, sir, I wasn't complaining. I'm not angry with anyone."

"If it pleases you, I am ready to offer my services."

"I am not worthy, Your Most High Excellency—"

"Love!" he cried out, turning his head to one side, "now come to my aid!" And he turned to Angelica and continued, "Oh, Miss, do not deny me your favor!"

"What do you wish?"

"I will reveal to you the secret that is oppressing me . . . I am terrified! . . . I would like to reveal my heart to you, but my tongue will not obey my wishes—"

"If you wish to do me the honor . . . my situation—"

"It is not within my power to reveal to you the reason for my alarm . . . It began on that very day when a tragic event took place in this house—"

I wasn't here when Grandmother died; I was with Maria at the fair; only Sister was at home, thought Angelica, and she flushed.

"I saw a divinity whose charms cast me into this misfortune."

"I don't know about that, sir!" answered Angelica angrily. "Perhaps my sister Sophia—"

"At least it is within your power to allow me to gaze upon her for the last time!" said the patient staring fixedly at her.

"Excuse me sir!" Angelica cried out, and after curtseying with a scornful smile ran out of the room.

"It's terrible!" she shouted after slamming the door. "He wants me to arrange a rendezvous for him with Sophia."

"There you see, my dear," said the treasurer entering the room. "Didn't I tell you?"

"I'm very glad, my dear sir, that you have introduced your daughter into higher circles; she will suit anybody!" shouted the treasurer's wife.

Meanwhile, the patient was saying something aloud and the words "and then get me a doctor as soon as possible" were clearly heard.

The treasurer rushed in. "What is Your Most High Excellency's desire?" he said softly.

The patient, leaning back on the pillows and looking at the ceiling, continued, "My weakness is abating—"

"Thank God, Your Most High Excellency!" said the treasurer, clasping his hands and bowing.

The patient went on, "My strength is being restored by a certain hope . . . Of course Sophia is safe. Oh, if only my presentiment were to come true! Almighty Being! What gratitude will I bring to You when I hold in my embrace my most precious Sophia! Hark! I hear her voice!"

"Sophia! Sophia!" shouted the treasurer, running into the bedroom and grabbing Sophia by the hand, "Go, take his most high excellency his medicine!"

Sophia, a good-looking, modest girl with blue eyes still shining from the tears brought on by her stepmother's scolding, was pushed into the patient's room by her father. She stopped and covered her face with her kerchief.

"I am still alive, dear Sophia! Still alive! Do not grieve!" cried the patient stretching out his arms. "Oh, she is in such a frenzy! And it's all out of love for me! . . . Oh my heart is torn with pain and anger!"

"Where do you think you're going, Sophia!" whispered the treasurer trying to hold back his daughter who was trying to flee.

"Please excuse my Sophia, Your Most High Excellency, she is a bit shy."

"Do not be alarmed, my most precious! Life has been granted me . . . Give thanks to Providence! . . ." (Damn! That fool of a prompter is no help . . . How does the rest of it go?)

"Father! Let me go!" cried Sophia, struggling to free herself.

"I am alive," continued the patient, "alive because that's what's most precious to you—"

"Listen you fool!" whispered the treasurer into his daughter's ear.

"And now help me to rise, my dear Sophia! My weakness will not allow me to—"

"Allow me, Your Most High Excellency, to help you up!" And with these words the treasurer lunged forward to help the patient sit up, but Sophia fled from the room.

Sitting up on the sofa, the patient stared at the treasurer and continued to whisper something to himself; suddenly he seized a pillow, lifted it up, and shouted, "So! Or perhaps you, barbarian, have come here to finish your foul deed?"

"Your Most High Excellency! Most gracious sovereign! . . . I have done nothing—" said the treasurer, shaking like a leaf.

"And where is the Sovereign?"

"It's not for us small fry, but for Your Most High Excellency to know such things," answered the treasurer, bowing respectfully.

"How can it be that the Sovereign has given you power over me?" The patient was shouting again.

"I wouldn't dare even think such a thing, Your Most High Excellency, I am a man who carries out orders, the mayor is in charge of everything—"

"I shall go to him immediately!" shouted the patient, and suddenly leaped up from the sofa, threw his coat over his left shoulder (his arm had been removed from the sleeve for the bloodletting), grabbed the treasurer's hat, and rapidly strode out of the room. In the foyer the servants jumped to their feet, the messengers and the orderlies came to attention; at the gates, the sentries presented arms and the signalman flashed the sign to the guard post nearby on the square.

Striding rapidly down the street, his most high excellency headed for the square.

CHAPTER VIII

Meanwhile, in the town the administrative activity was remarkable; the precision was wonderful, the orderliness exemplary. In everyone there was a zeal worthy of the attention of higher authority: in the council chambers and in the courtrooms all were in proper uniform and wearing swords; regulations came to life—before Peter the Great's symbol of justice[12] truth and righteousness were being dispensed according to the law and cases were being discussed and decided, rather than yesterday's gossip. In the town hospital doctors were taking the pulse of each patient and their prescriptions were no longer the same for all sicknesses, nor was the diet the same for everyone. The garrison troops were drilling on the square, policemen were all at their posts, and the mayor was busily signing reports, referrals, memoranda, housing assignments, and orders consigning prisoners to exile. His work was interrupted by the theater impresario who came in bowing deeply.

"Greetings, my friend! What's this? A new theater announcement?"

"By no means, Your Excellency; it's a small petition."

"Ivanov! Take this and read it!" ordered the mayor as he continued to sign papers. The chief clerk began to read: "Entitled a petition on behalf of the free citizen Yakim Kozyrin, son of Prokhor, and concerning which the following items pertain: Item 1. Being an actor by trade and having become a director, that is to say, the manager of a traveling company, I have presented on stage various productions, to wit, comedies, operas, and tragedies, to the public's complete enjoyment at fairs and in the provincial cities of the Russian Empire, having obtained in every case permission from the local authorities, at my own expense with various scenery and costumes. Item 2. Last year at the Rostov fair there entered into the troop under my direction the citizen Cornelius Zaretsky, son of Ivan, with the purpose, as agreed to by contract, to subsist at my expense and play tragic roles, and, when the need arose, comic ones as well, and in the case of the absence or sickness of an operatic artist in the troop—the retired bass from the cathedral choir—he, that is, Zaretsky, would also sing. In spite of this, he, that is, Zaretsky, on arriving in this town, has absented himself from his duties and has taken from me, the owner, various costumes, to wit, a pair of velvet trousers, a frock coat of blue cloth with red woolen lining and three stars on it made of foil and sewn with gold thread, a green silk waistcoat, and, in addition, took, in advance, a sum of money in the amount of 120 rubles, which I request the police to seek out and, proceeding according to law, return the abovenamed items and money to me. To be delivered to the town police authorities. This petition was composed and copied from the words of the petitioner by the petitioner himself. To which petition is affixed the signature of . . . etc."

"But, my friend, you didn't say in the petition how old the man is, what distinguishing marks he has, whether he is married or single, and where he is registered as a citizen! These things are essential to the police; from this information we would compose an official inquiry on him and send it to that town."

"Your Excellency! Here is his passport."

"Doesn't matter, my friend," said the mayor, continuing to sign papers. "It all has to be included in the petition. You see, my friend, rather than drawing up and copying out petitions yourself, you'd be better off going to someone who knows how it's done."

"Let me write it for you," said the chief clerk. "It'll only cost you a trifle."

Suddenly a commotion was heard in the street.

"Find out what's going on out there!" shouted the mayor as he continued to sign papers.

A constable and some patrolmen rushed out and did not return: curiosity and duty drew them after the crowd of people rushing toward the square and crowding around a stranger in a three-cornered hat. Only his flashing eyes and gesticulating hands could be seen. In a terrible, frenzied voice he was declaiming:

"Magnificent city! . . . What grandeur to rule over it, to shine above it like the majestic day! . . . To plunge all boiling passions, all unsatisfied desires, into that bottomless ocean! . . . An abyss! . . . Fling into it all that man holds dear! Conquerors, cast down your victories! Artists, your immortal works! Epicureans, your love of pleasure! Discoverers, your seas and islands! . . . Oh Doge! . . . What sort of bliss is it to stand on that terribly exalted pinnacle, to look down into those stormy depths where the wheel of the blind deceiver spins out human events! What rapture to drink first from the cup of joy! . . . What magnificence to restrain the rebellious passions of people with a slender bridle, to turn the inflated pride of a vassal to dust with one breath! . . . Break down the thunder into simple sounds and you can put children to sleep with them; pour them together into one sudden bolt and the majestic sound will shake the universe!"[13]

"Your Excellency! Your Excellency!" shouted the returning police clerk breathlessly, "There's a terrible disturbance in the town; some hothead is raising a row in the square—"

"What!" shouted the mayor as he grabbed his hat and sword from the table. "Call out the entire force! . . . Tell the garrison commander to march his troops to the square! . . . Follow me! . . ." And with these words the mayor rushed out like one possessed.

Meanwhile, the stranger continued: "Is it possible that I, I, Fiesco, could have killed my own wife! . . . Oh, I curse you! Do not look like pale apparitions upon this game of nature! I thank Thee, Almighty God! There are things that cannot frighten a man because he is a man! . . . Is it to be the fate of the one who is denied divine ecstasy to suffer the torments of the devil?"[14]

"That's him! That's him!" shouted a voice in the crowd standing around him with their hats in their hands.

"That's him! He killed his wife!"

"Silence! . . . Where are you going?" continued the stranger as he grabbed a frightened, retreating Jew by the collar and flung him back into the crowd.

"Seize him! Seize him!" a police official shouted as he made his way through the crowd.

"May your tongue turn into a crocodile!" roared the stranger, hurling himself at the police official, "Begone to the bottomless inferno!"

The police official cringed, respectfully fell silent, and came to attention; it was not the stranger who frightened him, but the three stars shining on his chest.

"Seize him! Seize him!" came the mayor's breathless voice from a distance. But the crowd had surged back from the stranger, who grinding his teeth was shouting, "Avaunt! Avaunt, human countenances! Oh, if all creation were to fall between my jaws! Oh, Man! . . . With what joy does this vile creature stand up and thank the gods that he does not share my fate!" continued the stranger while pointing at a law clerk, who having pushed through the crowd had just appeared in front of him. "Upon me alone all the fury of hell has fallen! . . . Brother!" he continued in a pitiful voice while striking a tattered and barefoot Jew on the shoulder, "I thank Thee, Almighty God, that yet another is struck down by that thunder!"

"Zaretsky!" a new voice rang out in the crowd. It was the theater impresario. "It's him! It's him!" he shouted, making his way through the mob and seizing the stranger. "He's drunk! I recognized him by the soliloquy from Fiesco! A fine place to declaim speeches! . . . Here's my costume and my stars! A good thing he didn't pawn them for drink!"

The policemen, jolted out of their trance by the impresario's words, swarmed all over Zaretsky.

"Tie his hands behind his back!" shouted the mayor triumphantly. "Take him to the police station for questioning!"

The unfortunate Zaretsky was led away. His incoherent, disjointed words, spoken with eyes flashing, could no longer be heard above the noise of the crowd that was following him.

CHAPTER IX

Poor Zaretsky was brought to the police station. A crowd of people had surrounded the building; they were very noisy and were shouting, pushing, and shoving. The mayor took his seat and gave orders for the criminal to be brought in and for the chief clerk to prepare to record the interrogation. Two patrolmen led Zaretsky in; behind him came the theater impresario.

MAYOR: Your name?

ZARETSKY *(aside):* Oh, my God! A mistake! And on stage during the performance! He's supposed to say, "Your name, sir?" *To the mayor:* Konrad of Turin.

IMPRESARIO: He's drunk . . . Your Excellency, he's repeating his lines from the drama *The Free Judges.*[15]

MAYOR: Shsh! No one is to interrupt my words! Your rank?

ZARETSKY: Baron of the Empire and member of this tribunal.

MAYOR: What? New tricks? So be it! *To the chief clerk:* Write it down. *To Zaretsky:* Why did you come to this town?

ZARETSKY *(aside):* Lord! He doesn't know his part. He's even getting me mixed up! *To the mayor:* To defend my innocence and take up my post!

MAYOR: I'll give you innocence! You, my friend, will take up your post in prison!

ZARETSKY *(aside):* The devil knows what he's saying! They've given a fool the part of the free judge! *To the mayor:* What is my crime?

MAYOR: What? What is your crime? You can't deny it my friend! The whole town witnessed it . . . Tell us how and for what purpose you and Mr. Treasurer conspired to have you play the role of the governor general! Well?

ZARETSKY *(aside):* He's talking nonsense! Me play the governor general? *To the mayor:* Where, then, is my accuser?

IMPRESARIO: But Your Excellency, in his drunken state he's reciting the parts he has played in the theater.

MAYOR: Shsh! All the better, for what the sober man has on his mind, the drunk has on his tongue. *To Zaretsky:* Answer the question: for what purpose? Ah? Wasn't it to rob the treasury and make off together? . . . Oh . . . Yes! I almost forgot. *To the policemen:* Please proceed immediately, without the slightest delay, to arrest the treasurer. If he gets away, you will be responsible. Do you understand? *To Zaretsky:* Well, tell us, for what purpose? Well?

ZARETSKY *(aside):* That's not the way it goes! *To the mayor with surprise:* What sound in your voice!

MAYOR: Speak! What have you got to say?

ZARETSKY: That this is too noble a tribunal to be punishing delusions or laying snares.

MAYOR: Snares! What impudence!—

ZARETSKY *(interrupting):* Yes snares! All Germany knows of the ties of friendship, family—

MAYOR *(interrupting):* Ties of friendship and family! Aha! At last! *To the clerk:* Write: "Ties of friendship and family!" Write it down! So that's it! Now everything is clear!

ZARETSKY *(angrily aside):* He's spoiling it, he's ruining it! He didn't let me finish!

MAYOR: And what did the treasurer promise you for this?

ZARETSKY *(aside):* Instead of "Did you promise that?" the devil knows what he is saying! *To the mayor:* And I have kept my word; he was my friend—

IMPRESARIO: But Your Excellency, he's reciting his lines from *The Free Judges!*

MAYOR: Shsh! Silence! I'm not a free judge but a government one!

ZARETSKY *(continuing):* . . . my guest, but I drove him away; he stretched forth his hand to me, but I destroyed him—

MAYOR *(interrupting):* A belated repentance!

ZARETSKY *(aside):* He's completely mixed up! How does it go? Oh, yes! *To the mayor:* Must he die twice, twice endure the ordeal of death? No matter who you may be . . . if this is your verdict, then you have the heart of a cannibal! *Lunges at the mayor.*

MAYOR *(jumping up in terror):* He'll kill me! Seize him! He'll kill me! . . . Clap him in irons! Drag him off to prison! Put him in fetters! . . .

IMPRESARIO: Your Excellency! He's drunk; he's acting this way because he's drunk. Please listen, he's not speaking his own words; it's a role—

MAYOR: A yoke around his neck! And tomorrow bring him here in irons for a second interrogation and a personal confrontation with the treasurer! Banditry in broad daylight!

CHAPTER X. CONCLUSION

The "virtuous criminal" secretly visits Zaretsky in prison. Finding him delirious, she throws herself into his arms and, in the voice of Angelica, cries out, "Roland! Look upon my grief for you! . . . Be at peace, my darling!"

And he answers, "Greetings, greetings, noble daughter of savage Sacripant,[16] greetings! . . . What! Have you run away alone from your father?"

Seeing there's no hope for restoring any reason to poor Roland-Zaretsky, she says sadly in the voice of Angelica, "Unhappy one!" and quickly leaves the prison in order not to be late for rehearsal.

When rumors about these events reached the real governor general, he laughed heartily over them and then ordered Roland-Zaretsky moved from the prison to an insane asylum, and the treasurer transferred to another town.

Until this day, whenever the treasurer's wife quarrels with her husband, she tells him to go and see his son-in-law in the crazy house in Moscow; while Zaretsky unceasingly declaims his lines. First he imagines himself to be the ambitious Fiesco laying his criminal hands upon Gianettino, beating the wall with his fist, cursing his fate over the body of Rosabella;[17] then, throwing himself into the sea, he falls out of bed to the floor unconscious. Then suddenly regaining consciousness, he is the Marquis La Fast and is pledging his love to Sophia; next he is defending his innocence and his rights as an imperial baron before the Free Tribunal. But in the role of Roland the Furious he outdoes himself: all the madmen in his ward forget their manias—the musician stops playing on his invisible keys, the hallucinator forgets to grasp by their tails the devils who are sitting on his nose, the poet drops his imaginary pen, the orator stops trying to cough up the word that has become lodged in his throat—and all attentively, silently, their mouths gaping open, marvel at the frenzied art of Zaretsky.

Travel Impressions and, among Other Things, a Pot of Geraniums

A Story in the Form of a Tale

BEGINNING WITH THE END of June a heat wave had set in Moscow. No one could recall such hot weather; the air hovered over the iron roofs like white fire; you could have poured water on the white-hot stones of the pavement just as though you were in a bath house—everywhere you looked it was like a huge Russian bath—without the exit to the dressing room, where you could go to cool off. It was impossible to breathe; your insides melted.

A week went by, then two, there was no mercy; the sky remained clear, only rarely appearing to be covered over so that you would think to yourself, "Look, a life-giving cloud, there will be a fresh breeze!" It was nothing of the sort, just dust churned up by a whirlwind, and once having been churned up, it now stood motionless.

Alexander Fyodorovich's friend, Sergei Fyodorovich, was the best indicator of the heat's intensity. He had become accustomed to temperatures of 118 degrees in the Transcaucasus region, and Russian heat waves of more than 70 degrees seemed to him barely above freezing when compared to temperatures in the Caucasus. During all his previous summers in Moscow he had felt refreshed, but this summer, at the beginning of July, he suddenly said, "It's hot!" He removed his Persian silk shirt, took off his deerskin jacket, and decided to go without his summer overcoat.

"It's bad, a bad sign," thought Alexander Fyodorovich, and he made up his mind to leave white-hot Moscow for cool Petersburg. With this happy thought in mind, he immediately set out for the posting station.

This story was first published in the journal *Syn otechestva*, no. 1 (1840): 35–84. It later appeared in a collection of Veltman's stories that came out in 1843. (A. F. Vel'tman, *Povesti* [St. Peterburg: M. D. Ol'khin, 1843]). The translation is based on the latter edition.

"Is there any space available for tomorrow?"

"There is on number 8."

"Is that a four-seater?"

"A four-seater, but there is one other person going with you—a maiden."

"A maiden! What rotten luck! Well, nothing can be done. Sign me up."

More than likely a foreigner, thought Alexander Fyodorovich as he left the office, for a Russian maiden, even one bent over by the weight of years, would never, not for anything in the world, consider spending three days and three nights alone with a man she knew, not to mention a stranger. That would trouble her for the rest of her life, cause her to blush every time the post was mentioned in conversation. No, we don't care for ambiguous situations, and it is well that we don't. Thus our patriarchal ways: there can be no purity where there is even a shadow of a doubt. In such cases people will immediately say: "It's a bad sheep that goes off alone in the forest; she's not God's victim, but the wolf's."

Having assumed that his traveling companion was definitely a foreigner, Alexander Fyodorovich appeared the next day at the posting station with his suitcase. While they weighed and loaded the baggage, he strolled about the office and the yard, occasionally going outside the gate, awaiting the arrival of the foreign maiden. Alexander Fyodorovich imagined that she would surely arrive in a cab, that she would be wearing a hat of coarse cambric covered with a green veil, and have on a linen or a calico dress with a wide flounce and an apron or *tablier* with pockets. In one hand she would be carrying a large umbrella *à la Taglioni,*[1] and in the other a huge handbag *à la meshok.*[2]

In impatient expectation, Alexander Fyodorovich sat down on a curbstone in order to divert himself with some sort of impressions, and, in accordance with the requirements of the times, investigate some aspect of life. He turned his observant eye to the left, along the side street, and in the distance, near the Myasnitsky Gates, sought some object worthy of attention. Suddenly, quite near him, a voice rang out, "Please, your honor, help the victims of a fire!" It was a young peasant woman in a white smock with a baby in her arms.

"Where did you come from, my dear?" asked Alexander Fyodorovich, giving her a ten-kopeck piece.

"From a long way off, your honor."

"Have you been in Moscow long?"

"We have just arrived, and we don't know how to get to the square. Lord, what a great city—you can't tell which is a house and which is a church; you just keep going along and crossing yourself."

Alexander Fyodorovich wanted to laugh at this rustic simplicity, but he recalled that the times demanded we laugh at nothing and express pity for everything. Fortunately the conductor announced that everything was ready and requested the passengers to take their seats. Alexander Fyodorovich made his way up the iron steps of the so-called French *diligence,* entered the rear door, and sat down in the stuffy passenger compartment still wondering about his fellow voyager.

"Madame, would you please take your seat?" shouted the conductor to a woman sitting on the porch. Alexander Fyodorovich had paid no attention to her, taking her for a person who had some connection with the office.

"Right away, my good man," she said, and picking up a little bundle and a huge flowerpot from the bench, she came up to the coach.

"Hold this, dearie, while I climb in."

"Really, Madame, do you plan to take this flowerpot with you?" said the conductor.

"Am I supposed to leave it with you?"

"What would I want with it? I'd just heave it out."

"Heave out your own property, and we'll take care of ours," she said, and with difficulty clambered up into the coach, dragging behind her a geranium plant whose many branches were supported by wooden stakes.

"So this is the foreign maiden," thought Alexander Fyodorovich, looking over his fellow voyager from the coarse locks under her cap to the well-worn shoe on an enormous Saxon foot with its very prominent big toe. She was thin, bony, and wrapped in ten square yards of modest calico, the bodice *décolleté.* Her age was difficult to determine, although under her cap it could be seen that her plait was no longer than a mouse's tail and that it was already time to trim her grenadier's mustache.

"Are you going to 'Petey'?" she asked, sitting there holding the pot of geraniums on her knees with both hands.

"To 'Petey,'" answered Alexander Fyodorovich.

"Lord have mercy on us!" she pronounced when the stage started to move; she would have crossed herself, but the stage had begun to bounce over the pavement in such a way that her head was hitting the roof and the pot was jumping around so much she couldn't take a hand off it.

"Oh, it's the devil's own carriage!" cried Alexander Fyodorovich's traveling companion, while for his part, he could not but marvel at the stupidity of her attempting to take along a pot of flowers.

When the coach came to a stop at the toll gate at the city limits, it was immediately surrounded by peasant women and young boys carrying rolls which they began to thrust insistently through the windows and into the hands of the passengers, shouting: "Hot rolls! Sir, Madame, buy some for the trip!"

The coach was now rolling smoothly along the highroad, and Alexander Fyodorovich's companion had calmed down a bit.

Alexander Fyodorovich was wearing his hair in the latest fashion, *à la moujik,* and he had on a conservative summer jacket. In the words of

Pushkin, "a dozing overcame him," thus permitting the modest maiden to inspect her traveling companion and draw both favorable and unfavorable conclusions.

"Ugh! What impossible heat!" he cried, when he had awakened from his reverie, weak and sweating as if he had just stepped out of a steam bath.

"Terrible heat!" pronounced his honorable traveling companion, assuming that Alexander Fyodorovich's complaint was addressed to her. After this courteous attention, probably wishing to find out whether her traveling companion was worthy of the honor, she turned to him and asked, "With your permission, Sir, what might your rank be?"

A bird is recognized by his flight, a human by his questions.

"I am a *raznochinets*,[3] Madame; I do not have the honor of knowing your name," answered Alexander Fyodorovich.

"Minodora Pamfilovna."

"Minodora Pamfilovna," repeated Alexander Fyodorovich.

"And what trade do you pursue?"

"Literature."

"Do you have your own factory?"

"Of course."

"What sort of product do you make? I've heard something about it, but I don't know exactly."

"We make poetry and prose."

"What sort of material is that? Something new, French no doubt."

"Paper[4] material, motley and striped."

"But surely that's simply cheap Russian homespun cloth. What's it used for?"

"Poetry now has no use at all; it's not selling, it's gone out of fashion, anyone can make it by hand, and it's used for wrapping."

"It's not worth it, my dear sir. You'd be better off in some other trade."

"I don't know anything other than reading and writing."

"Glory be! What could be better! Become a government clerk."

"I don't know how to write in the official style; there everything is written in a special way."

"You're no hand at curlicues? But sir, you'll learn, they'll teach you. And what people! I saw them for the first time when they came to inventory my late father's goods—may God spare me from ever going through that again! They left us nothing but the clothes on our backs! Turned us out like beggars!"

And here the maiden Minodora Pamfilovna began to sigh deeply, almost to the point of tears.

"Why did they have to inventory your goods?"

"Who knows? Somehow, you see, papers were served on my late father—as though he had mortgaged everything, everything: twenty souls, the house, all mortgaged! They themselves, of course, had mortgaged their souls to the devil!—God forgive me. Please hold this," continued Minodora Pamfilovna, handing the pot of geraniums to Alexander Fyodorovich. Obeying the accustomed impulse to be of assistance, he took the huge pot from her hands, feeling certain she was transferring her precious burden to him only for a moment. But Minodora Pamfilovna was untying a little bundle containing white bread, caviar, and a few rags; she covered her face with a handkerchief and, shedding bitter tears, began to complain about her fate.

Meanwhile, the pot of geraniums was weighing heavily on the arms of Alexander Fyodorovich.

"Do you wish to take this back?" he said, handing the pot to her when it seemed she had calmed down. "I'm afraid I might damage your flowers."

"Oh, don't worry about that—you hold them—you're doing a good job."

"Excuse me, but your flowers are making my arms tired," said Alexander Fyodorovich, and he placed the pot at her feet.

"Oh, my God!" screamed Minodora Pamfilovna angrily. "It really is heavy! If you put it on the ground it would shake the whole earth! As for me, I'd rather have my soul shaken out of this cursed carriage!"

"What expensive flowers!" said Alexander Fyodorovich.

"Yes, they weren't cheap."

"Please let me have them: in Petersburg I'll give you a dozen pots in place of them."

"How kind of you! Imagine, a dozen!"

"Even a hundred if it pleases you, only let me throw this trash out, because during the night those stakes are liable to put out your eyes and mine."

"Well now, such lavish generosity I humbly thank you! Well, I have no need of other people's goods—it may be trash, but it's mine. What's a person to do! How is one to put up with this! There was a time when a person would have considered it an honor to be of service, and not just in such trifling matters. He would have considered it his good fortune that he was being spoken to! To trash everything is trash . . . but a well-brought-up man shows respect to ladies . . . observes the amenities . . . knows how to behave . . ."

These and other refined admonitions to Alexander Fyodorovich would have continued for a long time, but the coach had come to a stop and the conductor, having opened the door, inquired, "Will you be dining here?"

"It wouldn't be a bad idea to grab something," said Alexander Fyodorovich. "We've covered thirty versts—and it's been over four hours!"

About twenty people had climbed out of the three coaches that had pulled up at the inn. The whole company of travelers, cursing the heat, crowded into the anteroom, or, if you will, the common room of the inn where a round table was set. One traveler with a pipe, another with a bundle of provisions, a third with a bottle of Madeira for the road were sitting at the hospitable table; others were relaxing on a sofa that was stained to look like mahogany and covered with coarse woolen cloth. A robust lady with two rather robust daughters of marriageable age climbed out of the two-seater in which they had been riding along with their cushions, bundles, manteaux, and various traveling supplies, and ordered cutlets. Two German *jüngermanner* ordered a bottle of light Berlin beer; a Frenchman, who was taking his elderly sick wife back to Paris in order to remedy the ravages wrought by the Russian climate, ordered a portion of soup and a pitcher of water; a merchant from Rybinsk ordered them to serve him up a bottle of kvass, but since they had no good, simple kvass, agreed to a bottle of murky liquid that went by the name of carbonated kvass and was foaming from the raisins that had been put into it. Two merchants' sons decided to treat themselves to Kronoff honey; all the remaining assortment of people shouted with one voice, "Beefsteak! A half portion of tea! A glass of vodka!" At the same time, the tavern opposite the inn was also full of people demanding portions and half-portions of tea. Here, Russian peasant lads in colorful calico shirts and white aprons were quickly filling teapots from the continually boiling samovars. But things were different in the inn: here, a long beanpole of a servant in a frock coat with a food-stained sash and a dirty apron was having difficulty repeating the words, "Right away!" not to mention filling the orders of the travelers who had poured in. He was especially attentive to a certain burly landowner who, above all the other voices, loudly sounded a full chord: "Dinner!" This word expressed the dignity, the importance, and the prosperity of the traveler, whereas the demand for a bowl of soup or a slice of roast with cucumbers indicated a man on a small budget who only needed "a bite to eat" to be satisfied. When the beanpole finally had finished racing "hither and thither" and all had sampled the culinary productions of the establishment, each one pulled a long face, grimaced, swore, took another bite, spat, and asked, "How much?" The tall servant meekly announced either the fixed or the variable tariff and began to collect the money. "What!" shouted one young man, who had hoped to avoid buying dinner by ordering a glass of milk. "What! Twenty kopecks for a glass of milk in the country!"

"And why not, sir?" answered the servant-beanpole. "We sell one glass, but ten pitchers turn sour."

"It's terrible! I'm going to complain! . . . It's robbery!" repeated the young man.

"As you please," said the servant.

In the meantime some sort of beggar standing in the doorway, turning his eyes on everyone, in a pitiful voice produced the following sounds to which no one paid any attention: "*Mein bester Herr, mein gnädiger Herr! Ihre Excellenz, Herr Graf!* Please give something for the road to a poor man with a family . . ."

As soon as Alexander Fyodorovich got out the door, he was met on the porch by new demands from the peasant women who had surrounded him:

"Please, sir, buy these remaining soft-boiled eggs!"

"That's enough, Karpovna, the gentleman would prefer to buy a couple of meat patties from me."

"Sir! Buy a basket of strawberries," squeaked some little girls.

"Buy something from me, from an old woman, it'll be both a purchase and a charity."

It was impossible not to buy something.

Squeezing himself through this berry market, Alexander Fyodorovich thought that the coach was ready to go. Nothing of the sort; the other coaches had already left, but near the one in which he had been riding with his fair maiden/traveling companion, one of the drivers was tossing a coin while the others stood around him like addicted gamblers waiting to see who would drive the coach, who would hitch up the three-horse team, and who would tie on the extra horse. The lottery was settled. Then they began to haggle over the hiring of the extra horse; after that a quarrel arose over dividing up the earnings for the trip:

"Uncle Vanya, I'll drive for thirty kopecks."

"You agreed to twenty-five; I won't add a kopeck—I'll drive myself!"

"You're cheating me out of five kopecks!"

"How can you say that?"

"Yes, you're cheating me! Hand them over! Who do you think you are in that fancy shirt? We wear homespun, but at least it's our own."

After interminable wrangling the horses were finally hitched up, and Alexander Fyodorovich climbed into the coach. Minodora Pamfilovna had been listening to a conversation between the Frenchman and his wife.

"Tell me please," she asked, "what language could that be that they're speaking? I can't make head or tail of it."

"They are French."

"French? Actually real live Frenchmen? I've never in my life seen real Frenchmen . . . In Moscow I once asked to be taken to Kuznetsky Bridge[5] to have a look at them, but I never got to do it. But this is what I'd like to know: Do the French still have that same Napoleon who was in Moscow or is there another one?"

"Another one," replied Alexander Fyodorovich, without even smiling.

"And what happened to the first one?"

"He died, as is the custom."

"They used to say he was the Antichrist and that he would live three hundred years . . . Imagine, such stupid people! And they also said that when the time of the Antichrist was upon us, people would not die until the Second Coming."

"Heaven forbid! To live three hundred years! What could one do with so much time on earth?"

"To tell the truth—that is, by way of example—I have neither relatives nor friends, neither kith nor kin; my only care is to water the 'gerany' and break off the dry leaves. God forbid that it should wilt, for then I wouldn't know what to do on this earth!"

As she said this, Minodora Pamfilovna was ready to burst into tears.

"Get yourself another geranium and the grief will pass," said Alexander Fyodorovich.

"Another? . . . Not on your life! I'd rather crawl into my coffin, pretend I'm dead and be buried alive!"

"A most remarkable geranium! Surely it must be an heirloom?"

"An heirloom if you like."

"And all your sweet memories are connected with it?"

"In my life there was nothing sweet," said Minodora Pamfilovna in a mournful tone.

"Then what's so special about it?"

"Oh God—well, it's simply mine, my own property . . . at least it's something that belongs to me."

"Please don't be angry; I am ready to ask your forgiveness for daring to think—"

"Daring to think! Just because we don't have mountains of gold, you dare to think!"

"You have misunderstood me," said Alexander Fyodorovich, and wishing to soothe Minodora Pamfilovna's wounded pride, he continued, "In your time you were no doubt beautiful and charming and had a multitude of admirers—"

"Skirt chasers!" cried out the maiden Minodora Pamfilovna. "What do you mean? That I could have allowed men to chase after me! That some empty-headed fool would dare try to get romantic with me! They start acting tender and winking, and the well-born young lady melts with joy that she has acquired herself a lackey!"

"How stern you are!" said Alexander Fyodorovich. "However, this cold-bloodedness does you honor."

"Where did you get the idea that I had fish blood! All the same, I will never allow myself to be humiliated by a man . . . A well-born young lady must be modest and never show in any way that she loves someone . . . How shameful! Imagine! 'I am helpless, I can't hide it, I love you' . . ."

"But surely you must have been in love, and doubtless were loved in return?"

"A fine question! Are you my confessor or what?"

Paying no attention to Minodora Pamfilovna's remark, Alexander Fyodorovich continued to probe insistently for the secrets of her heart.

"And if you loved and were loved, then there had to have been some means to express this mutual love; it would have been impossible for the one who adored you to hide his feelings—how else could you have known he adored you?"

"For everything there is a refined manner . . ."

Minodora Pamfilovna suddenly seemed to catch herself, realizing she was carrying on an immodest conversation with a strange man about love, and she began to complain about the unbearable heat, the flies, the mosquitoes, and the shaking of the coach which was then riding over a roadbed of crushed stone. But one only had to turn one's attention to these minor torments of the road to begin to take them for extreme torture, especially with a pot of geraniums in your hands. Minodora Pamfilovna's complaints became more and more frequent and finally she turned to Alexander Fyodorovich.

"This is terrible!" she complained, shaking her head to drive away the flies. "Cursed things! And you can't get rid of them . . . What unbearable heat! Foo! Oy! My soul has been shaken loose! . . . Lord! . . . How can they be so determined . . . They have no pity . . . All they care about is themselves . . . Let everybody else perish . . . That God should send such a misfortune! And you're not to raise your hand against a mosquito!"

The complaining and grumbling was followed by moaning. Alexander Fyodorovich understood where all this was leading, but he was in no way disposed to indulge Minodora Pamfilovna. But she kept moaning and sighing until Alexander Fyodorovich could endure it no longer, and shouted, "All right, please, give it to me. I'll hold your geraniums for a while, and you can shake off the flies and mosquitoes—only stop moaning!"

"I thank you most humbly! But I don't accept services that are such a burden to the offerer." And Minodora Pamfilovna went on groaning still more.

"What an impossible old woman!" Alexander Fyodorovich screamed to himself, but said aloud, "Whose fault is it if you yourself have tied a weight around your neck and then complain about it to other people?"

"I'm grateful for the advice, but I'm a little older than you and I don't require it!"

"I didn't dream of giving advice! As the saying goes, the one who acts honorably is spared by God from a loss!"

"Oh, may God forgive me! How heartless I am! I didn't realize you were doing me an honor. I should have acknowledged it with particular gratitude!"

Alexander Fyodorovich did not answer, and it seemed that the good relations between him and his traveling companion—the maiden Minodora Pamfilovna—had ended. Nothing of the sort. For a long time she continued to rail in an undertone against cruel people with hearts of stone and souls of ice; she complained of a splitting headache, that her arms felt as though they had turned to wood, that her whole body was worn out and racked with pain.

And all this was proceeding *crescendo;* suddenly streams of tears burst forth and the sobbing, wailing, and groaning ended with a sudden "Oh, my God, I'm dying! Oh, for God's sake, take this for a minute!"

Frightened, Alexander Fyodorovich snatched the pot from the hands of his exhausted traveling companion, and she collapsed in the corner of the carriage; under her cap her head drooped like a wilted lily and her arms hung down like ivy.

Fortunately for Alexander Fyodorovich, the coach had just stopped at an inn. "You should get out, rest, and drink some tea," he said with sympathy.

"Whatever gave you the idea that I would go into a tavern?" answered Minodora Pamfilovna, her head raised proudly.

"Crazy woman!" thought Alexander Fyodorovich, climbing out of the coach and following the others to the inn for a "spot of tea."

At the very moment when the horses were ready to depart and all had taken their seats, a light carriage pulled by three lathered horses rushed up and stopped in front of the inn.

"Well, did we catch them?" the driver asked a merchant who was climbing out of the carriage with difficulty.

"We caught them!" he answered, hardly moving his tongue and blinking his puffy eyes.

This was one of their fellow passengers, Ilya Fedoseyevich or Kuzma Tikhonovich, God knows which. At the last station he had wandered off somewhere and, in accordance with the post regulations, no one had noticed he was missing and he was left behind, eminently safe and sound. He was, however, hard to miss. Fleshy, less than five feet tall, and dressed in a frock coat, he sported a beard at least half a yard long and had had his hair trimmed using a bowl. When the coach had stopped at the previous station, all the passengers had headed for the inn on the right, but he had climbed out, hatless, and headed straight for the cook-shop on the left, where he was in his element. The conductor shouts "All aboard!" but Ilya Tikhonych or Kuzma Fedoseyich—God knows which—doesn't dream of hurrying but plods along at his own pace, heavily placing his unsteady legs before him one after the other in order not to veer to one side.

"Who is that drunken old man?"

"That drunken old man is worth 300,000 rubles."

"Oho!" said Alexander Fyodorovich as he took his seat in the coach for the further torture of listening to the groaning of the accompanying damsel of his dreams.

It was already dark; Alexander Fyodorovich tilted his hat down over his eyes and, curling up in the corner of the carriage, prepared to go to sleep. Nothing of the sort—it was quiet at first, but suddenly there were groans.

"Would you be so kind as to stop groaning? It seems there are no flies now nor is the heat unbearable, and the road is rather smooth."

"I would be pleased not to groan, but I can't stand it! My feet have swelled up, my corns ache like the plague—it means a sure change in the weather—and my cursed shoes are too tight!"

"What's stopping you from taking off your shoes?"

"What do you mean! How shameful! Not for anything would I take such a disgrace upon myself!"

"Disgrace? What disgrace?" repeated Alexander Fyodorovich irritably.

"That I should remove my shoes in the presence of a man!"

"May you and your maidenly modesty go to the devil!" thought Alexander Fyodorovich, burying his head in his pillow. He was vainly rolling a hoop in front of him while trying to forget himself in sleep. Before his eyes whirled the groaning Minodora Pamfilovna and the green geranium leaves. The more he tried not to think about that insufferable person, the less this allopathy helped. It was necessary to apply the rule of homeopathy:[6] *similia similibus curantur.* He began to think about Minodora Pamfilovna and to speculate: "What sort of mysterious connection can there be between her and the pot of geraniums? Is it possible that a heart can so passionately love an inanimate object, cherish and coddle it like her own child? No, it's not possible; the inanimate object would have to have its own language, a language understandable only to the one who has secretly entered into friendship with it, caressed it, cared for it . . . But then Minodora Pamfilovna's geranium probably does talk to her about something and somebody, occupies her, amuses her with stories about the past, vouches to her for someone's heart as a pledge . . . Otherwise Minodora Pamfilovna would not love the geranium, except, perhaps, if it produced, instead of leaves, interest on some sort of capital . . ."

Reasoning to himself in this way, Alexander Fyodorovich gradually reconciled himself to his traveling companion; for the first time he became interested in knowing her life story, but sleep overcame him.

When morning came the stage had arrived at Tver. Alexander Fyodorovich went into the inn and ordered tea. He was concerned about his companion, who, it can be said, had neither eaten nor drunk anything for the whole trip. After pouring a glass of tea, he took it out to her in the coach, almost certain she would refuse this offer of refreshment. But he was mistaken; her eyes lit up with joy when he said to her, "Would you like to take some tea?" Extending her lips forward in anticipation, she savored the salutary decoction, the medicinal drink, the subtle opiate that dulls the spirit and produces throughout the whole body a *chinaism* or numbing of the senses.

"Well, how grateful to you I am!" said Minodora Pamfilovna. "It relieved my soul! I never thought they would have such good tea here."

"The best!" said Alexander Fyodorovich. "Genuine Koporsky."

"It's very aromatic, probably made with herbs."

Alexander Fyodorovich, taking advantage of his traveling companion's favorable mood, tried to encourage her talkativeness.

"This will at least be better than the groaning," he thought. But it couldn't be done by employing ordinary speech. Alexander Fyodorovich began to speak to her in a lofty, bookish style.

"I am sure this blossom reminds you of something pleasant in your life? A devotion to such a thing is a sign of a sensitive soul."

"But of course," his companion, the maiden Minodora Pamfilovna, answered with a sigh.

"And surely a sensitive, beautiful woman would have experienced lofty and noble passions during her ardent youth?" continued Alexander Fyodorovich.

These words touched Minodora Pamfilovna's heart. She stretched her neck, gently bowed her head, pursed her lips, sighed deeply, and said, "Oh, it's true!"

After this two small tears appeared in her eyes.

"But could it be that your memories are sad ones? Perhaps some ungrateful man, unable to appreciate your lofty, unspoken love, deceived you?"

"Deceived me!" she suddenly pronounced in a proud tone with a scornful smile. "Deceived me! No, that person has yet to be born who could deceive me."

"Oh, I'm sure no one was capable of attaining such a position as to deceive you . . ."

Alexander Fyodorovich didn't know what to say to strike a responsive chord in Minodora Pamfilovna, so he decided to speak at random. "But . . . often fate deceives us . . . I myself have experienced the vicissitudes of the heart, unhappy, hopeless love . . . the cruelty of fate . . ."

"Oh, that's terrible!" said Minodora Pamfilovna. "Terrible! I know that from experience! Imagine, my dear departed father was well off; we lived in style. Although I was not a raving beauty, I was not a wallflower either. I was capable of attracting attention; suitable men sought my hand. I was brought up strictly—no one would have dared to trifle with me."

"But you must agree, it's impossible to resist the urgings of the heart," said Alexander Fyodorovich. "The heart finds for itself the object of love . . . One is destined to love but once in life."

"Of course sympathetic love is permissible; I cannot call myself such a misfit as not to have experienced sympathetic love."

"It goes without saying that to a completely worthy person, attractive—"

"Without the slightest doubt; I'm not some sort of—"

"Oh, a lofty, noble soul could not be otherwise," interrupted Alexander Fyodorovich, fearing that Minodora Pamfilovna's touchy sense of dignity might become disturbed and the frank conversation come to an end.

"Oh, if you have experienced love," he continued, "you must understand the agonies I have experienced . . . It was terrible."

"Terrible!" repeated Minodora Pamfilovna. "A young landowner, a retired cavalry captain, used to visit us most of all; a man impossible to describe—so charming, clever, well-bred, modest—in a word, a high-class gentleman and, moreover, a man of property. I would never have guessed the reason for his frequent visits, made under the pretext of playing chess with father or hunting on our land, had it not been for Ulyana Tikhonovna, the sister of a neighboring landowner, who opened my eyes. 'It's not for nothing,' she said, 'that Peter Matveyevich frequents your house—he surely has some reason, for where could he find a better bride than you?' It was as if the scales fell from my eyes. I began to notice that, in fact, Peter Matveyevich did have something on his mind; at times he was so sad that I was seized with pity; why, it seemed I would have been glad to give up my soul to console him, God is my witness!"

"It's terrible!" said Alexander Fyodorovich. "One's first, passionate love pierces the heart like an arrow."

"The first! But what other kind is there? I don't know how things are done in your set, but with us it's 'with the first one the fast begins.'"

"Goodness me, of course I was speaking of the first and last love."

"Well, that's different."

"You wouldn't believe how much suffering! It's awful!"

"Oh, it was awful!" repeated Minodora Pamfilovna. "Whenever he didn't come you would sit by the window, waiting—would he be coming soon? Indeed, it may have seemed very stupid and deadly boring to sit with your hands folded like a girl in a portrait, but you could sit that way for a whole lifetime. A cloud of dust appears on the road—you think: he's coming! And you run to pretty yourself up, come out . . . and what do you think? You wait and wait, but it was only a whirlwind that kicked up the dust. You get angry from irritation, but then he, as if for spite, suddenly appears at the door. Now, whether you are dressed or not, you begin to bustle about—nothing fits right—and you bury your head in a pillow and cry and cry! God is my witness! It seemed that in his presence I completely lost my tongue, and there was nothing but a dark mist before my eyes. You trip over things, you run into the door post; as for pouring tea for him, the Lord deliver me! Instead of putting the tea in the teapot, you put it in the rinsing cup, place it on top of the samovar, and sit there like a fool. You must admit it's not for nothing that love is a feeling: I certainly felt it enough!"

"Oh, nature has endowed you with a sensitive heart," said Alexander Fyodorovich. "It's even evident in your concern for that plant. True, sympathetic love cherishes not only the plant as a whole, but even a little leaf that recalls a mutually returned affection. Look how I have saved this precious leaf, given me by the object of my adoration." And Alexander Fyodorovich opened his wallet, in which, as in a herbarium, there was preserved a rose leaf completely covered with writing.

Minodora Pamfilovna looked at it, was deeply touched, and sighed heavily.

"Perhaps this is as precious to me as that sacred geranium is to you!" said Alexander Fyodorovich, likewise sighing deeply.

Minodora Pamfilovna bent her head to one side, looked away, and with her lips pursed modestly, attempted to blush with the glow of bashfulness.

"Oh, how curious you are!" she said.

Suddenly a persistent cry was heard alongside the coach: "Please, sir, please, something for the poor!"

It was the children of the village through which they were passing. Running at a trot they followed the coach for about half a mile. Looking at them, Alexander Fyodorovich felt both irritation and pity. He recalled he had some change in his pocket, took something out, and threw it on the road. The coin flashed brightly in the sun.

"What was that you threw?" asked the man sitting on the other side of the window, a merchant from Armenia.

"By mistake—a ruble instead of a kopeck."

"Well, now you've set them a task: they'll be killing themselves running after every coach, hoping for a big handout."

"Yes," thought Alexander Fyodorovich, "thus fate flings good fortune at the feet of one man and makes others chase after it in vain: she bestows abundance on one while tempting thousands of others!"

And Alexander Fyodorovich sighed still more deeply; he was still thinking, first about the boy jumping about with the ruble in his hand and teasing the others with it, and then about the coaches they would chase after shouting: "Please, sir, please, something for the poor!"

"Excuse me for interrupting your story," he said, turning to Minodora Pamfilovna.

"But I have forgotten where I stopped . . ."

"It seems you stopped at the place where two hearts inspired with mutual love understood each other . . ."

"Oh, yes. Well, you see, I think I already told you that the landowner from another part of the village, Ivan Tikhonovich, almost every day—yes, every day—burdened us with his visits. Worse than bitter horseradish! Skinny, ugly, a regular Adam's skull with a wig, and yet he fancied himself a lady's man and was always offering to tell fortunes with the cards. Peter Matveyevich would arrive and there he would be sitting! Out of politeness, Peter Matveyevich would sit down to say something and he would stick his nose in, interrupting the conversation, and everything would be spoiled. And what was worse, my father, half jokingly, half seriously, was thinking about giving him my hand in marriage! 'Well, Minochka,' he used to say, 'if Ivan Tikhonovich should ask for your hand, would you marry him?' That I should marry that toad! My late father loved me dearly, he never forced me to do anything in word or deed, but he wanted this union: a close neighbor, the properties adjoining; it was a chance to unite the estates; we had little plowable land, and he didn't even have a tree to hang himself on. I didn't want to hear of it: a fine match, the devil and a child!"

"That was awful!" said Alexander Fyodorovich.

"Indeed, how awful! Repulsive! Whenever he came to dinner, I couldn't eat a thing; a fine husband!"

"And then your heart was already dedicated to an object of devout adoration."

"Oh, no, it seems that such was not to be my fate! Our union was never to be consecrated!"

"Really!" said Alexander Fyodorovich with surprise. "Do you mean that you never declared your love to each other and never confessed to each other the feelings of your enflamed hearts?"

"How could that be? According to our customs, that can only take place after the betrothal, when the priest has given his blessing."

"But I'm speaking of an understanding; do you mean that you never even exchanged a tender look?"

"We were about to, but that devil Ivanovich prevented it. A few days before my name day, Peter Matveyevich dropped in to eat with us after a hunt, and immediately Ivan Tikhonovich shows up. Before dinner, my late father said to me, 'Minochka, pick some nasturtiums for the salad,' and I went out into the garden. Peter Matveyevich volunteered to help me, and Ivan Tikhonovich, the cursed monkey, was right on our heels. What could I do? Tell him to go to the devil? Well, we went out; I was beside myself, burning all over. Suddenly Peter Matveyevich asks: 'What kind of flowers do you like, Minodora Pamfilovna?' I was so embarrassed I didn't know what to answer; I couldn't remember the name of a single flower. The word *geranium* came to mind, and in order not to stand there like a fool, I blurted it out—even though I couldn't stand their smell. My favorite flowers were peonies . . ."

"Yes," thought Alexander Fyodorovich, "it's the same with people: you are expecting help from a rich relative, and you get it from a poor stranger."

"It's a wonder, by God!" continued Minodora Pamfilovna. "Now I can't bear to look at peonies."

"Well, was Peter Matveyevich surprised that you chose such a modest flower?"

"Not a bit. 'It does honor to your taste, Miss Minodora,'" he said. "But Ivan Tikhonovich had to stick his nose in: 'How is it,' he says, 'that you don't have a single pot of geraniums?' 'There were some, but they dried up,' I say (May your throat dry up!) . . . So we picked some nasturtiums; it never entered my head that the words of Peter Matveyevich had any significance—

only my heart wanted to jump out of my breast. And what do you think? Oh the heart is a true prophet! I had just returned from mass on my name day when I look—and there in the garden stands a pot of geraniums!"

"No doubt this very one here?" asked Alexander Fyodorovich.

"Exactly. I stood there like a post, trembling, my knees knocking together; I could hardly breathe. I asked everybody at the house, 'Who brought the geraniums?' No one knew anything . . . And I thought to myself: who else could have had the delicacy to do such a thing but Peter Matveyevich . . . It wasn't for nothing that he asked me which flowers I liked."

"It was obviously a declaration of love," said Alexander Fyodorovich.

"I didn't take it any other way, and I put the geraniums on the window sill in the best room."

"Well, after all that, all that remained for him to do was to fall down at your feet and say:

My love, my angel of protection!
O, you who are beyond compare,
My life has need of your affection,
But where may love its secret share?

"Really? I thought so, too, but that devil Ivan Tikhonovich, like a fly in the ointment, was following me around like a tail; as if by design he seemed to have become a permanent fixture at our house! And Peter Matveyevich, modest and well-mannered man that he was, was not about to make a declaration of love in the presence of an outsider! He was not one of those tricksters who is ready to pay court as long as there are thousands involved. I had already noticed that Ivan Tikhonovich was not to his liking; yes, I was already imagining that I could have torn him to bits! Imagine, the guests had just arrived for my name day party when Ivan Tikhonovich goes over to the geraniums, sniffs them, and says 'What pretty geraniums you have, Minodora Pamfilovna!' I was simply fuming; and then his sister, Ulyana Tikhonovna, the brazen hussy, insolently pours oil on the fire—shamelessly chasing after Peter Matveyevich! 'Apparently they were a gift?' she asks. 'Your gift, Peter Matveyevich?' At that, everyone turned to look at me and Peter Matveyevich. I was dying with shame! But I didn't miss the chance to ask her as we went out into the garden: 'Where did you get the idea that Peter Matveyevich gave me the geraniums?' 'From the fact,' she said, 'that he is head over heels in love with you.' 'But how can you dare say such a thing, how can you slander me so?' But she says, 'That's what I said and what I will keep on saying.' The miserable hag! Here I lost my temper and began to let her have it. And what do you think? Going into the room, she picks off a healthy leaf, crumples it up and sniffs it. 'Oh, how gloriously it smells! Where did you get such geraniums, Peter Matveyevich? From your own garden?' Peter Matveyevich turned white and red by turns . . ."

As darkness fell Alexander Fyodorovich was overcome by sleep, and he heard nothing further of what Minodora Pamfilovna was saying. However, the two stations he slept through more than made up for the loss, since in his dream Alexander Fyodorovich found himself at Minodora Pamfilovna's name day party, and he witnessed how she fought with Ulyana Tikhonovna over Peter Matveyevich and how she thoroughly drubbed her. Since in dreams, as well as in reality, it is sometimes strictly forbidden to willfully and with one's own hands commit violence, Minodora Pamfilovna was haled into court, as was likewise the witness to her misdeeds, Alexander Fyodorovich. And so they are being driven there together; the road is long and terribly rough. In despair, Alexander Fyodorovich reproaches Minodora Pamfilovna. Why did she have to invite him to her name day party?

"And why did you have to fight with her? Wouldn't it have been better if you had simply beaten her?" he said to her.

"You're right," she answered, overflowing with tears. "It would have been better to simply rip her head off without any ceremony, without violating decorum."

"And, of course, then I could have sworn before the court that it was not her head you ripped off, but some kind of garden vegetable—a pumpkin or a melon—because Ulyana Tikhonovna's head in both outer appearance and color exactly resembles a ripe pumpkin or melon, and consequently I could have been deceived by the appearance—"

"Would you care for some tea?"

"Mercy! Tea at a time like this!" shouted Alexander Fyodorovich, but having reawakened, he looked around, yawned, and said: "It's morning already, I must have some tea!" Jumping out of the coach, he asked the name of the station. It was the village of Zimogorie, near Valdai.[7]

"Aha! Tea with Valdai rolls!"

Alexander Fyodorovich had hardly taken a step away from the coach when he was surrounded by Zimogorie maidens with bundles of rolls tied together with string.[8]

"Take some rolls, sir! May you eat them in good health, my prince!"

"How many bundles will you take?"

"Ah, my prince! These are fresh ones!"

"What's this? My prince, are you buying from her? After all, I met you first."

Alexander Fyodorovich took a bundle, but they forcefully hung ten more bundles on him, saying, "Eat them in good health, my prince!"

And it did not end with that. The crowd of girls followed Alexander Fyodorovich into the station where he intended to drink his tea.

"No, my prince, no matter what, take some," continued the girl who referred to herself as the first he had met, "It's not fair, here, take some, my prince."

"What am I supposed to do with your rolls? I don't need them!" shouted Alexander Fyodorovich.

"Eat them in good health, my prince. I'm not asking for money." And placing all her rolls on the table in front of Alexander Fyodorovich, she left.

Surrounded by huge piles of rolls, Alexander Fyodorovich drank his tea and watched how the girls attacked two merchants who were sitting at another table also sipping their tea, one hand resting on the knee, the other holding a saucer between beard and mustache. But they enjoyed drinking their tea, not eating what usually goes with it; therefore the roll sellers vainly surrounded them repeating, "Governor, take at least one bundle of rolls!"

"Off with you, sweetie," one merchant kept saying in an angry voice.

As Alexander Fyodorovich was preparing to leave, the fair maiden who had forcefully thrust her rolls upon him was still standing at the door with her arms folded.

"Take back your rolls," he said to her.

"No, my prince, eat them in good health."

"Well, my princess, here are ten kopecks, only stop pestering me," said Alexander Fyodorovich as he hurried toward the coach, for the horses had been ready for quite a while.

At a loss as to how to get Minodora Pamfilovna to repeat all that he must have slept through, Alexander Fyodorovich began by railing against Ulyana Tikhonovna.

"It's awful! What a woman!" he said. "I would have broken that Ulyana Tikhonovna in three pieces!"

"Yes, sir, that's the way it was: she spread rumors that I was having an affair with Peter Matveyevich! The man had to stop coming to our house. And suddenly I had two misfortunes: I was deprived of my happiness, and then God took my father's soul; if that wasn't enough, the property was seized, the house sealed up, and I was sent begging! . . . And this . . . this is all the property I have left . . ."

Here Minodora Pamfilovna began to sob bitterly.

"When the officials started sealing up the place . . . in a daze, I rushed to get the pot of geraniums: 'Lord! The geraniums will surely die without water!' and I snatched it up . . . snatched it and ran . . . Fortunately no one noticed, otherwise there would have been trouble over it . . . I would have lain down right there and said, 'You can bury me, but I won't give it up!'. . . What we didn't have in that house! . . . And they took everything! A whole closet of crystal and china! . . . Two trunks full of clothing . . . all kinds of household goods . . . What a farm it was! We had everything: three cows, a whole coop full of chickens. In the cellars was enough food for a whole year—everything you would need: pickled cucumbers, all kinds of jams, stewed apples, three vats of cabbage, so many barrels of beer and kvass—March-brewed—I would really like to have a glass right now—I tried some in Moscow at a kvass stall—

nothing like the real thing! You can't buy kvass like that; and there were times when I turned down our own! And now . . . God has seen fit to—"

Minodora Pamfilovna was already beginning to cry. Alexander Fyodorovich tried to disperse the rain cloud by means of diversions.

"Was it a long time ago?" he asked.

"It's been eight years now, or perhaps even ten."

"Where have you been living all this time?"

"With various people: a guest at one place, then another; it's fine to be a guest but better to be at home. At first they make a fuss over you, then you see you are becoming a burden; worst of all are the good-for-nothing servants. Anything to drive you out of the place. I also tried being a housekeeper—no one has to go to school for that—but I had to put up with such nonsense from the servants that only God could save me! No, that wasn't for me! If you tried to stop them from putting their paws in the master's pocket, they'd give *you* a housekeeping! Out of spite they would smash the china, gobble up everything that was supposed to be locked up and you would have to answer for it. Not a trace of honesty about them, and conscience had disappeared long ago . . ."

"Then why are you going to Petersburg now?"

"Well, you see, an old debtor of my deceased father lives there; year after year he has been saying: 'I'll pay, I'll pay,' and he was supposed to pay twenty-five rubles at a time. The total amount was considerable—five hundred rubles; now for the second year in a row he has paid nothing. And there is another important matter in 'Petey.' I met a judge from our town; he told me that someone is suing Ivan Tikhonovich for the land my father sold him. The case has reached the senate, but Ivan Tikhonovich has so cleverly manipulated the affair that he has gotten the opposition charged with illegal possession of my late father's estate. So here I am going to Petersburg; I myself will present a petition to the minister; perhaps, if it's God's will, all will be returned . . ."

"May God grant it," said Alexander Fyodorovich. "Who knows? Perhaps also your old love will return and Peter Matveyevich will once more seek your hand."

"And declare himself faithful to the grave!" said Minodora Pamfilovna sighing deeply. "He's still a bachelor!"

"How could anyone forget you?"

"How could he remember! So much time has gone by, how could I interest anyone?"

"Now enough of that! Feelings are not affected by age and years."

This conversation, with some details about happy times, continued all the way to Petersburg, where, thanks to the heat, the continual squabbling of the drivers over hitching up the horses, the fact that three horses were used instead of six, and finally the habit of both horses and drivers following the proverb 'slowly but surely,' the stage arrived on the evening of the fourth day. Having no other choice, Alexander Fyodorovich decided to take a room in the hotel adjoining the stage office.

"Where will you be staying?" he asked his traveling companion.

"As yet, I have no idea; wherever the Lord leads me."

"Do you have friends, or will you rent a room?"

"How can I rent a room? I only want to find Ivan Tikhonovich; I'll find out from him where Prokhor Zakharovich—the debtor of my deceased father—lives. I'll go straight to his door; then it will be up to him to either give me the money or provide me with food and lodging."

"But how are you going to find Ivan Tikhonovich at night? And you can't just stay here in the office."

"Actually, I don't know what to do. I'm new here; Moscow's another matter—there I know people."

Alexander Fyodorovich began to sympathize with Minodora Pamfilovna's helpless plight. He offered to let her use one of the rooms he had taken.

"No, I humbly thank you!" she answered in a rather angry tone.

"Why not?"

"Where did you get the idea I would stay with you?"

"Ah, I understand," said Alexander Fyodorovich. "In fact you do have to beware of the slander of evil tongues; I myself would be horrified if anyone should think I'm living with you, but I'm offering you a separate room."

"That's another matter; in that case I accept."

According to Alexander Fyodorovich's instructions, Minodora Pamfilovna was shown to a small room costing two and a half rubles and he ordered them to serve her tea and dinner at his expense.

After wishing Minodora Pamfilovna a good night, Alexander Fyodorovich returned to his five-ruble room, which was decorated with soot-covered paintings, a huge grandfather clock, and two enormous square pictures, each three yards across; on one of these some Petersburg Teniers[9] had produced a four-part scene: the first a tree, then a fish swimming in the water, then a fisherman armed with a pole, and finally a mountain with a setting sun. Like the gates, doors, and shutters of Moscow, the furniture was stained to make it look like oak, and it was covered with *semistuff*.[10]

Alexander Fyodorovich ordered tea. The tea was brought and looked as if it had been brewed from tobacco.

"And the cream?"

"Do you want cream?"

"Yes, I want cream."

"There isn't any; it soured."

"Get some—I don't care how!"

The man left, returned with the cream—milk with flour stirred up in it.

"And the biscuits?"

"Do you want biscuits?"

"Yes, I want biscuits."

He left and came back with the biscuits.

"Good Lord! My dear man, these biscuits are ancient! Where did you get them?"

"From the baker, sir."

"Not true; probably from the Egyptian Museum, where they have been kept under glass with a label saying, 'These white flour biscuits were baked three thousand years before Christ for the Asian campaign of the Egyptian Pharaoh Sesostris.'"

"Not at all, sir. There are no better biscuits in Petersburg."

"There are, my good man."

"No, sir!"

Having ordered the man to take away the home-brewed tea, the ersatz cream, and the Egyptian biscuits, Alexander Fyodorovich lay down on the bed and, as if enervated from a steam bath, slept the sleep of a Russian folk-tale hero. Phantastus the Greek, a brother of Morpheus, immediately appeared before him in the form of an officious Italian *cicerone* and proposed they take in the sights and attractions of Petersburg. And lo and behold, he led him through the marvelous streets of a magnificent city, such that no fairy tale can depict nor pen describe. Alexander Fyodorovich could not believe his eyes.

"Can it be possible," he asked Phantastus, "that all of Petersburg was carved out of a single stone?"

"How many do you think? After all, it's not some sort of collapsible burg you could carry away in a cart."

"So many people!"

"Excuse me, but what you see scurrying about the streets are not real people."

"What?"

"Real people and all other animate things are shown by my brother Morpheus."

"Then what is this?"

"It's all a simple mechanism."

"But look, that gentleman is speaking."

"Speaking? Not at all—in order to speak, one has to think: listen for yourself."

"I don't like to listen to conversations that are not my concern."

"Go ahead, listen, don't be afraid, you won't understand a bit of it. And there's another would-be man who lives in space and not in time. And here's a most excellent specimen made for mechanical love; look at the fine, incomparable workmanship."

"Enough," said Alexander Fyodorovich. "Show me the picture *The Last Day of Pompeii.*"[11]

"Here it is."

"You can't see anything but darkness. Where are the people?"

"It's not my job to show them; they're animate."

"What good is a *cicerone* like you to me?"

"That's strange; to you only the animate is of interest? And what about, for example, all those who are *without souls*[12] because of their love for someone? I think that even you yourself occasionally enter my domain when it comes to love for children."

"May God prevent it! Be gone, send me your brother Morpheus."

"I regret," said Phantastus, "that you still have not seen all of my domain."

Phantastus disappeared and Alexander Fyodorovich found himself in some sort of chaotic side street; on both sides marvelous buildings and structures soared upward, a mushroom wearing a sword was leading a tower wearing a bonnet by the hand, and a young man in a semi-frock coat and a semi-beard was bustling about having semi-conversations with everyone and casting semi-glances through his lorgnette. A girl with drumsticks instead of arms beat a tattoo on a piano; four swans wearing glasses danced the quadrille with fashion illustrations wearing Paris creations. A full Russian moon, *chapeau bas,* chased a pale sentimental French moon in a cloudy dress; a convoluted wind whistled popular airs from all the latest operas; and a spirit with disheveled hair hovered over the object of his adoration and looked at her in the mother-of-pearl moonlight.

"What can I do for you?" said a voice near Alexander Fyodorovich. "I am Morpheus."

"Show me *The Last Day of Pompeii.*"

"In reality or in the picture? But I'm afraid to show it to you in reality, because it would surely engulf you in lava, and you would wake up from fright in the hotel in the other world. It would be better to look at the picture and not to get upset because all the principal streets of Pompeii are in a state of artistic horror and confusion. Look, the figures are so animated that it seems they are about to step right out of the canvas: a son with his decrepit father is trying to escape destruction, another is dragging his enfeebled mother out of danger, a suitor tries to pull his bride out of that hell, and so on. But where are they to run to? I don't know; it would be better just to remain there in their effective poses until the last day of Petersburg. The whole picture is not illuminated by ordinary light but caught in a brilliant flash."

"That's all very well, my dear Morpheus, but the picture is not in your line."

"What?"

"Just that; all the figures in the picture must have *taken leave of their souls*[13] from horror."

"That's sophistry, sophistry pure and simple; that might be true in the real world, but in art it's another matter. Would you care to consider contemporary animation? Here, for example, is a useless object, but it is animated, it stands out, it tempts you, it attracts you by its appearance, by the play of light and color, by its thickness or thinness, by its name or title; it so attracts you that you buy a completely useless item because it is the going thing. This means that you animate, you give life to the thing. For example, look at literary animation: how difficult it used to be to become a writer . . . Why? Because it was considered an important matter, having consequences, resulting in either glory or humiliation; but now from dishonor itself honor is extracted: an intelligent man will politely say that you are a fool, but then, in order to spite him, ten fools will shout that you are a genius, and you will enjoy the fame of being a genius, of being acclaimed by 99 percent of the people, while the 1 percent will involuntarily keep silent. Very well and good! For life is a dream, and the more the variety—"

"But after sleep comes the awakening, and after the awakening, reality. What sort of reality can there be after a dream that resembles life?"

"As far as reality is concerned, it's not my affair; not one of my thousand brothers works on the reality side."

"Can it be that I am asleep and dreaming all this? Perhaps you can show me Babylon instead of Petersburg?"

"What for? The impression would only be the same."

"What a swindle!" shouted Alexander Fyodorovich. "How can I get back to the hotel?"

"Transportation is not my job," said Morpheus. "Why don't you ask one of these beings?"

"Hey, cabby, take me to the hotel by the Obukhov Bridge."

"Climb in, sir."

Alexander Fyodorovich took a seat in the cab, and as is usually the case, they drove off. They went on and on; there was no end to the street. The further they went, the darker it got. Finally the gloom around them became darker than midnight during an eclipse of the moon. Suddenly the shaking carriage stopped and a voice said: "We have arrived, your honors; would you please step down?"

Alexander Fyodorovich shuddered and looked around; next to him sat Minodora Pamfilovna while the conductor was at the carriage door, letting down the folding stairs.

"What's the meaning of this?" asked the surprised Alexander Fyodorovich.

"We have arrived in Petersburg," said the conductor.

"Where, at the hotel?"

"Yes, there's a hotel here, too."

"You slept soundly," said Minodora Pamfilovna.

Alexander Fyodorovich could not believe his eyes, but the dream was becoming reality: everything that had happened before he had gone to bed in the five-ruble room was happening again, only in another hotel nearby. Minodora Pamfilovna really did not have a place to stay, nor did she have the money to rent a room, and he offered her the small two-and-a-half-ruble room. It even seemed to Alexander Fyodorovich that he had been in his five-ruble room before. Just as in his dream, they brought him cheap *Wan-chu-so-dzi;* instead of cream, skimmed milk; instead of cakes, dry biscuits from the reserve supplies of Rameses.

Trying to decide which was more distinct, dream or reality, Alexander Fyodorovich once more fell into a deep sleep, but this time neither Phantastus nor Morpheus tried their tricks on him.

The next day, having awakened rather late, he sent for a carriage; while waiting for it, he called on Minodora Pamfilovna. She was calmly trimming from her plant leaves that had dried up during the journey.

After wishing her a good morning, Alexander Fyodorovich asked her, "What do you intend to do?"

"I don't know myself. I'll have to find out from Ivan Tikhonovich where Prokhor Zakharovich lives, but not for anything would I call on Ivan Tikhonovich personally. He's a bachelor."

"If you wish, I will go and see Ivan Tikhonovich. Do you have his address?"

"Here's a note," said Minodora Pamfilovna, taking out of her reticule a handkerchief with a scrap of paper tied up in it.

"If Ivan Tikhonovich were to come and see me, I could better ask him about everything myself."

"Very well, I'll bring him to you: surely he'll consider it a particular pleasure to see you again."

The man who was sent to see about a carriage returned and reported to Alexander Fyodorovich that they were asking twenty-five rubles per day, along with the proviso that he not drive out of town. The rate seemed outrageous to Alexander Fyodorovich, and he set out on foot in hopes of finding a cheaper price. Passing Haymarket Square, he stopped to watch a fat merchant's wife dressing down a cabby (she was calling him a crook and a pirate).

"What have you done to her?" asked Alexander Fyodorovich.

"Look here, sir, she hires me to take her to Police Station Bridge; I asked a half ruble—cheap enough, not even a quarter per hundredweight—and she offers me a five-kopeck piece. What am I, a freight hauler?"

"Crook! Pirate!" the merchant's wife repeated, walking away.

"You're in the right," said Alexander Fyodorovich to the driver.

"Why sure, sir, what if a springer should snap—and that springer's worth more than she is—that's the truth!"

"And how much to take me to Police Station Bridge?"

"For you, sixty kopecks."

"Why should it cost me more? I'll give you a quarter per hundredweight just as you said."

"It can't be done, sir, it'd hardly be worth it."

"Take you somewhere, sir?" shouted the other drivers who had crowded around, but Alexander Fyodorovich had already taken his seat and was on his way to Police Station Bridge. Arriving there safely, he found a carriage for hire for fifteen rubles (with the proviso that he not drive out of town) and set out for Ivan Tikhonovich's address.

At the gates of a huge seven-story building, he jumped out of the carriage and went into a small courtyard where he felt he was at the bottom of a deep shaft from which the sky could hardly be seen. His gaze traveled upward from the ground floor to the main entrance to the upper rows of windows, each row smaller than the preceding one.

By a narrow staircase that zigzagged its way from floor to floor, Alexander Fyodorovich made his way skyward, noting the apartment numbers and the names on brass plates affixed to the doors. Reaching the seventh heaven, Alexander Fyodorovich knocked at the door on the right, No. 100 it would seem. A key turned within, the door opened a crack, and a sturdy maiden asked, "Whom do you wish to see?"

"Ivan Tikhonovich so-and-so."

"He lives here, but he's not home."

"When can he be found at home?"

"He goes out very early in the morning and returns at about eleven at night."

"Then it would be more convenient to see him at eleven p.m.?"

"And who shall I say is calling?"

"You don't have to say anything."

Alexander Fyodorovich returned to the hotel, changed, informed Mindora Pamfilovna that he wouldn't be seeing Ivan Tikhonovich until late that night, and then went out to make some calls.

At about 10:30, having spent a typical day in the capital, Alexander Fyodorovich once more knocked at the door of apartment No. 100. The same maiden answered.

"Is Ivan Tikhonovich at home?"

"Oh, it's you; I thought it was one of ours. But then you would have shouted, 'Anna!' Come in, I'll light a candle."

Alexander Fyodorovich entered the tiny dark foyer and waited while fat Annchen struck a light. Soon she appeared from her miniature kitchen with a candle.

Alexander Fyodorovich looked around the tiny foyer; besides the entrance and the door on the left into the kitchen, there were yet three other doors; here a drunken Vanka would have no cause to complain that "there are so few doors in the world."

"Come this way," said Annchen, leading Alexander Fyodorovich to the left-hand door of the two that were in front of him. He entered a rather empty room from which there was a passage into another room.

"Ivan Tikhonovich should be returning soon," said Annchen as she placed the candle on the table. "What time is it?"

"Well, my watch has stopped; I probably forgot to wind it," said Alexander Fyodorovich, looking at his watch and taking a seat by the table.

"I'll see what time it is," said Annchen, going into the other room. "No, Grigory Ivanovich took his watch with him; but never mind, in Peter Sergeyevich's room there's a clock." And Annchen went into the other part of the apartment.

"Soon it'll be eleven," she said, returning.

"Are you German or Finnish, Annchen?"

"I'm from Reval."

"Have you been serving Ivan Tikhonovich for a long time?"

"I am not serving Ivan Tikhonovich," answered Annchen. "He is living here with his nephew, Grigory Ivanovich."

"Then you are working for his nephew?"

"Oh no, I only do Grigory Ivanovich's wash, shine his boots, prepare his tea, and make his bed; but for Peter Sergeyevich I also do the cooking."

"Aha! Then you are the servant of two masters. How much do you get per month?"

"From all three, fifteen rubles."

"Do you live well?"

"What do you mean 'well'? I could go mad from boredom; they all go out early in the morning and I sit here all day by myself with no one to say a word to. Grigory Ivanovich and Peter Sergeyevich are such quiet ones—except when they come home angry—then they never shut up, rake you over the coals for nothing. Now Yakov Matveyevich is a good man and likes to joke; whenever he comes, he's always in good spirits, talks and talks until it's time for bed."

"Then Yakov Matveyevich is also your master?"

"And what else?"

"But who serves Ivan Tikhonovich?"

"I just shine his boots and bring him water for washing; he has his tea with Grigory Ivanovich—"

Suddenly there was a knock at the door and a voice shouted, "Hey, Anna!"

"Oh, it's Peter Sergeyevich!" cried Annchen, and she rushed to open the door.

"Why the candle?" and with these words somebody went through to the middle section of the apartment.

"Who broke the glass case?" the same voice shouted angrily.

"The cat did it, Peter Sergeyevich," answered Annchen in a sad voice.

"And what were you doing? Why did you let the cat in here?"

"The devil let it in! It jumped through the open window!"

"I don't want to hear any more about it. The new glass will come out of your wages."

"I was going to pay for it myself so that you wouldn't find out; I thought it wouldn't cost much—but twenty rubles—I don't earn that much in a month—"

"Fool! . . . All right, I'll pay half, but from now on—"

Another knock was heard.

"Damned cat! Because of it I'll have to work for nothing!" said Annchen while angrily opening the door.

"Take my coat, Anna! Why the light? What a miserable stump of a candle! Oh, what's to be done with you!"

"What was I to do? After all, I told you we were out of candles, and you said yourself you would buy some wax ones; now we'll be sitting in the dark when this stump burns out."

"How stupid you are, Anna! Not even to think of buying tallow candles!"

"And what was I to use for money? Peter Sergeyevich gives me money to buy food; as soon as I come back, he demands an accounting. Am I to tell him I bought tallow candles for you?"

"Anna!" came the voice of Peter Sergeyevich, "Let's see the bill!"

"There, you see?"

Another knock at the door. Annchen hurried to open it.

"Perhaps at last it's Ivan Tikhonovich," thought Alexander Fyodorovich.

Someone wearing an official's frock coat with his hat down over his eyes passed silently by Alexander Fyodorovich, and paying him no attention, took the candle from the table and disappeared into the next room, slamming the door behind him. Alexander Fyodorovich was left in darkness.

"Anna!" came a shout from within. Annchen hurried to answer the call.

"Why don't you come when you're called? Go out and buy me a jar of cabbage soup."

Annchen rushed headlong out the door for the cabbage soup; meanwhile, someone had quietly opened the door and entered the room where Alexander Fyodorovich was sitting in the dark, contemplating the disadvantages of one master having three Russian servants and the advantages of three masters having one German servant.

In a low, groaning voice, the one who had just come in also called out, "Anna!"

But Anna did not reply.

"This must be Ivan Tikhonovich at last," thought Alexander Fyodorovich. "It couldn't be anyone else."

Feeling his way, Ivan Tikhonovich placed his hat on the table; then he removed his dress or frock coat and was about to hang it right on Alexander Fyodorovich's nose. Not wishing to be a clothes rack, Alexander Fyodorovich sprang up from his chair.

"Is that you, Annushka?" whispered Ivan Tikhonovich, groping in the dark with his hand.

"No, it's me," answered Alexander Fyodorovich.

"Oh, is that you, Grigory Ivanovich? You got home early today: I thought you weren't home yet."

"What's that you're saying, Uncle?" came an angry voice from the next room.

"I was just saying that you got home early."

"And what about it?"

"Nothing."

"Ivan Tikhonovich, this gentleman has been waiting to see you for a long time," said Annchen, coming into the room with a candle in her hand.

"Oh, my goodness, excuse me!" cried Ivan Tikhonovich, snatching his coat from the chair. He was a small man, about fifty years of age.

"I have a message for you. A certain acquaintance of yours—Minodora Pamfilovna by name—is here—"

"Oh my goodness, Minodora Pamfilovna! She's here! . . . Permit me to ask, do I have the honor of speaking to her spouse?"

"Certainly not; I met her in the coach on my journey here."

"Please do me the honor of taking a seat . . . Well, how is Minodora Pamfilovna?"

"Thank the Lord . . . She requests you to come and see her; she is staying in the hotel by the Obukhov Bridge . . . I don't recall the room number—"

"Certainly, certainly! . . . And could you furnish me with your address?"

"I am staying at the same hotel," said Alexander Fyodorovich, handing his card to Ivan Tikhonovich and taking his leave.

"Well," thought Alexander Fyodorovich as he was leaving room No. 100, "this is not our dear Mother Moscow."

The next day, at about eight o'clock in the morning, Ivan Tikhonovich suddenly appeared.

"Excuse me for bothering you," he said, "but I asked to see Minodora Pamfilovna and no one here knew anything about her."

"Then allow me to be your guide," said Alexander Fyodorovich, who was curious to see the meeting between Ivan Tikhonovich and Minodora Pamfilovna.

"Minodora Pamfilovna, Ivan Tikhonovich is here to see you."

"Minodora Pamfilovna, is it really you!" cried Ivan Tikhonovich, approaching the hand of his former object of adoration.

"How could you be expected to recognize me now, Ivan Tikhonovich! Please sit down—"

"What a pretty little room you have, and what a coincidence! Your favorite flower—the geranium—on the windowsill . . . Remember, Minodora Pamfilovna, I had the pleasure of presenting you with geraniums on your name day—"

"No, I don't remember, Ivan Tikhonovich," pronounced Minodora Pamfilovna, suddenly turning red. "Who told you that I liked geraniums?"

"You yourself were pleased to say so, Minodora Pamfilovna," said Ivan Tikhonovich significantly after noting her embarrassment. "But why bring up the past . . . All kinds of things happened . . . In ten years, Minodora Pamfilovna, a person can change . . . heh, heh, heh! I, too, have sins on my soul!"

"I asked you to come to see me, Ivan Tikhonovich, in order to find out where Prokhor Zakharovich lives," said Minodora Pamfilovna dryly.

"Poor Minodora Pamfilovna!" thought Alexander Fyodorovich as he bowed and left the room. "What a shattering revelation! It would have been better for you never to have come to Petersburg and never to have seen Ivan Tikhonovich for the rest of your life . . ."

Alexander Fyodorovich's further melancholy thoughts were interrupted when he met an acquaintance in the corridor, then he went out to pay some calls, and from there to the Pavlovsk Railroad[14] in search of new impressions. He bought a metal token and took his seat in the carriage with a palpitating heart . . . Ooh! The Bogatyr[15] puffed and hissed, his nostrils belched smoke, and flames shot out of his ears. He hurled himself forward, pulling behind him a whole retinue of carriages and wagons, rushing pell-mell along the iron rails. In each carriage there were some thirty-two people, about four hundred in all. When the train began to move, about fifty heavy iron wheels began to clatter and rumble, and it felt as though the earth had gone lame, trembled, melted, and begun to float.

In thirty minutes the Bogatyr flew to Tsarskoe Selo. The worthy passengers stepped off into a gallery for a change of tokens, then seated themselves in new carriages, and the steam engine Arrow whisked them on to Pavlovsk in six minutes. The people streamed into the gallery and park, which was already rather crowded.[16] Some headed for the buffet to drink schnapps and eat cold piroshki; others preferred to dine at table, drink tea, or refresh themselves with various snacks and beverages; still others crowded around the bandstand to listen to the *restauration* waltzes of Herman's nervous orchestra.

Suddenly a light rain began to fall. Everyone crowded into the gallery. An hour passed, then another, amid monotonous variety. Then the crowd rushed off to the office to buy tickets for the return trip. Seized with fear that he would be too late to get a ticket for the ten o'clock train, Alexander Fyodorovich fought his way to get to the window before the stream of tickets ran out, forcefully thrust two rubles and sixty kopecks toward the vendor, and received a metal tag indicating the time of departure and the number and section of the carriage.

Soon the steam engine Smoldering Fire, Stormy Spirit began to get up steam at the platform. A bell rang once, and the passengers crowded around the gates; it rang twice, and everyone took his seat, the late ones rushing to the carriages; it rang three times, and the carriage doors slammed shut. The conductors, emitting on their whistles the drawn-out piercing notes of a hawk, were seating people and taking tickets. Stragglers who came running up too late groaned, and the whole procession of the fiery furnace began to slowly clankety-clank its way out of the station; faster and faster it went, hurtling along and showering hellish sparks along the way. An Englishman who had sold his soul to the demon of speed drove the engine. In a sooty white jacket and wide breeches, he appeared to be heated to incandescence. The uninitiated Orthodox Christians, who were met along the way on both sides of the tracks, crossed themselves in horror at the sight of the quick-legged dragon that ran rapidly along the rails like an annulated, many-stomached *Polynoe fulgurans.*[17] They looked with pity at the poor people with whom the bellies of the monster were filled.

At the Tsarskoe Selo gallery it was necessary to switch to different carriages. In order to bolster his forces, which had been depleted by the great number of new impressions, Alexander Fyodorovich asked for a swallow of bitter vodka: they gave him some aromatic stuff that was undoubtedly made with ipecac. He ate a pastry that had been fried in castor oil and suffered for the rest of the trip. By the way, it may have been train sickness—something like sea sickness. But to his good fortune, a new strong impression made him feel better; a woman sitting in the same section of the carriage suddenly groaned in a most unusual way, and soon there appeared—contrary to the rules—an extra passenger—and without a ticket.

Meanwhile, the train entered the station. Alexander Fyodorovich hastily jumped out of the carriage and, fearing any new impressions, took a cab home.

While helping Alexander Fyodorovich undress, the servant at the hotel said to him, "The lady who arrived with you in the coach sends you her compliments; she has moved somewhere else."

"Really?"

"Such a strange person!"

"What do you mean?"

"It seems that all she had to her name was a pot of geraniums."

"What's to be done? If you have no other possessions, then you might as well be thankful for that."

"Yesterday she spent the whole day fussing about with it—she made me sick! I should get her a scissors to trim off the dead leaves—ten times she asked for water to sprinkle it—she sat there blowing dust off the leaves. 'What is it with you and that geranium, Madam?' I asked. 'There's no treasure I would take for that geranium,' she said. And today she up and left without it! 'You forgot your geranium pot,' I said. 'Keep it,' she said. 'What do I want with it—it will only be a bother to keep watering it,' I said. 'Then throw it out,' she said. 'The devil take it!' So I threw it out."

"Aha! The tale is ended!" thought Alexander Fyodorovich. Poor Minodora Pamfilovna! What a disappointment for your faithful, ardent love! For ten years you watered that precious flower with your tears, that precious flower that recalled the time of your heart's hopes . . . And suddenly a few words from Ivan Tikhonovich, meaningless to anyone else, exposed the ten-year deception of your heart! For so many years you kissed each little leaf, like a promise of love, and imagined in your dreams how Peter Matveyevich, on the eve of Saints Minodora, Mitrodora, and Nymphodora's day, stealthily climbed over the garden fence with a pot of geraniums, placed it among your flowers, sighed deeply, and disappeared . . . How sweet were those dreams, those beneficent veils screening a miserable life! And suddenly along comes Ivan Tikhonovich and says, 'It was I, Minodora Pamfilovna, I was the one who . . .' Ugh! What a picture! Ivan Tikhonovich, repulsive little Ivan Tikhonovich, is climbing the fence with the pot of geraniums in his hand; he steals along, fearful of making a sound, and places it in the middle of the flower bed, sighs deeply, whispers, 'This is for you on your name day, my most precious Minochka,' and disappears. What a difference in one and the same geranium!"

Thus reasoned Alexander Fyodorovich as he was falling asleep, but he had hardly fallen asleep when the scene changed—and for the better. From out of nowhere there appeared a tall man with a red mustache.

"Could you please inform me," he said, "where Minodora Pamfilovna has gone?"

"With whom do I have the honor of speaking?" asked Alexander Fyodorovich.

"I am Peter Matveyevich."

"Really? Where have you come from?"

"For ten years I have been imprisoned in a pot of geraniums by that evil sorcerer, Ivan Tikhonovich. For ten years Minodora Pamfilovna has been fussing over that pot, not knowing how to free me, while the whole secret consisted in merely smashing it against the wall. But for the last ten years it never occurred to her to do it. Then yesterday the evil sorcerer Ivan Tikhonovich suddenly reappeared before Minodora Pamfilovna, abducted her, and pitilessly locked her up in his heart—so unexpectedly that she did not have time to take the pot of geraniums with her. Fortunately for me, some benevolent spirit smashed the pot and I am free; otherwise I would have remained on the window sill for the rest of my life, or I would have withered away in the flower of my youth for lack of care. You know where that evil sorcerer Ivan Tikhonovich lives—be my second, let's go to him—I'll challenge him to a duel for abducting Minodora Pamfilovna; besides, my own honor has been slighted by this affair."

Alexander Fyodorovich could not refuse such a request, and he immediately accompanied Peter Matveyevich to Ivan Tikhonovich's apartment. They knock. Annchen opens the door. They enter and hear the voice of Ivan Tikhonovich; he is singing something.

"Shall I announce you?" asks Annchen.

"Shsh! It's not necessary."

They sneak up to the door. Ivan Tikhonovich is singing, "I have locked you up in my heart . . ."

"Ivan Tikhonovich!" shouts Peter Matveyevich, suddenly bursting into the room, "Either you immediately release Minodora Pamfilovna, or it's a duel!"

Ivan Tikhonovich turns pale, is speechless, gets frightened, and suddenly turns into a mouse, but Peter Matveyevich turns into a cat and begins to chase him around the room.

"Oh, that damned cat!" screams Annchen. "She'll break the glass case again! Here, Kitty!"

The cat pays her no attention; Ivan Tikhonovich becomes exhausted, and the cat seizes him with its paws. Suddenly Ivan Tikhonovich squeaks and is quick-witted enough to turn into a cat; he leaps out of the claws and right onto Annchen's neck. Peter Matveyevich is about to reach for Annchen . . . but she cries out, "What do you think you're doing?"

"I am trying to catch Ivan Tikhonovich, my dear; be so kind as to—"

"Get away from me!" Annchen screams and rushes for the door. Peter Matveyevich rushes after her, she from him, he after her, she from him . . . away they run, with people chasing them . . . Stop! Stop! . . . They disappear from sight . . .

Only Alexander Fyodorovich saw them—both awake and when asleep.

A Traveler from the Provinces; or, A Commotion in the Capital

Proclaim, Oh Muses, how a youth lacking humility
Is arrogant,
Lacking modesty is impudent, lacking direction,
Is impetuous,
Lacking purposeful schooling, of the arts
Is ignorant,
Lacking constancy, depraved, lacking firmness,
Is frivolous . . .
Ever sure of himself, yet helplessly heading
For the abyss;
And notwithstanding its faults, crown this creation
With beauty!

Tilemikhida[1]

I

From the tale "Roland the Furious" and the comedy *The Inspector General*, and from other tales and comedies about travelers who arrive from the capital, it is well known, even too well known, what a commotion can be produced in provincial towns by the arrival of vice governors, governors, or inspectors general. It will therefore be fitting to describe in proper form how a similar commotion took place in the capital because of the arrival of a traveler from the provinces, and how the quid pro quo, or the *this* instead of the *that* was received.[2] It is, of course, true that the arrival of such personages as those mentioned above will not normally produce a commotion in the capital; consequently, it would have to have been produced by the arrival of

This story first appeared in the journal *Moskvitianin* (1841) part 1: 131–218; the present translation is based on Aleksandr Vel'tman, *Povesti i rasskazy* (Moscow, 1979). According to L. Ia. Ginzburg (in V. G. Benediktov, *Stikhotvoreniia* [Leningrad, 1939]), Veltman's satirical treatment here of the sudden rise and fall of a poet's fame was suggested by the career of V. G. Benediktov.

some sort of genius. And this is precisely what happened. At a time when there is the most wild craze for geniuses, then, of course you find them where you can or produce them if you have to. And so they produced them: all Europe became full of geniuses—calculating geniuses who immediately understood that owing to the ease, rapidity, and convenience of transportation, one could manage without wings, and that instead of soaring in lofty ethereal space, one could be hauled about by carriage, train, or ship in agreeable company. Consequently, instead of their ancient wings they grew contemporary beards and began to ride about the capitals in public conveyances, some with their violins, some with an entire orchestra, some with their portfolios, some simply with just their hands and feet; there were others with their tongues, or perhaps their throats, and several who had only their European airs. Our poor contemporaries were enthralled by the geniuses and threw money at them, just as in the old days when they were enthralled by mountebanks at fairs.

The genius with whom we are concerned here had arrived in the capital on this occasion not from the European wilds but from the Russian sticks, and therefore those who are not interested in Russian geniuses we request to read no further nor to expect from us a tale in the European manner that expounds some sort of idea.[3]

Having announced this to all who may have no interest in us, let us begin:

The house of Apollon Ivanovich was a house into which only "our geniuses" had entrée. He himself and his brother were filled with erudition; his spouse, Deanira Diogenovna, and her sister-in-law were filled with poetry and the *graces.* Apollon Ivanovich, his brother, Deanira Diogenovna, the damsel Elena, or, according to the latest pronunciation, *Ehleg'n,* and all the visiting geniuses were referred to as "our family."[4] Their *salon* was in the best taste, furnished and arranged not in the old-fashioned symmetrical way with a sofa and a round table and twelve chairs along the sides, but according to the new system of the regenesis or *palingenesis* of taste. Scattered around the flowery patterned rug in a pleasant, poetic disorder were various seating devices: vis-à-vis lounges on springs with little wheels on their legs so they could conveniently be moved toward each other; they also had screws for raising and lowering, delicate arms on which you did not dare rest your weight, and backs you could not lean against. On the mantelpiece stood a bronze clock with the figure of Napoleon in a glass case; on tables with crane legs and on little mushroomlike pedestals—also randomly scattered about—there were lying, as if forgotten, some sort of eternal work project of the lady of the house, an open leather-bound book with gilded pages bearing the author's own signed dedication, a pile of English almanacs, German philosophers, and French novels, and, in addition to all that, the lady's album that was intended to serve as a comment book to be used by all those who were worthy of her attention. Into this room came both our geniuses and the traveling European celebrities: those with singing violins, with throats under contract to the English, with portfolios of artistically smeared sketches; those with their reacquired beards, with their omniscience, with their mother's milk barely dried on their lips. Here then, in the not too distant past, we find Apollon Ivanovich, pacing back and forth and impatiently awaiting the arrival of someone to talk to, since he didn't care to talk to the members of his family. His brother was sitting in a rustic sleigh,[5] concealed behind the open pages of *Le Voleur*[6] as if behind a screen, and occasionally laughing to himself in such an interesting way that Apollon Ivanovich couldn't help asking, "What's so funny, brother?"

"Nothing, brother," Yuly Ivanovich, who didn't like to go into such details, would invariably answer.

Deanira Diogenovna and her sister-in-law sat at their work and maintained a deep silence so as not to exhaust their supply of thoughts and impressions before the arrival of the geniuses and, more important, to conceal them from each other: it very often happened that one of them would pass off as her own some lofty idea of the other, and rivalry over an idea can be just as intense as rivalry in love.

"What can it mean? Neither Pavel Alexandrovich nor Vasily Grigoryevich has come," said Apollon Ivanovich.

"That must be Pavel Alexandrovich now," said Elena suddenly, after turning her head toward the door. "Oh no, it's not him!"

"It's Vasily Grigoryevich," said Deanira Diogenovna.

"How perceptive you are!" said Apollon Ivanovich. "It is indeed Vasily Grigoryevich."

Vasily Grigoryevich, a short-waisted man in a frock coat and carrying a cane, his hair *à la moujik*, nodded his head in the doorway, clumped across the parquet floor to the rug in his huge heels, took first the hand of his host, then that of the lady of the house, bowed with a saccharine smile to Elena, and sank wearily into an armchair.

"Are you at all interested in politics?" asked Deanira Diogenovna. "It seems that you were concerned about the fate of Don Carlos?"[7]

"Oh, by no means! On the contrary . . . I have just been surprised, amazed, overwhelmed! I swear to you! It was extraordinary, incomprehensible! To have such a mastery of the Russian language, to so ennoble it, so to speak . . . so to speak, to sweeten, to radiusize, to aristocratize! I am beside myself!"

"So that's why I'm seeing double!" said Elena, very pleased at her own cleverness.

"I . . . I . . . Oh, please don't ask! It's impossible, you yourself must hear it and feel it! That's poetry!"

"What are you saying? What are you saying?" asked Deanira Diogenovna. "Has Pavel Alexandrovich written some new verses?"

"No, a new poet . . . This is a poet, *Mesdames,* indeed a poet!"
Deanira Diogenovna smirked, and everyone else laughed.

It should be pointed out here that in "our family," Vasily Grigoryevich had been considered the prose genius and Pavel Alexandrovich the poetry genius. They were both men of means, and therefore the literary section of "our family" was able to function without desperate competition. But here, unfortunately, another aspect became involved: one of them would definitely have to be made an *actual* member of the family. Unhappily, they had both chosen the same object for their affections—namely, Elena. A terrible rivalry arose over the question, should her praises be sung in verse or should she be described in prose? At first she inspired them both, but then she suddenly elevated the poet to the position of leading candidate, the one who fulfills the self and the universe; at the same time she began to treat prose disparagingly and even went so far as to tell the prose genius, the spinner of Russian tales, right to his face—a clever dig—that he was in no way inferior to the best French novelists because his tales seemed to be copied word for word from Balzac, Eugène Sue, and other such geniuses. At this point, however, seeming to have perceived that prose can have little influence on the feminine heart and inflamed by rivalry and the desire for revenge, he turned out some doggerel in which each couplet began with the question "Dost thou know?" and ended with the refrain "Dost thou love?" He secretly submitted them to the judgment of Deanira Diogenovna, who had always preferred distinguished prose to mediocre verse.

"Wonderful!" she said.

Vasily Grigoryevich blushed with pleasure at the thought that, having acquired the knack, he would now eclipse the fame of the poetry genius.

"As an intelligent man," continued Deanira Diogenovna, "you can always write pretty poetry, but it will be the poetry of an intelligent man, not a poetry genius. Do not divert the pen of a prose genius with such trifles."

Trifles! Oh how this hurt the prose genius. His first stratagem for destroying the poetic fame of the rival so loved by Elena had failed. Vasily Grigoryevich took another tack. The poetry genius had been revealing his creations only to "our family," and being proud, had no desire to give them up to profanation by the world—therefore Vasily Grigoryevich began to praise his works to the skies and at the same time protest their concealment from the public.

"For heaven's sake!" he said, "To hide such treasures! Not to share the inspirations of your soul with suffering mankind! To refuse to be the representative of the country's literary glory! This is . . . this is . . . egotism! This is contempt for one's fellow man! This is . . . this is . . . this is the Lord knows what!"

At first Deanira Diogenovna and the entire family opposed this call for the sharing and revealing of genius. Even Elena, with emotion and very much to the point, said:

Keep thy holy inspirations
To thyself, O great poet!

But then she added with a sigh, "But then really why not publish . . . The astonishment of the crowd is worth something."

"No, you are *our* poet," said Deanira Diogenovna proudly. "The rabble will neither appreciate you, nor understand you."

"If my works are worthy of praise, then I want to hear it only from you," the poet said proudly, allowing his gaze to encompass the entire group, but especially singling out Elena.

However, Vasily Grigoryevich continued to express his disagreement so sharply and vehemently that finally "our family" began to waver.

"Well, if you think about it . . . why not?" said Apollon Ivanovich.

"Of course," added Elena.

"Well, if I do decide to publish, it will only be a small number of copies—just for our friends."

"Wonderful!" exclaimed Vasily Grigoryevich.

As a result of this decision, the poet carefully copied out on English paper his "Verse Fragments," had them bound in morocco with gilt edges, sent them to the censor, and, finally, a small number of copies of the "Verse Fragments" were printed and distributed to "our family" in a *gros de Naples* binding.

It was night. Vasily Grigoryevich was sitting at his desk wearing a little skull cap; throwing his bathrobe off his right shoulder, he began to write a sarcastic, merciless review, pouring out on the paper his heartfelt pity for the unfortunate poet who had published the unfortunate "Verse Fragments." By morning it was finished, recopied, sealed in an envelope, and mailed to Petersburg, destined to appear in the pages of a journal of literature, industry, fashion, invective, and other such things.

The sin having been committed, Vasily Grigoryevich suffered through an entire month waiting for his article to appear in print. Daily, he made the rounds of all the bookstores and bookshops: had the issue with its lethal attack on the poetry genius been received? Finally it arrived. Vasily Grigoryevich read it, trembled with pleasure, said aloud: "Now we'll see!" Then he put the issue in his pocket and went off to see "our family," on the way preparing exclamations of protest and anathema for journalists who are unable to appreciate genius. Entering the drawing room, he wanted to pull the journal out of his pocket and exclaim: "Would you look at this blasphemy!" but his hand was unable to reach into his pocket; he flushed red for his whole body was ready to betray him . . .

"Lord, it's hot!" he exclaimed and dropped into an armchair.

A day passed, then two, then a week, and not a word—as if neither the journal nor the review of "Verse Fragments" had ever existed. It was an excruciating situation for Vasily Grigoryevich. In the very next conversation about Russian literature he began to reproach all the journalists for not promptly announcing to the public the good news that the "Verse Fragments" had appeared, then he began to reproach all Russians for their indifference to their own literature.

"Surely there must be some exceptions," said Deanira Diogenovna.

"Not one!"

"But what about me?"

"Not even you."

"Why not?"

"Why not? Do you really want to know? I'll prove it to you. Do you have here at least one Russian book? Do you subscribe to even one Russian journal?"

"Your reproaches are in vain: are we the readers at fault if there is nothing worth reading? And the Russian journals consist of nothing but distortions of everything European, crude Russian productions, and vulgar invective. Ask Derzhavin:

May we take flight as on eagle's wings
And reach the sun through soaring thought?

"Invective!" exclaimed Vasily Grigoryevich. "The truth hurts. That's why we call even commonsensible criticism invective."

"Invective! Invective!" repeated Deanira Diogenovna, and she continued:

The slave's unable even to praise,
He tries his best, but can only flatter![8]

At this moment Apollon Ivanovich's brother entered the room with some journals in his hands and some wrinkles on his forehead.

"Poor Pavel Alexandrovich!" he said as he sat down.

"What do you mean?" asked Deanira Diogenovna.

"He's not sick is he?" Elena interrupted with alarm.

"No, thank God."

"It has already been three days, and we've seen nothing of him."

"Have you been to see him?"

"No, I haven't, but that's not the trouble . . . but this . . ." And Yuly Ivanovich began to look for something in the pages of a journal.

"What's that? A Russian journal?" asked Deanira Diogenovna.

"Yes, a Russian journal . . . Listen to this!"

Vasily Grigoryevich began to squirm.

"This is very much to the point," said Deanira Diogenovna. "Let me take a look at the criticism section and I'll prove to you that it's not criticism but simply invective."

"So you have already read this journal?" asked Yuly Ivanovich.

"No, but judging by the others, I am sure you will find the same thing there."

"So they have given it to him in the other journals, too? Poor Pavel Alexandrovich! Listen to what they said about his 'Verse Fragments.'"

"A review of his 'Verse Fragments'? Oh, read it! This is interesting!"

"Right away!" said Yuly Ivanovich, after placing the journal on his knees and wiping off his glasses.

"Wait a minute, brother, let Vasily Grigoryevich read it! He reads better than you do," said Elena impatiently.

With trembling hands Vasily Grigoryevich picked up the journal and began to read his own article.

The members of "our family" were horrified.

"It's the work of an ignoramus!" said Elena.

Vasily Grigoryevich did not wish to support this opinion, but he did not dare to defend the critic, and therefore he bit his lip in silence.

"There's criticism for you! That's how we appreciate genius! How can you defend Russian journals, Vasily Grigoryevich? Do you admit you were wrong?"

"This is unheard of!" said Vasily Grigoryevich with noble indignation.

"I was the first to say that it wasn't a good idea to publish—that he should not publish! Genius will find recognition even without publishing."

"Can you expect the rabble to understand the language of ideas?" said Elena proudly. "What a pity that Pavel Alexandrovich isn't here."

"Brother, go to Pavel Alexandrovich's and bring him here. I am sure that he himself will laugh at his critics."

"I'll go," said Yuly Ivanovich.

Pavel Alexandrovich, his pride wounded, was lying in bed; the fatal issue of the journal was lying on the table. This was how Yuly Ivanovich found him.

"*Bonjour!*"

"*Bonjour!*"

"Have you read it?"

"What do you mean?"

"What? Well this . . ."

"Those swine . . ." the poetry genius said evenly.

"*À manger le foin,*"[9] added Yuly Ivanovich, trying to pour soothing balm on the mortally wounded pride of the poetry genius. However, it was only with difficulty that he persuaded him to go to see "our family," where, by the way, the ladies had been braiding him a wreath of home-grown laurel, and, when he entered the *salon,* they all rushed up to embrace him. Deanira Diogenovna, playing the role of triumphant Fame in a lady's cap, placed the wreath on his head and pronounced a short, dignified speech:

"Your fame cannot be tarnished by envy and ignorance! Accept this crown of glory, bestowed upon you by those who respect your genius . . . ," and so on.

"The ignoramus cannot diminish legitimate praise," said Apollon Ivanovich.

"And it's not praise, if an ignoramus gives it!" added Vasily Grigoryevich with irritation, while looking with alarm at Elena who had taken the hand of the poetry genius and squeezed it in an expression of tenderness.

The poet had completely revived, and, in an exasperated outburst of anger, he said: "These people are ignoramuses who can only judge the taste of hay."

Vasily Grigoryevich was stung by this second defeat. In the general attention being paid to his rival he had been forgotten. After the crowning of the poet, it seemed that Elena had decided to no longer conceal her poetic feelings toward him. In despair, the prose genius, complaining about an upset stomach, declined to stay for dinner and went off to dine at Yar's.[10] No one was there yet, except for a young man who, having ordered beefsteak and a glass of wine, was sprawled out on a couch and declaiming some sort of verses. He paid no attention to Vasily Grigoryevich.

"Well, where's the wine? How long do I have to wait?" he repeated several times.

"Would you be willing to wait until they serve me?" asked Vasily Grigoryevich.

From this they struck up a conversation: one word followed another, about literature, writers, poets.

"Our climate is too cold for poets," said Vasily Grigoryevich. "By the way, could you tell me whose verses you were just reciting? They seemed to breathe some sort of oriental languor . . . The poet must have been acquainted with the East . . . Could it be Pushkin?"

"Oh no, that was one of my friend's southern poems."

"Good Lord! Who is he? Ordynin? It's the first time I've heard the name . . . Excellent poetry! Please repeat it; I am a writer myself and I can appreciate works of genius."

The young man began to recite the following:

On a hill crowned with myrtle,
Where leaps the waterfall wild,
On a bed of fragrant roses—
The refuge of mountain nymphs—
A fair youth inclines his head

Over a tender passionate maid;
Their feelings burst into flame,
Her soul melts in rapturous bliss!
And with his kisses he interrupts
Her passionate whispering,
While, like divine nectar,
He drinks in the maiden's soul!

"Oh, that's excellent! Wonderful! I know of nothing better in that style!"

And with his kisses he interrupts
Her passionate whispering . . .

"Incomparable! What did you say the poet's name was?"

"Ordynin."

"Please be so kind as to introduce me to him. I am beside myself! Hey! Bring some champagne! We must drink to the poet! How does that go?"

The breath . . .
. . . like divine nectar,
He drinks in the maiden's breath.

"He drinks it in like nectar! That's poetry!"

"Oh that's nothing; you should hear his ode on Napoleon. Magnificent!"

"Really? On Napoleon? Let's hear a few verses—please!"

"I can't remember . . . He sees him as an unbridled steed . . .

Above the earth he gallops,
Neighing like thunder . . .

I can't remember—"

"Oh, that's a pity! To the health of the new poet! You must come to see me tomorrow. Hasn't he made anyone's acquaintance here yet? I will introduce him into the best homes . . . Once again: to the health of the new poet! You must dine with me tomorrow! Please! My address: near St. Nikola's, the second side street, just ask for me, everyone knows me . . . And so I'll be expecting you; until then, good-bye!"

II

Vasily Grigoryevich, who was thirsting to *annihilate* the poetry genius, was eager to besiege him with all manner of poets and would-be poets. He rode about Moscow proclaiming the appearance of a new, original poet, while the young man from Yar's ran back to his hotel room on the uppermost floor.

"Ah, you're at home!" he shouted upon entering the dingy room, where a young man in a bathrobe, his hair cut *à la moujik* in an attempt to imitate the latest fashion, was lying on the bed. He was chewing on a cigar and had a pencil and sheet of paper in his hands.

"Listen, my friend, tomorrow we are invited to dine with a well-known Moscow literary figure . . . I made his acquaintance and recited 'On a Hill Crowned with Myrtle' for him. Oh, how I recited! It was wonderful! He was so carried away that he ordered champagne and we drank to your health . . . He memorized the lines and said that by tomorrow all Moscow would be talking about the new poet . . . Well, are you pleased with me?"

"Oh, that's too bad!"

"What do you mean?"

"You should have recited something from my epic poem . . ."

"From your epic poem! But I haven't memorized anything else but those verses . . ."

"Listen to the continuation:

> Having plunged his dagger into the foe,
> The warrior back to his village rode.
> T'was a night of howling wind and raging rivers;
> Suddenly from the distance comes
> What sounds like the crying of a babe . . ."

"Oh, that's enough reciting! Let's get down to business: how are we going to dress for dinner tomorrow? I will feel awkward in this jacket."

"You can wear my frock coat."

"And you?"

"I have ordered a new outfit; it's fortunate that it will be ready by tomorrow."

"Where did you get the money?"

"Right here."

"Bravo! It came from home?"

"Yes."

"Well, admit it now, didn't I show you how to write a convincing letter?"

"Sure! I would never have been able to tell such lies to my mother and father!"

"What do you mean? Who lied? Has not half what you wrote already come true? Tomorrow you will be dining with a famous literary man; after that he will introduce you to other literary men, and they will introduce you to others, and then to all of Moscow, Petersburg, all of Russia, and so on. Your fame will resound from pole to pole and from the nadir to the zenith . . . You're an odd one! Just give me the money you promised: we'll have to hire a carriage for tomorrow in order to set the right tone . . . Don't worry, you just write some verses. I'll take care of everything."

The young men went off to a confectioner's such as that of Renommée and Luguét, while we, in the meanwhile, will say a few words about who they are and why they have come to the great city of Moscow.

We do not know under what circumstances they left the parental nest to try their fledgling wings; but we do know that when one of them arrived in Kharkov to take the examination for admission to the university, he was already a *poet in his soul.* Here he made the acquaintance of our other young friend who had already managed to take the examinations for admission to all the departments and schools of all the Russian universities, but without much success. At Kazan University he took the mathematics examination but failed; at Dorpat he tried philology—and also failed; at the University of St. Vladimir, he sought admission to the law school, but he did poorly; at Moscow he was refused admission to the philosophy department; and finally, here at Kharkov, he tried for the medical school but was again refused. Knowing the names of all the branches of knowledge (his name was odd: Aigolova),[11] he made his living as a private tutor—living in the country with the families of his pupils. However, he did not care for this life and decided to go back to Moscow and give lessons there. Since traveling by oneself can be boring—and he was out of funds—he sought out a traveling companion. At this point he came across the one who was a *poet in his soul.* After smoking their first pipe together, they were already friends and brothers.

"But look, Brother, what can you learn here? Here! In the philology department! You, a poet in your soul! Do you want to write verses in the Kharkov dialect? Congratulations! Enough of this! Let's go to Moscow. There they speak the real Russian literary language; there they have all the educational opportunities, whatever a poet needs: journals, cultured society, libraries—in a word, everything."

The poet was convinced by his friend's words and so they took off for Moscow in a stagecoach that was still mounted on runners. They had to go slowly because it was rainy and muddy, and the poet would like to have flown to Moscow. He remained angry the entire trip:

"Bah! A man's time and talent could perish in this mud and boredom! Onward, onward to the capital! To the enlightened city!

There, where from morn til eve
I'll play and while away the hours
And when the inspired moment strikes
My pen will delight my fellow man!"

They were finally approaching Moscow.

"Where will your honors be staying?" asked the coachman.

"At the best hotel, of course!" the poet answered proudly as he took in the panorama of Moscow with a sweeping gaze and then rapturously declaimed:

Oh Mother of Russian cities!
Oh mighty capital of the mind!

"Do you feel," he continued to his companion, "how the soul becomes filled with delight in the presence of this spectacular view? Oh, it's just overwhelming! It's poetry! No matter which way you look, Moscow stretches out before you, even to the very sky; it's as though it has covered the whole earth, and having run out of space, has gone beyond its earthly limits and been extended into the azure world above! It's enchantment!"

"Bravo! A wonderful notion! Put it in verse!"

"But of course! I shall write my poem 'Moscow' in octaves à la Tasso . . . What activity, what movement, what variety of people, classes, tribes!" continued the poet as they rode through the streets. "How many new impressions for a poet!"

Having arrived at the stagecoach office, they hired two cabs: one for themselves and one for the luggage, because the poet had brought from home not only his clothing but also his feather bed. After loading up, they headed for Tversky Boulevard and the best hotel.

"Is this the very best hotel?" the poet asked the doorman.

The doorman glanced indifferently at the travelers, one of whom was wearing a jacket covered with lint, while the other had on a short, thoroughly greasy, calico caftan, and asked: "May I be of service, gentlemen?"

"Give us your best room."

"You mean one that's a little cheaper? Well, all the cheap ones are taken; you'd be better off finding yourself an inn."

"Listen, you long-eared beast, I said the best room!"

"But, sir, the best room has parquet floors, silk upholstery, expensive mirrors, even a piano . . . If we let just anybody in, they might pay for one night but cause a year's worth of damage: we wouldn't get the mess cleaned up and the trash removed even if we worked overtime."

"Bah! Let's go to another hotel, brother."

"And such a beast is permitted to exist in the world!" said the poet with indignation as they got into the cab.

When they arrived at the second hotel, the poet did not demand the best room but simply a room. After they had been examined from head to foot and their worth thus determined, they were conducted through a series of passageways and corridors and up a dark, filthy staircase to a lofty height and shown a dingy room with two beds and a kitchen table with two chairs in front of the window.

"It's the seventh heaven!" exclaimed the poet looking out the window. "Marvelous! What a view! All the wonders of the earth are at our feet—in clouds of dust and ashes! Here I shall meditate on the transience of it all and sustain myself on poetic thought! Hey, bring us something to eat!"

"Do you wish to order an entire dinner or by the portion?" asked the servant.

"By the portion? No, not by the portion, but by the half portion!"

And when they had been brought a very small portion of soup in which there remained only the memory and recollection of the soups of previous days, the poet declaimed:

> Though the portion's extremely meager,
> As a favorite of Mnemosyne's daughter,
> I feed on feelings—thus I'm eager . . .

But the poet's companion angrily continued:

> But this soup tastes like sea water.

"You ask for a half portion and you get a half portion—no more, no less," said the servant.

After the meal, our travelers were in a hurry to go out.

"Where are you going?"

"What about you?"

"I'm going to the university; I have friends there."

"I'm going to take a look at Moscow."

"Let me have fifty rubles; I've got to order some clothes . . . As soon as I get a *situation,* I'll pay you back right away."

"Here you are," and with these words the poet reached into his pocket and began to count out fifty rubles . . . "There's a ten, a five, another blue one, another, a white one . . . Oh what knavery! There's only fifty rubles left! You'll have to wait until I sell an episode from my epic poem."

"Make it just ten rubles for now; I guess I'll just have to put off my order . . . But don't you have another jacket?"

"Only my new one; but I do have a frock coat."

"Excellent! But I'll need a better pair of breeches to go with it . . . Excellent . . . only they're a little tight; well, in extreme circumstances, I can squeeze myself into them."

"Good-bye!"

"So long!"

The poet went out to look around Moscow. He made his way to Tversky Boulevard, looking about him, reading the signs . . . Suddenly he saw the words *Library for Reading.* Well, a library for reading! He needed to get some books to read . . . A stroll, some reading, some writing, and again a stroll; after a stroll one needs food for the intellect. And so the poet found himself amid intellectual food; he signed up for a month's membership, paid a deposit of twenty-five rubles, and requested the latest novels.

"These are the very latest!" answered the bookseller as he handed him a copy of *The Library of Fiction.*

With *The Library of Fiction* under his arm, the poet headed for the Kremlin. He went straight to the Bell Tower of Ivan the Great and began to mount the steps.

"There is a charge for admission!"

Having paid five kopecks at each landing, it cost him more than a ruble to reach a height from which the people looked like absolutely insignificant creatures. In a state of rapture, the poet stood gazing for a long time at the expanse of Moscow and at the people crawling over the surface of the earth below. It was already evening. A full moon arose over the Rogozhsky gates, but the poet in his state of oblivion called out to the moon's crescent, then to the lofty sky around him, and finally decided to descend to the earth and make his way on foot to his own lofty abode.

His companion had not yet returned and the poet desired to read. He reached for *The Library of Fiction*—but it was nowhere to be found! He had left *The Library of Fiction* up in the sky! Thus ended the poet's reading. Boredom then gave birth to poetic thoughts, and these had to be recorded on paper—but there was no paper! This was no problem for the poet; he tore off the blank half-page from his birth certificate, sharpened his pencil with his teeth, lay down on his bed, and began to pour forth on the paper his "longings induced by solitude." He had covered the half sheet with writing, but the outpouring of his soul continued; he turned the sheet over and filled the other side, first from side to side, then diagonally. He fell asleep without noticing it. The candle, which had been placed on a chair close to the bed, also began to nod, bend over, and suddenly, as if awakening, flare up, lighting the entire room, burning brightly, spreading itself over the wooden chair. Fortunately, Aigolova returned and put out the small conflagration without disturbing the poet's sweet dreams.

The poet liked to sleep until noon. When he awoke, his companion had already left, probably having gone out in search of a *situation*. The poet went out to explore Moscow once more but was bored by himself and so returned home. He waited, sitting by the window, smoking one pipe after another. Only when he once again fell into a deep sleep, his pipe in his mouth, did his companion return. Thus he spent several days—sleeping, walking, waiting in vain for his companion, who only returned to the room to sleep, allowing for this the hours from two until eight in the morning.

On the fifth day, after awakening, drinking his tea, and smoking his pipe, the poet wondered: Should he refill his pipe or should he go out? Suddenly the servant, who had been clearing away the dishes, handed him a bill.

"What's this?"

"It's a bill, sir. We have a policy here of settling with our lodgers on the first of the month. For five days lodging at five rubles per day, for fifteen portions of tea and for the other meals, it will be forty-seven rubles in all."

"All right," said the poet, taken aback by this unexpected and unequivocal demand for money.

"So please, sir—"

"Later, as soon as I get change."

"What do you have? We surely can change it."

"No, I'll get change myself . . . tomorrow."

"Then I will have to inform the innkeeper."

The poet was in despair; he thought for a moment. Suddenly he had a happy thought—to sell his poem to some journal or bookseller. He quickly got his notebook out of his suitcase, put it under his arm, ran into the street, jumped into the first cab he saw, and ordered the driver to take him to some journal editor.

"I don't know where any such man lives," said the driver, "You should ask at the policeman's booth."

The policeman thought for a while, shifted his weight from one foot to the other, and rested his elbow on his halberd: "Jernol, Ed? There's nobody by that name on my block."

"It's where they sell newspapers."

"Newspapers? The Moscow ones? I don't know . . . I haven't lived here very long."

"Then take me to a bookshop."

There would be no difficulty in finding a bookshop, for Moscow has many of them.

"But, sir, what kind of bookshop? Where they sell books, or where they buy them?"

"You see, I need to sell a manuscript," answered the poet.

"Well, why didn't you say so! Now that's what is called a book trader . . . Last week I found a book and brought it there; I thought I could sell it, but no; they said I should take it to the flea market—and glory be! I got thirty kopecks for it!"

"But that was a printed book—a single copy."

"A handsome book; it had a red cover."

"Is it far to the book trader's?"

"It's right nearby."

The driver whipped up his horse and soon, having turned right at the church of St. Nicholas, they found themselves at a flea market where, with some difficulty, they drove through the crowd to a stall where used books were sold.

The poet had hardly gotten out of the cab when he was greeted by the bookseller:

"What can I do for you?"

"Do you buy manuscripts?"

"Why not? What do you have there?"

"Well, I want to sell a verse epic."

"Written out by hand?"

"By hand."

"That is, you wish to print it?"

"Of course I wish to print it."

"And what would be the price?"

"A thousand rubles."

The bookseller closed the notebook and handed it back to the poet.

"You might try one of the bookstores."

The poet set out for the bookstore for which he had just been given the address.

You can always tell a person trying to sell his work by his appearance. In spite of the dignified tone he tries to assume, it is obvious that what he is carrying under his arm is for sale. The most unlikely item for sale is that which is written because it is not sold by weight nor by measure; it does not have an attractive appearance nor an appealing fragrance; you cannot sample its taste in order to decide whether to swallow it or spit it out. Buy it! But what are you buying? Half a ream of scrawled sheets of paper! That's all you've gotten for your money—and what's the use of it? Can you eat it? Can you wear it?

"Would you like to buy an original work . . . an episode from a long epic?" asked the poet, after he had looked around and then approached an impassive-looking bookseller.

"What's this, verses?"

"Verses!" answered the poet with self-satisfaction and expectation.

"No, we're not interested in verses; now if you had written a fortune-telling book, we might be interested."

The poet was struck by this reply.

"Where do they publish journals around here?"

"The journals do pay for verses," said the bookseller.

This rekindled the poet's hopes. He got the address of a journal and went off to call on the editor. He ran into the outer office; there was no one there, so he quietly opened the inner door.

"Who's there?"

The poet entered the room.

"What can I do for you?"

"Do you buy verses here?"

"No, here we sell verses."

"Excuse me," said the poet as he headed for the door.

"That's all right."

Thoroughly disillusioned, the poet went back to the hotel, threw his notebook into one corner, his hat into the other, sat down by the window, placed all five fingers of his left hand on the top of his head, and tightly squeezed his hair in his fist; only by this means was he able to smooth out the wrinkles on his youthful forehead. Then he placed both arms on the windowsill, bent his head down to rest on them, and began to weep. These were his first tears of homesickness, the first time he felt the cold dew on his heart.

There had to be some way to ease the pain. Who could better console him at a time like this than his mother and father?

"But how can I write to my father? What can I say?" thought the poet. "Father, I know, will be angry since I haven't written since I left home; he thinks I am in Kharkov taking the exams, and here I am in Moscow. He gave me five hundred rubles for my expenses for six months and now, after a month and a half, I don't have one kopeck left! What am I going to do? It's not my fault! This could not have been foreseen! I made the trip to Moscow without thinking . . ."

With these thoughts the poet sent for some writing paper and sat down to write a letter. At this point his companion returned.

"What are you working on now?"

"Oh, go to the devil!"

"Well, see if you can rhyme it; I'm leaving."

"What do you mean, rhyme? This is a case of the most ugly prose: the innkeeper wants his money, but there is none!"

"So you are composing something on that account?"

"Yes, a sentimental epistle to my father—that he should send money; if he doesn't, I'm going to jump through that window!"

"A fine son you are! Instead of comforting your parents, you will reduce them to despair!"

"Oh, what's the use! I'm fed up with life! Comfort them! What do I have to comfort them with? Comforts cost money, and where am I going to get it? Five hundred rubles for six months—wonderful! Didn't I myself get accustomed at home to being well fed, to eating five-course dinners, drinking coffee and tea with sweets, and then, suddenly, 'Take this, young man, for bread and water and for patching your clothes and boots!' "

"Exactly! That's the truth!" said Aigolova after listening to the poet's complaints.

"Where are you going? Wait, help me; I don't know what to give as my reasons for coming to Moscow. Listen to what I have written: 'My dear parents! My heart was filled with the most cruel suffering on parting from you. After leaving, I had a pleasant trip to Kharkov; new sights, new places passed before my eyes! I was enchanted, and my soul was enveloped in a cloud of new impressions! God's creation was being opened out before me like a scroll of time . . .' What do you think?"

"Pure poetry!"

"'Suddenly the rains came. The damp weather, together with the change of climate and the water, had a terrible effect on me, and I fell desperately ill. The sickness required great expenditures, so that I have unexpectedly spent all the money I was furnished with . . .' "

"You're lying! All that, my friend, is lying, the most unpleasant kind of lying to one's parents."

"But what am I to do! It's not my fault; as though they would believe that I spent all the money on food."

"You shouldn't lie."

"But what should I say so they will send me money?"

"I told you that you should comfort your parents. The beginning was well written, as far as the words, 'God's creation was being opened out before me like a scroll of time'—cross out the rest. Write: 'Having arrived in Moscow—' "

"What do you mean 'having arrived in Moscow'? I was sent to Kharkov! They will wonder what I'm doing here."

"All right, wait a minute . . . Write: 'Having arrived in Kharkov, I began to study for the exams and make the acquaintance of all the best professors. They took a liking to me, and when they found out I was already writing poetry, they said that with my poetic abilities I must go to Moscow because only there do they have a department of higher poetry; besides that, in poetry and literature the Moscow dialect is used, since it is the best and most free of provincialisms. Not wasting any time, they all advised me to depart immediately for Moscow, especially since the exams were to start very soon. Convinced by these reasons, I immediately left for Moscow where I arrived safely by stage. Oh, my dear parents, you will not believe how overwhelmed I was when I entered our noble capital!'—here you stick in some verses."

"Wait a minute . . . Let's see . . ."

> The churches' gilded spires,
> The belfries' lofty towers...

"The devil! I can't think of a thing!"

"Well how about adding this?"

> All this my soul inspires,
> Thus my rapture lasts for hours.

"No, that won't do!"

> All this my soul inspires . . .

"Wait a minute . . . hours, cowers, bowers . . ."

> All this my soul inspires . . .

"Yes?"

> To sing of love among the flowers . . .

"No, it's no good!"

"Well, enough of this; when you recopy it, you can add what you like. To continue: 'Oh, if you could only see Moscow! Our town is like nothing when compared to it. What magnificent buildings, what splendor everywhere! And how they appreciate talent here! Imagine, I only had to present myself, and everyone immediately recognized that I was a poet; all the literary men offered me their acquaintance, all the journals requested my verses—'"

"Just a minute, brother, that's lying!" said the poet as he put down the pen.

"Were your lies any better? You were about to reduce your mother and father to despair! Continue: 'In a word, I have become a celebrity here; my verses are on everybody's lips, they all are surprised that at my age I have already written a huge epic. You will be surprised, my dear parents, when you hear that I spend every evening at parties and balls given by Moscow's highest society, by the Maecenases of enlightenment. It's impossible to refuse them, but it's frightfully expensive. While I am going full speed ahead in my pursuit of happiness, dear parents, I still must replenish myself, and this requires funds. To maintain acquaintances, to dress properly, to have a decent apartment, to hire servants—all this takes money. Without this financial foundation, the temple of my happiness will collapse. And therefore, my dear parents, I request that you send by return post your parental blessing and a thousand rubles—more, if possible. In the case of further needs, if they should arise, I may once more be appealing to you with filial love. Your obedient son . . .' Sign it! And add a nota bene: 'And now I must devote myself to studying for the exams; as soon as I have more time, I will work on completing and revising my epic poem. The writers have been telling me that *I will get at least ten thousand for it.*' That, brother, is how you have to stir a parent's heart into action on behalf of a child."

"But look, that's really going too far!" said the poet.

"No, not really. Just let them send more money, for once you have the money you can acquire the influence, the honor, and the fame."

"But until they send it, how am I going to pay the hotel bill? What are we going to live on? We have to have fifty rubles by tomorrow."

"Do you have anything we can pawn? Do you have any silver?"

"Three silver spoons and also three teaspoons."

"Sell them! What do you need your own spoons for? I've never had a spoon of my own in my life. Everywhere you go you rent rooms and pay for your meals and they always furnish spoons. And what do you need that feather bed for? A bachelor who has his own feather bed and blankets! That's ridiculous! Everyone will laugh at you! You should sell the lot, turn it into money; meanwhile I'll be getting a situation, or you will be receiving money from your father."

These words were soon converted into deeds. The poet's companion, like a man experienced in such matters, immediately took charge of things. First, he found buyers for all those unnecessary items with which the poet's solicitous mother had supplied him. Second, he came to an agreement with the innkeeper to pay for the room and board by the month. Thus they gained some time to wait for the answer to the letter, especially when the inventory of items for sale was increased by the addition of a watch, table linen, and a shaving set, which the father had given the son so that, when it did become necessary for him to shave his beard, he would not have to waste money on a barber. Aigolova convinced the poet that all these things were unnecessary: that one cannot wear an old-fashioned pocket watch in the capital, that his beard had really yet to start growing, and besides, right now beards were in fashion, and consequently a razor was a completely useless item.

The university examinations were scheduled for July, and therefore the poet was in no hurry to prepare himself to answer questions that would be selected at random. According to his companion's theory, the best way to prepare for the exams was to wait until the last minute, or, in any case, until no earlier than a month in advance, and then not to eat or sleep so as to concentrate all one's mental faculties on committing to memory the entire gymnasium course of study, and then, for three days and three nights before the exams, not to think about them, but to eat, drink, enjoy oneself, and sleep to one's fill, and, after all that, to submit oneself to the examiners on an empty stomach.

According to this system, the poet could dispose of a whole month of time, and even sell it cheaply, if anyone wished to buy it, since it is said that time is one of the most valuable things in the world. In this manner three weeks went by as quickly as their first day in Moscow, the only difference being that the poet was continually visiting the post office and asking if there was a letter for him with five seals on it. Finally the letter was received, torn open, and the money counted out to the poet; he quickly picked up the money, signed the receipt, and headed for the door.

"You forgot the letter!" said the clerk as he was leaving. The clerk ran after him and gave him the letter. Jumping into a cab, the poet glanced at the envelope: *a thousand rubles!* He opened the letter: his father was glad to hear of his successes, advised him not to delay in getting admitted to the university, told him to be careful in making acquaintances; after that came more admonitions—not the best thing to be reading while riding in a cab. Putting away the letter, the poet began to consider how to expend the money prudently on essential needs. The first need—the one that seemed of *primary importance* to a man who had a thousand rubles to spend—was clothing cut in the latest fashion, for although he had left home with everything totally new, none of his provincial outfits would do in the capital because, first, the waist barometer in the capital was set at a few notches higher; second, the collars extended lower in the back; third, the lapels were not to stick out in the front; fourth, the buttonholes were not supposed to reach as far as the buttons; and, finally, the man of fashion had to have a Gallic *paletot*,[12] striped trousers, and lacquered boots with hooves.

All this was ordered on the way home at a foreign establishment where they sold ready-to-wear clothing. The order was to be ready by the next day without fail, and this turned out to be most fortunate. After stopping to eat at Chevalier's, the poet, happy and pleased with himself, returned to the hotel, lit a cigar, threw himself on the bed, and gave himself up to daydreaming. He was thinking about the various items of extreme necessity on which he would have to spend money. Suddenly a wonderful thought occurred to him: he would publish his epic poem and immediately begin to print it. He quickly grabbed his pencil and paper so as to finish the poem as soon as possible. It was at this moment that his companion came in and triumphantly declared that they had been invited to dinner by one of Moscow's famous literary men.

III

We have already mentioned that the prose genius Vasily Grigoryevich had gone out to beat the drum all over Moscow about the appearance of a new, original poet. On that very day he had managed to visit Princess Marya Alexeyevna, the Turusins, the Kolesins, the Berendeyev-Koshins, and many others. He had been to the Arbat, the Povarskaya, the Pokrovka, the Dmitrovka, to all the crooked lanes, on all the hills, at five soirees and ten balls; in a state of ecstasy Mademoiselle Elise urged her fellow poetry lovers, Madam Sofya Plokhonogova, Mademoiselle Esperance, and Mademoiselle Emable, to prepare their souls to be sacred vessels for the sweet feelings that the wonderful new poetry genius from the fragrant lands of the ardent South would pour into them.

"Have you seen him? Have you heard him? What's he like? Another Pushkin?"

Instead of answering, Vasily Grigoryevich recited for the younger generation some verses from Pushkin.

"Oh, that's every bit as good as Pushkin!" they were shouting in the drawing rooms.

"What are our poets compared to Derzhavin!" said the older generation.

Instead of answering, Vasily Grigoryevich recited some verses from Derzhavin.

And everybody exclaimed:

"Are those really the verses of the new poet?"

"Yes, Princess."

"Please introduce me to him!"

"That's genius!"

"Genius, unusual genius!"

"But where are you off to?"

"*Au revoir!* Tomorrow he's dining at my house."

"Give us a chance to meet him!"

"Without fail!"

Until three o'clock in the morning Vasily Grigoryevich was thus occupied in spreading the word about the great new poet; he made the rounds of all his friends, except for *our family,* where the poetry genius was reading the love in Elena's eyes, unaware of the plot that the prose genius was hatching against him. Meanwhile, on the next day, while he was still sleeping, our new poet and his companion were already getting ready to come to his house for dinner. The tailor kept his word: having picked out by size from his stock of ready-to-wear clothing everything that was necessary for a man of fashion—according to the latest patterns that he had received from Paris—he appeared at the hotel at twelve o'clock noon, helped the poet put on the freshly ironed clothing, said that everything fit, sat well, and that such a waist was a thing to behold. The poet wanted to look at himself in the mirror, but there wasn't one in the room. He angrily summoned the innkeeper, took him to task for the lack of a mirror, and demanded that he be given a room with mirrors. The new-fashioned clothing had to be supplemented in many ways: first, brightly polished boots, then a silk handkerchief, a new hat, Swedish gloves, and a stylish cane; in place of his watch, there had to be at least a bronze chain. At the Kuznetsky Bridge all these things were always available and only awaited the arrival of the poet—and the necessary amount of money. As he passed the optical shop, the poet perceived that his vision was weak and decided he needed glasses or at least a lorgnette. The oculist advised him to take both. Passing a wig maker's establishment that included a "curling parlor," the poet's companion said that the poet must have his hair curled.

"What you need is a wig!" said the *perruquier.* "Your own hair is coarse and thin; it must have fallen out as a result of a fever. It can't be curled, and that's all the better: all the fashionable people are now wearing wigs."

The poet could not resist such convincing arguments, and so, at three o'clock, the poet and his companion arrived at the house of the prose genius. In his wig and glasses not even his mother and father would have recognized him, not to mention recent acquaintances. What had happened to his extreme youth? Where did this dignity of *a man of fashion* come from?

Vasily Grigoryevich was comfortably seated in an overstuffed chair in a stylishly furnished room. He was reading a book while waiting for his guests. They had hardly come in the door, when . . .

"Ah, there you are!" he said, extending his right hand to the poet, his left to the companion. "You have interrupted my reading, and at what a wonderful passage: 'The friendship of a great man is a blessing sent from heaven.' I am very, very grateful. I have been looking forward to meeting you with such impatience . . . Your talent . . ."

The young poet, as we already have noted, was in a state of rapture. There was no need to pile firewood under him in order to set him ablaze. His *magnificent toilette* had transformed his provincial awkwardness into originality, or, as they cleverly put it these days, into *somebody.* The conversation immediately turned to literature in general, and then to poetry in particular. But this was soon interrupted by the arrival of two fashionable young men who had been thoroughly trained for drawing-room behavior.

"I recommend to you my friends," said Vasily Grigoryevich. "They are not writers, but men who appreciate genius: Prince Sinegorsky-Korka and Polpudov."

The "appreciators" of genius looked at our poet like astute judges of character and noticed there was something unusual about him.

During dinner the poet, inspired by the special attention being paid to his words and also enflamed by the vintages of Burgundy and Champagne, amazed everyone with his erudition, witticisms, and clever remarks—all acquired from his reading of the journals. In fact, he was a worthy pupil of all six sections of the journals: Russian literature, foreign literature, science and the arts, criticism, literary chronology, and miscellany. He could speak just as authoritatively as if he were quoting from a printed text about everything that had appeared in the past three years (that is, since the time he began reading the journals) in the *Library for Reading.*[13]

"Well, *mon cher?*" Vasily Grigoryevich asked his friend the prince as he led him to one side.

"*Mais, mon cher,*" said the prince, "this is genius, this is a miracle! I will invite him to my soiree on Sunday. My old folks claim that our generation has produced nothing; they challenge us to name at least one contemporary genius worthy of Lomonosov. I will present them with a genius in the flesh . . . Ask him to recite something from his works."

"Oh, he will definitely recite; he promised. I'll ask him."

And so Vasily Grigoryevich, with his friends following behind, approached the poet with an impatient desire for a sample of his creativity.

"I will recite something from my epic."

"Oh no, it would be better to recite 'Castalia's Font,'" said his companion.

Since we have all long ago been frightened off by the reading of epics, they were able to convince the poet to recite "Castalia's Font."

After sighing deeply, the poet sat down, turned his eyes toward the ceiling, and, inspired by both the praise and the champagne, began to recite:

> Oh burbling transparent spring,
> Flowing from your place on high,
> Nourishing this our fruitful vale
> With precious pearls of moisture . . .

"Wonderful! What a line: 'With precious pearls of moisture'!"

The poet continued:

In your silvery coils,
Blushing like a tender maid,
And strewing crimson roses,
Plays the radiant dawn . . .
When . . .

"Oh!"

"Ah!"

When the sun ascends his throne
And illumines all of nature,
Your crystal bursts into flame
And flows like liquid gold!

"What imagination!"

"Charmant!"

"Ah!"

But at night you are most dear to me,
Scattering your pearls in the moonlight;
When all is calm and is at peace
And all the groves are fast asleep . . .
Like a fugitive from daily toil,
I come to you, my beloved spring,
There to slake my spiritual thirst
In the coolness of your bubbling stream! . . .

"Bravo!"

There to slake my spiritual thirst
In the coolness of your bubbling stream!

The poet, now whipped up into a state of frenzy, was chanting like a shaman:

Let me drink at thy banks
And attain that harmonious state
Where my soul soars on high
And my song pours forth in torrents!

"Incomparable! Wonderful! Oh, how good that is! A Russian Hugo!" they all shouted as they stared at the poet as if at a wild beast, while he wiped the sweat from his brow and began to walk about the room waving his handkerchief.

Prince Sinegorsky-Korka invited the poet to a soiree at his house.

"You would be doing us an honor, and I hope you will enjoy yourself: there will be music, singing, and dancing. In Moscow's chosen society it's only a poet we've been lacking."

The invitation, of course, was accepted, and his companion whispered: "Didn't I say that everything you wrote to your father was the truth?"

Prince Sinegorsky-Korka played a prominent role in both the drawing rooms and in the feminine hearts of Moscow. Not only did the young maidens put on airs in his presence, but also the pretty, tender, enchanting, and captivating older women tried to play the role of innocent, maidenly victims, suffering in the shackles of marriage. To everyone with whom he graced his attention, he made the apropos announcement that Russia now possessed a genius of poetry and that on Sunday he would be reciting his works *chez nous*. On the very next day all the greetings and salutations in the twenty wards, hundred blocks, two hundred streets, three hundred lanes, and thousand drawing rooms began with the words: "Oh, have you heard?"

"Yes, I know, she's getting married to—"

"No, that's not it! A new poet has appeared who makes Pushkin look like a scribbler."

"Oh, I did hear that; they say he's something unusual, something in a completely new manner . . ."

"Have you heard?"

"Yes, I've heard."

"From whom?"

"From . . . from . . . at least twenty people," answered Mademoiselle Tekla hurriedly, since she did not want to say the name of Prince Sinegorsky-Korka because that would make her blush.

"Oh, have you heard? There's a new poet."

"Yes, the day after tomorrow he will be reciting his verses at the prince's, and I'm definitely going to be there."

"Do you know if it's by invitation?"

"Yes, I think so."

And there were other ways of beginning:

In the drawing room: "Have you seen the new poet? What a genius! He has really spread his wings! He soars like an eagle!"

In the servant's quarters: "Vanka, did you hear? They say a man with wings has appeared! I'd sure like to see that!"

In the drawing room:

"So you haven't seen him? I haven't seen him yet either."

"Where is he from?"

"He just came back from a trip."

"Oh my God, surely I saw him in the theater—in the front row of the orchestra . . . a new face . . . with a crowd around him."

"How did he look?"

"A tall man, his hair down to his shoulders, pale, with a languid gaze . . ."

"Oh, that must have been him!"

And on the street everyone was bustling about and asking each other about the appearance of the new poet.

"Something like the iambics of Barbier or Lamartine . . . but they say he's better."

"Vraiment? je veux apprendre le russe." ["Really? I want to learn Russian."]

"Il nous a lu 'La fontaine de Castali'—charmant! Il vous depeint comme la nature dore aux alentours et le ruisseau magique roule ses ondes de perles." ["He read us 'Castalia's Font'—charming! He describes how nature gilds the surroundings and the enchanting stream rolling its pearly waves."]

No less agitated than anyone was the civil councilor Lukyan Petrovich.

"Did you hear, Woman?" he said to his wife as he ordered her to hurry up and finish shaving him, get his wig, and help him get dressed.

"What are you talking about, Husband?"

"A miracle has occurred in Moscow!"

"What sort of miracle, Husband?"

"It's a man with wings, Woman."

"What are you saying, Husband? Who told you that?"

"Peter."

"Which Peter?"

"What do you mean, Woman, which Peter? Have you forgotten the name of my manservant?"

"Peter talks nonsense, and you listen."

"What do you mean, nonsense? He heard it with his own ears from Prince Sinegorsky's servants. Peter! Come here! Tell us what you heard."

"The prince's people have been saying that a man with wings is coming to the prince's house. The prince and the princess are inviting all their acquaintances to come see him. They say he will fly around in the main ballroom."

"It's odd that they didn't think of inviting us if there's going to be something like that to see!" said the civil councilor's wife in a voice that expressed her wounded pride. Her husband had been a civil councilor since the beginning of the century. "You're not going to go there and plead for an invitation are you?"

"What do you mean plead? As if paying a call on the prince means I am looking for an invitation!"

"Oh, that will be very natural! . . . And why all the curiosity, why such impatience!? You'll see, Husband, but it will be at your expense."

"Curiosity! I expect it's worth something to see a man with wings!"

"And do you believe, Husband, that he has real wings?"

"And why not believe, Woman? People are born joined together, like, for example, Siamese twins; why can't they be born with wings? It's a trick of nature. It could happen that during her pregnancy a woman could be frightened by wings, and so a child is born with wings. You yourself know what happened to Akulina Yakovlevna: she was frightened by a mouse, and her child was born with a mouse under the eye. Anything is possible."

"But still I don't believe it! The only men with wings are the angels in heaven."

Lukyan Petrovich thought for a moment.

"Well, we'll see," he said. "Anyway, the prince will surely invite us."

Meanwhile, while Lukyan Petrovich waited for his invitation, rumors were spreading like wildfire, here jumping a firewall, there leaping across a street. And as everyone knows, during the spreading of such flames, both old and new winds can be stirred up.

The news was even carried over the fence to Filat Kuzmich, a prominent, honored member of the merchant's guild who wore a gold chain around his neck.[14] It was that same Filat Kuzmich who had bought for himself a *princely palace*, only this one lacked certain armorial decorations. About this he said, "What do I care about the nobility! I am master here!" And he added Russian-style sleeping accommodations to the heating stoves in the princely chambers and moved in with his household of six people, which included Anisya Tikhonovna, Fedya, an old woman, two kitchen wenches, and a porter. In the past the former owner used to entertain five hundred guests at a time, burn up to two hundred pounds of wax candles in an evening, spend about a thousand rubles a day on food and twice as much on drink, whereas now the frugal Filat Kuzmich kept the gates locked and his watchdog barked through the opening at passersby, as if to say: "Keep on going or I'll be gnawing on your bare bones!" The only light was that provided by the almighty, except for the icon lamp and one tallow candle. The gilded furniture was kept under covers so that it would not be spoiled by lack of use. For food, there was *some soup of one's own and a marrow bone*. But as for the samovar, it was of noble proportions, requiring about three buckets to fill it; it was too bad the cups were so very small, each one containing about one swallow. Filat Kuzmich lived his life as though he were guarding someone else's wealth. The garden was much too large, so he had it plowed up and planted with cabbages and cucumbers. The conservatory he left as it was (for him it was the "conserve-a-tree"), only he wouldn't think of taking any of its fruit for his own use, but rather put the produce up for sale. He never used the front entrance; one time he was about to, but then he imagined that he saw the old prince's doorman standing there with his staff in his hand and shouting at him, "Hey there, you piece of trash, where do you think you're going?" Ever since that time, Filat Kuzmich kept the front entrance locked.

"Filat Kuzmich, have you heard what people are saying?" asked Anisya Tikhonovna, "They say that some sort of winged man has appeared."

"What's that?"

"What do you suppose it can be? It happened at Prince Sinegorsky's estate, and now they're bringing him here; I expect all Moscow will come running. Maybe you could get the prince's porter to sneak you on to his balcony or perhaps find you a place near the door so you could get a peek."

"Aha! Well then, Fedya! Get over there and ask the porter to come here. Tell him that your papa has a piece of business to talk over."

Fedya took off while Filat Kuzmich, after significantly clearing his throat, took out his wallet and said, "Just wait, we can arrange this."

The rumors had spread far beyond the city gates, even to the estate of Akim Ivanovich. It was a wonderful estate, the land was rich, but there was no time to plow it because it included that cursed forest which was the apple of Akim Ivanovich's eye and around which he set up skirmish lines to protect it. As soon as the weather got warm, Akim Ivanovich would go out to inspect his forest. "They've been stealing! I can see that they've been stealing!" he would say, and then order the whole village to construct earthworks and ditches around the forest—and the forest was about fourteen miles around. Then he wanted a ditch around the village, then around the entire estate, and thus he passed the summer.

When the man who was sent to Moscow to buy new spades and shovels had returned, Akim Ivanovich inspected the works and discussed the situation with his steward.

"Well, Brother Savely, if I were a rich man, I would surround the estate with a stone wall twenty feet high; that would fix it so no thieving devil could cart off my wood! . . . Aha! Look over there! Is that some peasant wenches trying to sneak away? Grab them and bring them here! Thieves! Stealing mushrooms! Show me what you've got there."

"These aren't mushrooms, but berries, your most high honor."

"Give them to me!"

And Akim Ivanovich took the pitcher with the wild strawberries they had gathered, poured them out into his hands, squashed them all in his fingers, and then smashed the pitcher on the ground.

"There's your berries for you! Stay out of my woods! . . . Get out of here! . . . Ah! Did you bring them?"

The steward, having just returned from Moscow, bowed down to the ground and reported that he had brought everything. In fact, he had brought—besides shovels, spades, and pickaxes—the news that Yany, the winged man, had appeared in Moscow. This news so alarmed Akim Ivanovich that he immediately set off for the city.

IV

May all our contemporary geniuses be as lucky or as fortunate: only toward evening on Sunday did the crowds begin to press against the fence surrounding the house of Prince Sinegorsky-Korka. They had come to see the winged man, just as in the olden days they had come to see an elephant or some bearded foreign emissary. Slowly the carriages began to arrive—first just a few; they rode back and forth several times, stopping and waiting, as if they couldn't decide to pass through the crowd. Then others, having seen the first ones and being curious about the reason the crowd had gathered, slowly drove up and gradually a line was formed. Meanwhile, people hawking apples, oranges, ice cream, toys, gingerbread, and poppy seeds began to circulate among the crowd. The only thing missing was someone with a samovar selling hot *sbiten*[15] or molasses with ginger, but alas these Russian treats can no longer be found in Moscow, their place having been taken by cheap tea and French confections made from potato flour and treacle.

So here on the street, in front of the house of Prince Sinegorsky, a regular parish festival was taking place—without police permission. One row of carriages stretched along the street, and another had penetrated into the prince's inner courtyard.

The young prince, having proposed to introduce the gifted poet to his mother and father, had invited only his own circle of friends, people who appreciated talent; in passing, he had also mentioned to certain *charmantes personnes* that there would be a literary evening at his house on Sunday. However, no formal invitations were extended nor intended. It is true that the old prince had whispered to some of his old friends: "Come and see us on Sunday evening; a young poet is going to recite his poetry. They say it's very good." And the old princess had also been whispering to various people: "Come and see us on Sunday evening; we are entertaining a famous writer . . . He will be reading some of his poetry." But they really did not intend to make it a formal occasion, all the more so since the old prince had no use for either the new enlightenment or the new literary lights and did not wish to honor some young smart aleck poet with a special reception including the full illumination of the house and formal invitations.

Evening came. The prince and princess went into the small sitting room and, not wishing to make it appear that they were expecting the poet, began the evening in their usual way.

"What is the meaning of all those carriages and that crowd of people?" asked the princess. "Go and find out!"

"But Your Excellency, they are waiting for the guest who is supposed to be coming here tonight," answered the servant.

"What is so unusual about that; is he really so famous that a crowd has gathered just to see him?" asked the princess. Suddenly the arrival of his excellency Prince Kuchuk-Kaimakanov with his princess and their daughters was announced.

"Their timing couldn't be worse!" said the lady of the house. The prince went to greet them.

"We just stopped by to see you; we were out for a ride when suddenly we saw this crowd of people . . . 'What's going on here? It must be a parish festival,' I said. 'Princess, let's stop and see.' 'Let's,' she said, and so here we are."

"We're very glad to see you!"

"How have you been?"

"Very well, thank God. What's new in Moscow? They say—"

"Marfa Grigoryevna Trusin with her daughters and her nieces!" announced the butler.

"Very well!" said the princess with a frown.

"I have come, Princess, to bid you farewell," said a magnificently dressed woman in a ringing voice as she entered the room followed by a crowd of graceful creatures. "Next week we are going to Petersburg, so that perhaps we might not have been able to—"

"Peter Sergeyevich Vesnevitsky and his spouse! Marya Yakolevna Gushchin!" Then came the Korovkins, then the Muzins, Puzins, and Zuzins, and soon the sitting room was filled with unexpected guests.

"Tell them to light all the candles in the main drawing room!" whispered the lady of the house to her husband as she seated the guests and attempted to conceal her irritation.

Meanwhile, there was a real crush outside in the courtyard and on the street; so many carriages had stopped that no one could get through.

"This beats everything!" shouted a police sergeant. "Giving a ball and not informing the police!" With the help of a constable he began to clear away the crowd and open a passage for the carriages.

The princess had just brought her guests into the main drawing room when suddenly the sound of movement in the hall was heard and everyone fell silent.

"Prince!" shouted Vasily Grigoryevich as he ran into the room, "I have brought the poet!" Behind Vasily Grigoryevich came the young poet—without his comrade because Aigolova did not care for aristocratic soirees.

Proudly raising his head, he clicked his heels in the doorway, and, because it was his habit to scratch his head with his whole hand, he nearly pulled off his wig.

"We are much obliged to you!" said the young prince as he took him by the hand and led him into the drawing room to present him to his mother and father.

The poet was overawed by the brilliantly lit drawing room full of people of the highest society; he began to feel dizzy and things swam before his eyes. In a rather original way, he bowed first to the princess and then to the prince. But when young Prince Sinegorsky let go of his hand and left him entirely on his own, standing there in the midst of that well-behaved public, his self-control completely disappeared. He was unable to move, rooted there in that circle with all eyes fixed on him. In fact, such a situation is unendurable for one who doesn't know that in such cases the thing to do is to squint or stare directly at them all so as to extinguish those bright sparks in their eyes, and then turn about on one leg and thus move out of that enchanted encirclement. Seeing eyes everywhere, the poet let his gaze follow the line of the cornice—all the way to the door . . . The door! The door of deliverance! One could go out through it!

All this, however, can be excused as *originality* in a person whom the public has proclaimed *extraordinary*.

"He's really quite good looking! And still so young!"

"Well, to me he seems more young-looking than actually young; that paleness and gravity in his face suggest wide experience in life."

"Did you arrive here in Moscow a long time ago?" asked the old prince as he went up to the poet.

"Oh yes, sir!"

"From far away?"

"Yes, from far away," answered the poet who had lost any conception of *time* and *distance* and was thinking only of *place*.

"Would you like to sit down?" asked the old prince.

Fortunately Vasily Grigoryevich moved in and loudly began to sing praises of the poet's works. This revived him.

"I hope," said the prince, "that you will afford us the pleasure of listening to something of yours."

"With particular pleasure! I would very much like that!" answered the poet, regaining his self-control and rapping out his words.

"Oh! 'Castalia's Font'! It's so charming!" said Vasily Grigoryevich.

"Please recite it," said the princess.

"Well, that poem is really not that good," said the poet, fixing his gaze on the ceiling while seeming to recall the lines. As was the custom in society, all attention was focused on him. In a whispering voice, he began to recite:

> Oh burbling transparent spring, . . .

The dignified matrons listened in thoughtful silence; the pretty young things listened, as usual, with an attentive gaze; the patriarchal heads of families, having removed the cotton from one ear, inclined their heads in the direction from which the spring of Castalia flowed; and the young society gallants were trying to catch something with their eyes and were not sparing in their praises: "Bravo! Bravo!" was heard whenever the poet pronounced something especially loudly or with feeling.

Vasily Grigoryevich could not restrain himself; with a glance at the pretty young things, he rapturously repeated: "Blushing like a tender maid! What a line! And how original! Poets are always comparing a blush with the red glow of dawn, but *monsieur* compares the red glow of dawn with a maiden's blush."

This observation made a great impression on the fair sex and also on its admirers. "*Charmant!*" proclaimed one melodious voice, and this was followed by assorted shouts of "Bravo! Bravo!" The audience's attention was now secured, and everyone was thirsting for more poetry.

"Don't you have a poem called 'Napoleon'?" asked Vasily Grigoryevich.

"Ah, Napoleon! Napoleon!" repeated all the admirers of the *hero of our age*.

"A comparison to Lamartin and Pushkin would be interesting!"

"Oh, he will not refuse our request to recite it!" said Vasily Grigoryevich.

The poet, spurred on by praise, wiped his forehead, boldly cast an inquisitive gaze on them all, and pronounced in a loud voice: "Who is he?" Everyone was taken aback by the unexpectedness of the question.

Who is he?
A giant, a new Atlas,
Who has lifted the world to his shoulders
And subdued it to his will
With his mighty conquering arm?

The poet paused as if waiting for an answer, but they all kept silent.

Who is he?
Like an unbridled steed,
Above the earth he gallops,
Neighing like thunder,
His nostrils breathe forth whirlwinds,
His mouth belches clouds of foam,
His gaze sends out sheaves of lightning,
He tramples kingdoms under his hooves!
Who is he?

"Bravo! Bravo! He's another Barbier!"

"He's better!"

"'Above the earth he gallops, neighing like thunder'! How about that!"

"Amazing!"

Who is he?
Under a flaming crown,
His feet planted upon the bosom of the earth,
He's arrayed in a fiery purple robe,
Woven from strands of lightning.
At his feet lie the slaves of slaves,
Neither dead nor alive;
His terrible gaze directs hosts of regiments,
His right hand reckons up the losses!
Who is he?
Who is he? That invincible leader,
The object of choruses of earthly praise,
Who snatches crowns from royal heads.
Who is he? Do not ask!

Fallen is the genius, fallen
Is he who tasted glory,
The storms have ceased, the thunder still'd!
All the world's enveloped in silence
And Adam's race is again at rest . . .
And once more the river of time
Flows smoothly down to sea.[16]

"*Incomparable!* Wonderful!"

The poet was in a state of rapture as he listened to the exclamations of admiration and wonder. No less exultant over his success was Vasily Grigoryevich—but for a different reason. *Everything is going according to plan,* he thought, rubbing his hands together.

"I give you the first poet of Russia!" he kept repeating as he squeezed the poet's hand.

"Yes," said the old prince, carried away by the general enthusiasm. "I don't think I have ever heard anything better!"

"Bravo! Our generation is victorious!" exclaimed the young prince.

The exalted poet, in an attempt to quell his internal agitation, began to pace the room while fanning himself with his handkerchief. The young girls were also walking about in pairs, trying to get as close to the poet as possible in order to get a good look at his features and his poetic eccentricities. From the next room came the sound of chords being struck on the piano; everyone quickly jumped up and rushed off in haste to join the circle around an incomparable singer of romances *whose fame was already established.* This young man had the *voice of a Stentor,* if you will excuse an old-fashioned comparison. The poet was left standing in the middle of the room, forgotten; he was trying to recall the best scenes from his long epic, since he felt sure they would again surround him and demand that he recite something else. As he was concentrating on the text of the third chapter, which consisted of no less than five hundred lines, he suddenly heard the enthusiastic shouts of "Bravo!" "*Charmant!*" coming from the next room; only then did he realize his total abandonment.

He felt hurt that no one had asked him if he wanted to hear the singer with the powerful voice, but it seemed to him that it would be impolite just to walk into the room without being invited. And so the young poet, his pride having been both stimulated and offended by the treatment he had received, left the house and went home.

V

Vasily Grigoryevich, the person responsible for spreading the fame of our poet, was already secretly celebrating the eclipse of his rival in an affair of the heart. He could already see how Pavel Alexandrovich's pride would suffer when before "our family" would appear the new poet about whom all Moscow was buzzing, and how Elena would not wish to continue to demean herself through her love for a star that had lost its brilliance.

You will recall how Vasily Grigoryevich had rushed in to "our family" and proclaimed that he was "surprised, amazed, overwhelmed," in a word, that he was "beside himself"; well, that was the day after the poetry reading at the Sinegorskys.

"I am beside myself!" he repeated.

"How can that be?" asked Elena.

"I . . . I . . . Oh, please don't ask! It's impossible! You have to see for yourself, to listen to him, to feel it!"

"This seems very curious," said Deanira Diogenovna. "I expect that finally you will tell us what it is that has so surprised you and so overwhelmed you."

"A great poet has appeared!"

"Ha, ha, ha! We have heard something about him. Just where are we supposed to find him if we want to see this greatness? By the way, he may only agree to perform for money."

"You may laugh, but I am not joking; I have seen him with my own eyes and listened to him with my own ears; I have made his acquaintance, and our first conversation was about you and your family."

"What do you mean?" asked Deanira Diogenovna in cold surprise.

"Well, my God, is it surprising that an educated man of letters, a poet, having come to Moscow, would not have heard of you and would not express a desire to make your acquaintance? Your house is the center of that educated society that evaluates and appreciates talent."

"Apparently you are attempting flattery," said Deanira Diogenovna.

"If you wish to consider the general opinion flattery, well, that's your prerogative. In any case our poet, who shares this opinion, has in fact requested that I arrange a time for him to be presented to you."

"I would be very pleased! It will be a pleasure to receive the great poet in my own home—you have been singing his praises so much and all Moscow is talking about nothing else," said Deanira Diogenovna with a smile, her last words attempting to disguise her feelings of gratified self-esteem.

"What kind of poetry does he write?" asked Elena, also with a smile. "Lyric, dramatic, satiric, or romantic?"

"I have heard some of his lyrics and some of his romantic poetry; however, he is also working on an epic, an epic that also includes drama. A true poet must be a master of all the poetic genres."

"So that's it!" said Elena dryly. Vasily Grigoryevich's comment had hurt her pride, since the poet of "our family" was considered only a lyric poet and everyone had advised him against attempting an epic or a drama and had said that his talent did not extend to those forms. But they did believe that their poet was capable of *lofty flight* and to Elena he was nothing less than a "general of poetry," and here someone had dared to suggest that he was no more than an *oberversmacher* with fledgling wings. Elena was ready to cry out with irritation: "Hand over your pen; you are under arrest; confine yourself to your quarters!" but she managed to hold herself back.

"So in your opinion, a lyric poet cannot be a genius?" she asked, in a voice that revealed her wounded pride.

"Mademoiselle *Ehleg'n*, you understand all things better than I, and therefore your question is completely superfluous."

"Why better than you?" she asked, fully satisfied with his answer.

"Because the gifts of nature, when they are developed to such a degree of perfection as they are in you, cannot be shared by many."

The prose genius knew very well how to gild his speeches and include the kind of precious words that would indulge her fragile and sensitive pride, and therefore the girl, whose natural gifts *were* developed to such a degree of perfection, was thoroughly pleased by this answer.

"And I must remind you that today you seem to be disposed to flatter everyone," said Elena with a pleasant smile.

"And I shall repeat to you what I said to Deanira Diogenovna on the same topic."

"Let us quarrel no further. When will you be bringing the new poet here?"

"It could be as soon as tomorrow, if I find that everyone here is eager to see him and hear him."

"Oh, we are all very eager to see him and hear him!"

With this the conversation about the poet ended. Soon Vasily Grigoryevich left, saying he had to attend to some affairs. And in fact he made several visits, hither and yon, to everyone acquainted with the house of Apollon Ivanovich, announcing that tomorrow evening the great poet would be giving a reading at Apollon Ivanovich's. This produced the desired effect. The next evening, at Apollon Ivanovich's, there was a repeat performance of what had happened at Prince Sinegorsky's. All their close—and not so close—friends, as if by chance, dropped by to see them. Pavel Alexandrovich, who for some time had been a daily visitor, was also there.

When Vasily Grigoryevich arrived with the poet, all the rooms were filled to capacity, as if it were a public auction. They were all talking about the new poet, and those who had been at the Sinegorskys' house proclaimed he was "wonderful!"

Deanira Diogenovna had hardly announced, with self-satisfaction, "He will be here tonight," when the poet came in the door; meanwhile, Pavel Alexandrovich took a seat in a remote corner so as to avoid such unpleasant questions as "Have you seen the new poet?" "Have you met him?" "A genius!" "An entirely new style!" Pavel Alexandrovich simply shuddered and turned pale.

Vasily Grigoryevich introduced the poet to the host and hostess. The poet was now self-assured; he bowed with the solemnity expected of a genius, looked over his audience with a confident gaze, and began to talk about literature, poetry, and the journals. They gathered around him, and soon he was being showered with requests to recite something, and, especially "Napoleon." The general admiration for the poet impressed Elena; she devoured him with her gaze, listened to him, but was unable to interrupt the flow of his words with her own comments, for his manner of speaking was so strange and new to her. Vasily Grigoryevich kept shouting, "Exactly so!" "Precisely!" "Absolutely right!" "How original!" and then proceeded to attack a student from Petersburg who had dared to disagree with a statement the poet had made. Poor Pavel Alexandrovich, pale from agitation, did not take his eyes off Elena. The poet began to recite his ode on Napoleon, and when, after the lines, "Above the earth he gallops, / Neighing like thunder . . .," the whole room was rocked with exclamations of astonishment, and Elena said, as was her custom, "*Dieu, comme c'est beau!*" Pavel Alexandrovich seized someone else's hat in his confusion and disappeared.

The next day he did not make an appearance at the house of "the family"; pacing the floor in desperation, he tried to compose a poem to the *deceiver*, but this, of course, has become an extremely difficult task, ever since Baratynsky wrote his "Disillusion."[17] If you should happen to be disappointed in love, then of course you will immediately recall the lines:

> Don't offer me your consolations
> Or promises of renewed esteem;
> The lure of yesterday's temptations
> Cannot revive my shattered dream![18]

However, it turned out differently for the poetry genius; he recalled these lines and cried out, "Oh, she is going to pay for my disillusionment!" and began the process of disillusioning himself. First, he vowed not to visit "our family" for a whole week, not to even leave the house so as to avoid running into the perfidious Elena; second, he decided that after this period he would treat her with an icy coldness; third, when his works appeared in print they would be dedicated to Mademoiselle Turusin, with whom Elena had more than once crossed swords in bitter intellectual debate.

Meanwhile, while the poetry genius was growing thin from his disillusionment, Vasily Grigoryevich was visiting "our family" every day and attempting to divert the favor of Deanira Diogenovna and Elena in his direction. When he appeared the day after the reading, he showered them with a thousand compliments in the name of the new poet.

"He has lost his head over you!" he said to Deanira Diogenovna. "'She is a woman of ideal intellect, a woman of charm and enlightenment!' . . .

Excuse me, but those are his words; I cannot keep them to myself because they are in such agreement with everyone's opinion, including my own."

"He has lost his head over you!" he said to Elena. "'She possesses ideal beauty, not the cold, classical beauty of a statue, but a beauty that is romantic, enchanting!'"

"He's very gracious," said Elena with lowered eyes. "From his words at least, it seems that, like me, he doesn't care for the classical Greek type of beauty."

"More than that, he hates it just as I do; we have the same tastes . . . How did he put it? . . . 'Woven from strands of lightning . . .' Do you remember the passage? What poetry! *C'est du sublime!* Those lines belong in your album."

"Oh, you make too much of my album!" said Elena incautiously.

"But tell me, how would you rank the talent of this new poet?"

"Really, I can't say. Let me hear your opinion, and I will agree."

Vasily Grigoryevich leaned toward her and said, "I don't envy anyone who is truly worthy of fame and admiration; therefore I would assign him to the first rank, at least at the present time. Envy is the vice of petty souls, of those of trifling ability who fear the appearance of great talent."

Having thus cast a shadow over the poetry genius, Vasily Grigoryevich, no earlier than the fourth day, inquired as to the meaning of the absence of Pavel Alexandrovich.

"He hasn't been to see us since that evening," said Deanira Diogenovna.

"He didn't stay for supper as he usually does," added Apollon Ivanovich.

"Imagine!" said Vasily Grigoryevich, "He didn't even listen to the ode on Napoleon to the end. I was hoping we could share our feelings of enjoyment, but when I looked for him he was not to be found. When I asked, they said he had left. Perhaps he wasn't feeling well."

"Perhaps!" said Elena with a certain agitation.

"Perhaps he is sick!" repeated Deanira Diogenovna. "We should find out."

"Who's sick?" asked Yuly Ivanovich, aroused from his reading of the *Debats*.

"Pavel Alexandrovich."

"How about that! I dropped by to see him yesterday; there was nothing wrong with him."

"Oh sure, according to you, Uncle, everyone is healthy unless they are unconscious," said Elena.

"I will go and see him right now!" said Vasily Grigoryevich, seeming to sympathize with Elena's concern. And he immediately left for Pavel Alexandrovich's house.

"What's wrong?" he asked as he entered his room. "No one has seen you for quite a while."

"Nothing," answered Pavel Alexandrovich dryly.

"Oh, by the way, what do you think of that young man's poetry? Not bad, don't you think?"

"Yes, of course, he has some ability."

"Yes, of course, some ability—no one would argue that; but what really infuriates me is this passion for bestowing on everyone the title of genius! I have just come from Apollon Ivanovich's . . . Oh what a to-do!"

"What do you mean?"

"They are still raving about him. That's all they talk about; they consider him the *nec plus ultra* of perfection. Mademoiselle *Ehleg'n* is beside herself. She spent all day yesterday memorizing his verses. When I went there this morning, I thought that perhaps this fever had cooled down—nothing of the kind! It was even worse . . . And I must admit, I did praise everyone who contributed verses to her album."

"And so?"

"Well, she would have asked the great poet to write something in her album, but, you see, she felt embarrassed about offering him an album containing all sorts of wretched doggerel."

Pavel Alexandrovich flared up; he wanted to say something but managed to restrain himself, while Vasily Grigoryevich, having torn the poet's heart into pieces, set out for the bookstore to pay a call on Russian literature.

"What's new?" he asked the bookseller as he picked up a copy of the *Northern Bee*.

"They're saying, Vasily Grigoryevich, that some sort of extraordinary poet has appeared; have you heard about him?"

"Of course," answered Vasily Grigoryevich carelessly as he scanned the pages of the paper.

"I have heard that he's been reciting his poetry in public. Is that true?"

"So it seems."

"Has he written a lot? Is there enough for a book?"

"An epic, a huge epic!"

"And where might he be living?"

"In a hotel . . . Hmm, what's the name of it? . . . Oh yes, he was talking about moving to the London. You must go and see him."

"Do you think he would sell the manuscript?"

"Definitely."

"Please, Vasily Grigoryevich, try to arrange it so he will sell it to no one else but me; I would like to go and see him."

"All right, all right . . . and what about my stories?"

"Surely it would be more to your advantage to print them yourself, Vasily Grigoryevich."

"No, I don't want to get involved in that. It's my job to write stories—and yours to buy and print them."

"Perhaps next year. Look, I've got twenty manuscripts lying around here now and no money to pay for the printing."

"But you do have money to buy an epic? A tale in verse? At a time when no one is buying poetry?"

"But this is an exceptional event."

"What do you mean by that?"

"It's a special case. Let's say, for example, that some event has taken place, like the battle of Borodino or the Khiva campaign;[19] well, a book would be just the thing—people would buy it out of curiosity. It's the same with this new poet: while the shouting continues, everyone wants to know what all the fuss is about."

"Do you have Ordynin's poems?" asked a man who had entered the store.

The clerk handed him a book with a yellow cover.

"Give me three copies."

Having paid good money for the three copies, the man left the store.

"How come you were asking me whether Ordynin would sell his poetry for publication when here it is already published?" asked Vasily Grigoryevich.

"Published, but without the author's name."

"Let me take a look at it."

"It seems there are no more . . . those three were the last ones."

"What do you mean the last ones, what's this here . . ." and Vasily Grigoryevich reached out and took from the shelf a yellow-covered book with the title *The Poems of I. O.* "Wait a minute, these miserable verses were written by Olsky!"

"I'm not sure how that happened . . . I bought them from a peddler as the genuine verses of Ordynin . . . Look how I have been cheated!"

"Wonderful!" exclaimed Vasily Grigoryevich in a fit of laughter. "Well, that's something! I am really going to enjoy this!" And he hurried about Moscow so as to share the delight produced in the public by Olsky's poetry.

As if it were planned, in the first house Vasily Grigoryevich visited, the whole family was sitting around the table while a certain *monsieur,* famous for his artistic reading, was loudly declaiming some verses.

"Sh! Sit down!" said the host as he pointed toward a chair.

"What's going on?" he asked.

"It's an ode on Napoleon, written by a new poet," said the host, "Listen!

Napoleon, that terrible hero
Unable to exist without war!
But where is he now?
Under that stone on St. Helena!"

Vasily Grigoryevich could barely contain his laughter. Covering his mouth with his handkerchief, he tip-toed out of the room without even answering his host's question about where he was going. After running out to the porch and leaping into his carriage, he, as they say, dissolved into laughter.

VI

Meanwhile, the young poet who had arrived from the provinces in order to produce a commotion in the capital by the force of his genius was no longer satisfied with an ordinary room in an unfashionable hotel; he had moved to the London, where he took the best, most luxuriously furnished room. This he considered all the more necessary because he was expecting visits from Prince Sinegorsky and Apollon Ivanovich who had both said they wanted to come and personally thank him for the pleasure he had afforded them.

In fact, the old prince, who respected not only breeding but also people's personal achievements, came to see him at two o'clock in the afternoon and found the poet in his dressing gown, lounging in a chair shaped like a sleigh, with a cigar in his mouth and a cup of coffee in his hand. One would not have believed that this was the same young lad who had just arrived by stagecoach with nothing but rapture in his soul; by no means: in a few days he had filled out, his face had changed, he had somehow acquired the self-importance of one of those spoiled young gentlemen to whom time and money mean nothing and for whom the purpose of living consists in their honoring the rest of mankind by their mere presence.

Having developed a very high opinion of himself as a result of the reception Moscow afforded him, the poet was about to favor his guest with his views on the change in the weather, but the prince, maintaining his own sense of dignity, interrupted: "Yes, the weather is damp . . . You have taken a very nice room," and left the poet to savor the pleasure of having been visited by a prince. Naturally the young poet had to inform his mother and father about everything that had so flattered his ego, so he, after placing a sheet of postal stationery on the table in front of him, opened the letter from his father that he still hadn't had time to digest completely.

After glancing once more at the beginning of the letter, he reached for his pen and began to write: "My dear parents, please excuse me for taking so long to reply to your letter. There has been absolutely no time: every day I have been invited to dinners or soirees by various members of Moscow's high society. Every morning, as soon as I get ready to sit down and write, someone pays a call on me. Just now Prince Sinegorsky, one of Moscow's grand *seigniors*, was here to thank me for doing him the honor of reading my poetry at his house. You should see how they are receiving me and praising me to the skies! You write that . . ."

At this point the poet paused in order to read the rest of his father's letter. Suddenly the expression on his face changed completely, and his hands began to shake. The end of the letter indicated that of the one thousand rubles being sent, his parents could only allow five hundred for their "dear son from Dmitry Potapovich and Fedora Yevseyevna"; the other five hundred was to be used to send them by return post three complete sets of the *Compendium of Laws with Appendices.*

The letter fell from the poet's hands, and, pulling at his hair, he began to groan in despair. Then he quickly opened his wallet: of the thousand rubles, only 350 were left! Again he grabbed hold of his hair with both hands.

Suddenly he heard someone quietly opening the door, and a voice asked: "Could you please tell me—"

"Who's there?" shouted the poet in fright.

"Excuse me, might you be the literary gentleman?"

"What do you mean? What literary gentleman?"

"That is . . . the one who makes verses . . ."

"Verses? Oh, yes, verses . . . That's me."

"Vasily Grigoryevich was telling me that you had a manuscript."

"A manuscript?"

"Yes, a manuscript of your verses . . . I would like—"

"Verses? What is this? Just who are you?"

"A bookseller . . . I, perhaps, could acquire the manuscript for printing."

"How do you mean 'acquire'?"

"Why for cash, sir."

"Oh . . . well, good; buy it, I'm selling . . . How much are you going to pay?"

"Please let me take a look; is it just a collection of poems, or is it a tale in verse?"

"Oh no, it's an episode."

"An episode? And just what is that? Something like a drama?"

"No, it's an episode from a long poem."

"Ah! You mean like a chapter; just the way they published *Eugene Onegin*—in chapters."

"Oh no, this is an episode, a complete poem, like an episode by Lamartine."

The poet produced a thick notebook full of rather illegible scrawling.

"It hasn't been recopied."

The bookseller opened the notebook at random and began to read:

> On a rocky cliff above the flood,
> Pensively gazing into the depths,
> Lost in thought, he watched the moon
> Hovering over the boundless deep.
> Meanwhile that pale orb
> Cast its light toward the horizon
> And spread its rays over the waves,
> Trying to penetrate the murky depths . . .

"Could you tell me what price you are asking?"

"A thousand rubles."

"The title doesn't seem appropriate; if you would consider changing it . . . A title can have great significance."

"How do you mean not 'appropriate'?"

"Well, people won't understand . . . An episode! God knows what that means . . . It would be better to call it a tale in verse."

"A tale in verse . . . well, that's so ordinary."

"Oh no, believe me, that will do very well."

"Well, all right."

"So, we'll make it a hundred rubles."

"What?"

"Well, that's for the manuscript; it will have to be recopied and handed over to the censor, and it will cost about a thousand rubles to print it. So I can't give you any more than a hundred for the manuscript."

"What do you mean? I'd rather burn it!"

"That's as you see fit."

"I will not give it up for less than a thousand."

"No one pays a price like that . . . That's more like what a novel brings—a novel in four parts, six hundred pages—but yours is a tale in verse, perhaps sixty pages at the most . . . Why, Pushkin himself sold his *Prisoner of the Caucusus* for two hundred rubles—you can ask anybody about that."

"Why should I bother?"

"Well, let's say two hundred rubles including all rights to publication in perpetuity."

"You can't be serious!"

"Well, if that's the way you feel—"

"All right, I'll let you have it for five hundred and not a kopeck less—and only on the condition that you furnish me with twenty-five complimentary copies."

"Well, you see, all that's included in the total: the author's copy has to be printed on good quality paper and given an attractive binding. Well, then, hand it over."

"Go forth, my creation!" exclaimed the poet as he placed the notebook in the bookseller's hands.

"So there you are, exactly two hundred rubles," said the bookseller, after taking out his wallet and counting out two hundred rubles in well-worn notes of various denominations.

"How come two hundred?"

"That's correct, it's exactly two hundred."

"I said five hundred, not two."

"Please, don't get upset; I swear on my honor that's the highest possible price. Would you please write on the manuscript: 'I hereby sell the rights to publication in perpetuity to the bookseller so and so.'"

"Well, I might be willing to come down a hundred rubles."

"But no, the price is already fixed. It will cost more than a hundred to print the twenty-five complimentary copies."

The poor merchant of verses sighed and gave up his creation, the child of his poetic inspiration, in exchange for a prosaic sum of money, and yet he was satisfied, happy. With his hands on his hips, he proudly strode about the room and thought: I can finish a poem or a tale in verse in about two weeks . . . that's about four hundred rubles in a month . . . in a year that would be forty-eight hundred rubles . . . almost five thousand! Not bad!

Having thus calculated the regular and reliable income he would earn from his writing, the poet put all the money he had into his pocket, an amount of 550 rubles, and went out to buy the *Compendium of Laws*. But unfortunately, this time he was unable to carry out his mission. As he was passing the Petrovsky Theater, a young man in livery—he was wearing a badge with a rooster on it and his coat had bright-colored epaulettes—stopped him.

"Would you like to buy a ticket, sir?"

"A ticket for what?"

"For the loge, sir."

Aha! thought the poet. *I have still not been to a theater, not even once!* "How much is it?"

"Fifty rubles."

"How come fifty?"

"But, sir, today they are putting on a special benefit performance—a ballet and a symphony; the price has been trebled. But I can give you a discount; some gentlemen ordered a loge, but they are not coming. They said to return the ticket, even if it means taking a loss: the ticket costs sixty rubles. I have the theater announcement right here."

The poet glanced at the announcement. It was terribly tempting: seven vaudeville acts and also a *divertissement!* He took out fifty rubles and gave them to the man.

"And for the announcement, sir?"

"Still more for the announcement?"

"But sir, I have something coming for my trouble in getting the announcement and for my services to you."

"Well, Brother, I don't have any small change."

"Well, sir, you can keep your small change, I had something a little bigger in mind. I can see you've got a really old fiver there—and no matter what else, I'll drink a bottle of porter to your health!"

Carried away with his thoughts about the theater, the young poet forgot about the *Compendium of Laws*, gave the man five rubles for the theater announcement, and continued on his way to Liuke's.[20] There he found Vasily Grigoryevich, and they got into a discussion about dramatic art and about the fact that at the present time Russia had neither a genuine tragic actor nor a genuine comic one.

From Liuke's, the poet, as was his custom, went to Yar's, where he happened to run into his companion. From Yar's they went home, and from there to the theater.

Meanwhile, at the theater, a new vaudeville act was appearing. The audience, in its enthusiasm for a rather risqué couplet, demanded that the new author take a bow; he was greeted with generous applause and shouts of "Bravo!" and "Author!" Every time he came out they yelled "Bravo!" and every time he disappeared into the wings they yelled "Author!"

Actually this itself was an interlude in seven scenes called *Bring out the Author.* It would have been extended by several more scenes, but for the fact that, fortunately, the audience lost its voice. The next act, also new, was a million times better than the first, but the audience was too tired to show its appreciation: their participation in the first act had exhausted them.

"Oh how delightful, how glorious it must be to write for the theater!" exclaimed the poet when he got home, and he immediately sat down to write a vaudeville in three acts. After working through the night, the next day, and still another night, the first act was ready. The action involved two lovers and a brigand. In the first scene a handsome young man is sitting alone in his room and complaining that it is his fate to be unable to love a woman. Suddenly he hears the sounds of a harp, runs to the window, and immediately falls in love. In a state of rapture, he turns toward the audience in order to share with them his joy that an *ethereal being* walks the earth and can be seen in the window of the house across the street. The second scene takes place in her room, where we see that there really is an *ethereal being* sitting at the window, playing a harp, and *lamentabile* singing a song complaining that it is her fate to be unable to find a heart that understands her. After heaving a heavy sigh, she looks out the window and exclaims: "Ah!" Then, addressing the window and the audience by turns, she triumphantly proclaims that her heart's need has been fulfilled and that she has found eternal love. Meanwhile the sun sets, darkness descends, and the *ethereal being,* leaving the window open so as to breathe the same air as her heart's chosen one, goes to bed. In the third scene, a terrible brigand, armed from head to foot, crawls in her window. He draws his dagger, sneaks up to the bed, looks at the sleeping girl, and turns toward the audience with the question: "Should I make love to her or kill her?" The audience doesn't answer and the brigand decides on the former course, while reserving the right to kill anyone who would dare not to fall in love or be loved.

At this point the poet stopped and thought for a moment: Would it be better to take this vaudeville, which he was thinking about calling "Love through the Window," and make it into a tragedy entitled "The Love of a Brigand," with songs, arias, duets, choruses, and ballet numbers? Having decided on the latter course, he was ready to continue when suddenly Vasily Grigoryevich came in and invited him to accompany him to a certain house where some people were dying to make his acquaintance. The poet wanted to refuse, but he couldn't. Vasily Grigoryevich prevailed on him to go, and they left.

Everything went very well. Once more the poet was surrounded, showered with praise, his verses greeted with shouts of approval in both French and Russian; those present also listened with attention to his views on literature and writers, both old and new. But he was upset by one bothersome old man. Staring fixedly at him, the fellow was digging around in his snuffbox, clearing his throat in a most irritating way, and insistently confirming every word the poet said. The poet tried to ignore him, but the fellow followed his every move. Finally, when the crowd had dispersed and everyone had left the poet by himself, the old man came up to him, took him by the arm, and led him into another room.

"You should be aware, my dear young man, that all these people who admire you so much do not understand at all the main thing for which you should be admired. They really misunderstand you, they are not capable of appreciating you—"

"That's very nice of you, but I must say . . . ," said the poet, at the same time trying to express his gratitude by fashionably rocking his body. "You are too kind!"

"A little extra kindness never hurts, my dear young man, especially when one needs to spare the young and the foolish. Wonderful verses! I was quite impressed! It was all, of course, intended as parody?"

"Well no, sir," answered the poet with a grin. "Parody means—"

"I know, I know what it means; it means to work over someone else's verses . . . That's really in fashion now; many geniuses have risen on that yeast. But you see, in the old days they parodied foreign authors, whereas now, in our bold new age, we parody our own. From someone else's large and elegant outfit it's an easy matter to stitch for ourselves a fashionable coat to fit our own small size, but you see, my dear young man, you have to sew it very carefully or else the seams will show."

"I'm not sure I understand what you mean."

"Sit down and I will explain."

And the old man forcibly sat the poet down next to him and, holding him firmly by the hand, continued: "For example, your "Castalia's Font" is a reworking of Derzhavin's "The Spring";[21] and your verses on Napoleon are . . . very familiar: 'a new Atlas who has lifted the world on his shoulders . . .' "[22]

"Pardon me, perhaps those lines are similar, but as to the rest of it—not at all!" said the poet, at first flaring up, then turning pale.

"I don't say they are exactly the same—no, and you do have the ability to pick out the picturesque, colorful images; you have taste and a certain fire, but that, my dear young man, is only your youth and nothing else. You are still living, functioning, and even writing by repeating what you have seen and heard. You have still not really thought about anything, tried anything, nor arrived at any conclusions; you have yet to earn the praises of your schoolmaster, not to mention those of society; you must mature, your eyes are still wide open, although you try to shield them behind glasses."

"My dear sir!" said the poet, flaring up.

"Now, don't fly off the handle, my dear young man, I am simply talking to you like a father; only a fool is angered by good advice. You would be better off listening to what I have to say. All these gentlemen are enchanted with your poetry—but of course this enchantment is nonsense. It is just taking advantage of your youth, leading you around by the nose. Within the confines of high society, you can't tell which way the wind is blowing. You see, it's like this: for the enchantment of the master of the house today, what was needed was not you, but that gentleman there with the star on his breast. It was necessary, first of all, to surround him with a crowd, and, second, to provide an amusing diversion. To have given a ball would have been inappropriate, and there was no occasion for a dinner party; consequently he needed some sort of bait and, if possible, something a little cheaper, because he is a real tightwad. At this particular time no European mechanical musician happened to be in Moscow, and so he thought about getting some Tyrolean singers, when suddenly this gentleman, a member of "our family" of geniuses . . . (the old man pointed at Vasily Grigoryevich) relieved him of the expense of hiring entertainment! It's still not clear why his honor is trying to pass you off as a genius, but he has been praising you to the skies, and these fools are all ears. So they book you in here like a circus act, but they advertise you as a genius. Is it surprising that they are all raving about your poetry? All the women and the girls you see here are enchanted by your youth and your enthusiasm. For all these young people, your verses are about as interesting as a sermon: they examine you with their lorgnettes, but they really have no time to listen to you. In high society, enchantment is not inspired but performed. The first 'bravo' was uttered by your benefactor, then it was echoed by our host in order to give significance to the entertainment he was providing for his guests. The ladies provided that meaningless high-society expression 'charmant!' and everyone else, in the course of your frenzied recital, let loose with his or her cheap exclamations: 'Bravo!' 'Wonderful!' 'Perfection!' 'Genius!' And why not? Everyone needs a pretext to begin the conversation when it is necessary to talk to someone about more interesting matters than your poetry. Look there, our host has already approached his interesting guest; listen to how he praises you—'Wonderful!' 'Very good!' 'Truly remarkable!'—and then he immediately moves on to Petersburg geniuses, then to the magnificent offices of the ministries; then, repeating 'Very good!' 'Remarkable!' he moves on to the departments and finally gets to the office that has jurisdiction over his own particular problem. So, my dear young man, you see what your fame is based on. But that's enough about you for the first time and for our first meeting; I see it has become tiresome for you to listen to me."

The old man shook the hand of the young poet, who was sitting there neither alive nor dead, got up, and went to the other end of the room where the host was sitting with his very important guest.

"Well, Ivan Ivanovich?" said the old man to the host.

"Wonderful! Incomparable! A genius, a true genius!" answered the host.

"Yes, Ivan Ivanovich, such ability should be encouraged, all the more so since he, as nearly as I can determine, is not a rich man. What do you think? Why don't we offer to publish his works at our expense?"

"Pardon me, sir! Is it our business to be publishing books? There are booksellers for that."

"Now then, Ivan Ivanovich, an advocate of our country's enlightenment could only say that in jest. Let me make the offer to him in your name."

And the old man got up as if really intending to go over and make the offer to the poet.

"No! No! No!" exclaimed Ivan Ivanovich as he caught up with the old man. "I'm not in the habit of wasting money on trifles! The hell with him! To make a big fuss over such miserable doggerel! It's none of my business. It's all right to listen to it to pass the time, to say a few words of praise to the young man, but that's all."

"It's a pity the young poet didn't hear your words," said the old man with a sigh. "They would have produced in him a fire of a different sort."

"But look now, get ahold of yourself! The boy declaims some nonsense, and you get carried away!"

"A pity!" repeated the old man. Meanwhile, the young poet had already disappeared.

VII

On the sixth day after the new poet had enraptured the members of our family, the poetry genius finally made his appearance. His face was gloomy, his hair disheveled, his manner cold, and his speech reserved. Everyone, as if trying to spare his pride, avoided mentioning the new poet. This made him even more irritable, and his coldness then irritated Elena. When she found herself alone with him, she could not resist reproaching him for his lack of attention to her.

"Oh, yes!" she said, "I forgot to ask you, what was your impression of the works of the new poet?"

"Such inexcusable forgetfulness!" said Pavel Alexandrovich with irritation, instead of answering.

"Indeed it was inexcusable!" said Elena sarcastically. "I should have greeted you with that question."

"Yes, and of course, one must exclaim: *Ah, mon Dieu, comme c'est beau!*"

"Yes indeed, and one must also add: *Ah, mon Dieu, comme il est beau!*"

"I hope you are enjoying yourself!" said Pavel Alexandrovich angrily while scornfully bowing to her.

"And I wish you *bon voyage!*" answered Elena just as scornfully.

After these words it was impossible for him not to leave. The poetry genius jumped up, cast a furious glance at her, carelessly dropped the Russian phrase "My compliments!" and left.

"My compliments!"—a most insulting expression at such a time and in such a situation. In high society it meant about the same thing that "Go to the Devil!" means in the street, if not something worse.

Elena had acted in a most undiplomatic way, and against her own interests, but that was in character. Having agreed to be the object of the poetry genius's affections, she could demand nothing less than slavish submission on his part. He must then seek inspiration not within himself but in her; he must find everything in her; he must write only about her, think only about her—and think only in accordance with her wishes.

Such imperiousness was the reason that several geniuses had already been frightened away from our family; they said that Elena was a very clever girl but that she was too headstrong. Meanwhile, the evil tongues of the town explained that for our family, a "genius" was what everyone else called a "suitor."

"Boor!" said Elena angrily, after Pavel Alexandrovich had left.

"But what has happened to Pavel Alexandrovich?" asked Deanira Diogenovna as she entered the room.

"He left."

"But where did he go?"

"Into retirement!"

"What's that supposed to mean?"

"I have dismissed him from the ranks of genius . . . He took it into his head that I should bow down to his greatness! He began to show his jealousy and dared to insult me!"

"I had always thought he wouldn't be a good match for you. In the first place he's not very well off, and then, well, he's simply stupid! All one has to do is praise him and his nose goes up. Tell me, please, how could you stand listening to those dreadful verses? What he needs is not a wife but someone who will eagerly listen to his compositions and then squeal with delight. Now Vasily Grigoryevich is an entirely different sort: in the first place he's rich, and in the second, he has no need to be dependent, neither on his relatives nor on his talent. I should think that out of love for you he would soon give up writing things in Russian. You will have to make up your mind, my dear—and soon; you know our circumstances: we will be spending this winter in the country."

"But it's not for me to be the one to propose!"

"Oh, but he would have proposed a long time ago if he hadn't noticed your preference for another."

"Well now, it seems there is no one to prefer to him."

"You must flatter him with a little special attention to make it easier for him to declare his wishes."

Elena did not reply, but hardly two weeks had passed before Vasily Grigoryevich was already promoted to an *actual* member of "the family." With this, any further need for geniuses also ended: about the new young poet not even a word was said. He, meanwhile, took the university exam and failed it—the first misfortune; next the innkeeper demanded the most unlikely thing imaginable: money—the second misfortune; and then his father wrote him asking why it was taking so long for him to send the *Compendium of Laws*—the third misfortune. And his friend Aigolova, who, in the case of misfortune, was always able to give good advice, had apparently gone off to be a tutor for some family in the provinces.

What was he to do? The worst of the misfortunes were the insistent demands of the innkeeper. In order to satisfy him, the poet sold his entire new outfit right off his own back—not near enough! Then the man took it into his head to prevent our young debtor from further increasing his obligations: he gave orders to serve him neither dinner nor tea.

Not expecting this, the poet at first upbraided the servant: When would dinner be served?

"Not ready yet, sir," answered the servant, a young lad with a good heart who felt embarrassed about telling him the truth.

"Well, how about something to snack on while I'm waiting?"

"But we don't have anything like that, sir."

"Damn!" said the poet with irritation. He was about to take a stroll on the boulevard, but then he remembered that he was now wearing his old, provincial coat—too embarrassing! He remained in his room.

Soon it began to get dark. The poet was getting hungrier and hungrier, but the servant did not appear. He went to look for him in the corridor.

"Well, my lad, what about dinner?"

"I'll go and find out," the servant answered and disappeared.

The poet went back to his room and lay down on the sofa in expectation; he waited and waited and then fell asleep. He found no relief in sleep. He dreamed he was in some sort of rich house, there was a multitude of guests, the table was set, the food had long been served, but no one showed the slightest interest in taking a seat. The poet was walking around the table and sighing. Finally they brought around the hors d'oeuvres. A man with a tray was passing through the crowd, the poet impatiently awaiting his approach. The man came nearer—but when the poet saw the empty plates he was finally being offered, he cried out in anger. They took their seats. Soup was being served; the man next to him began to eat heartily, but the poet still had nothing in front of him. He looked at the other people, but no one thought to give him anything. They brought dumplings; only two were left on the plate—the man next to him grabbed them both and swallowed them in one gulp. The poet was in despair.

"A bottomless pit!" he said, trembling with anger while looking greedily at the huge approaching sturgeon. But the sturgeon was getting smaller and smaller until only the tail remained, and that ended up on his neighbor's plate. Dish after dish was served; people were beginning to push back from the table to ease their full stomachs, but the poet was still tormented by hunger: either the dishes passed him by or they did not reach him or nothing was left on the plate.

In his grief the poet decided to eat a piece of bread—but there wasn't any.

"Waiter, bring me some bread!" he shouted. The man brought the bread; but as soon as the poet reached out, the chairs squeaked, everyone got up, and the waiter with the bread disappeared. Then the poet woke up, pale, worn out from hunger, and with a terribly dry mouth. Well, he thought, now it's time for them to bring the tea—but no one came. Sitting with his elbows on the table and his head clasped between his hands, the young poet sank into a state of oblivion.

"Well, sir, you must settle up!"

The poet raised his head; there were tears streaming down his face.

"All right, I'll settle up!" he screamed as he jumped to his feet. "Take it all!"

And he seized his suitcase, flung it at the innkeeper's feet, then took off his bathrobe and threw it in the same direction.

"There! Not enough? Well, take my shirt! Still not enough? Well, you can take my skin for shoe leather!"

"But, my dear sir, what am I to do? All right, I can wait a week, until, as you say, your father sends the money. But you will have to move to another room, since this one is rented by the month. I will take care of moving your things."

The innkeeper left. A servant came to carry his things to another room. The poet quietly followed behind him. They came to a small, dirty, dark room, where the servant deposited his things. After the servant had left, the poet looked around.

"Fine!" he exclaimed, smiling through his tears. "It's a prison and I am a debtor from whom payment will be extracted through hunger! I am going to be tortured on the rack of hunger . . . Wonderful! I'll imagine I am eating ambrosia and drinking nectar—the food of the gods!"

And he threw himself on the wooden sofa—more like a prisoner's bunk—and lay back and closed his eyes. At dinnertime a servant entered with a bowl on a tray.

"Would you like something to eat, sir?" he said.

"What's that?"

"Soup, sir."

"I'll try it! We'll see if it's as good as the ambrosia of the gods!" And the poet sat down at the table and began to eat the soup.

"My master is a really cruel man," said the servant. "I tell him it's time for you to eat, and he says you can go and eat with your friends."

"Good, then I will come to eat with him, since I know him better than anyone else."

"He won't give you a thing to eat for nothing."

"Then he's a monster!"

"Yes, the kind of monster who has pity for no one. You can see that I, a poor man, felt sorry for you and decided to share my portion with you."

"When I get rich, I'll pay you a handful of gold for that portion."

"No, sir, there's no need for that; this is what I would ask of you: you know how to write; teach me to write and I'll bring you food."

"Bravo! A thirst for enlightenment! Agreed!"

"Here's how your generosity will be repaid!" said the servant happily. "With your permission I will now bring you a roast and dessert!"

And he ran off to the dining room. Estimating which guests had the most roast meat left on their plates, he took two of them, dumped their contents onto one plate, and brought it to the poet. In the same way he produced dessert.

The next day the lessons began, and the pupil punctually fulfilled his part of the contract, bringing to his teacher the composite portions of breakfast, lunch, and dinner that he had gathered together in the dining room. Meanwhile, the poet was hurriedly finishing up his drama.

"You, my creation, will ease my hunger, slake my thirst, clothe my nakedness, and provide shelter for my homeless body!" he exclaimed when he had finished his drama and was preparing to take it to the bookseller.

"What's going on with my poem?"

"It's been printed," answered the bookseller gloomily.

"Well, here I have a drama for you . . . Do you want it?"

"No, sir, I don't."

"I can let you have it rather cheaply."

"I wouldn't take it if it were free."

The poet felt a stabbing pain in his heart.

"Then give me the author's copies of my poem that are coming to me," he said indignantly.

"Well, you can have all one thousand copies—they're just taking up space on the shelves!"

The poet silently took a copy of his epic and went back to his cell at the hotel.

"Happiness is nonsense, fame a chimera!" he kept repeating as he sat staring at a piece of paper, his pen in his hand, until his pupil came in.

"Why do you want to learn how to write?" he asked him.

"What do you mean 'why'? I have a friend who works as a waiter at a club; all he has to do is write down whatever comes into his head and the bookseller gives him a fiver for it, and then prints it; you see, it can really add up. He wrote a story about an old woman and a bear—it was really clever! Well, I know a story about a bear that's just as clever as his, and I'll write it up in fine style as soon as I learn how to write!"

"So you, too, want to be a Russian writer!" exclaimed the poet.

"Well, that wouldn't be bad. Everyone knows my friend; they even write about him in the *Library for Reading*. If he should decide to look for a position or something, well, he's already well known."

The poet thought to himself: *Now I understand the old proverb, "It's a poor soldier who doesn't want to be a general." It's probably also true that a clerk who doesn't want to be a writer isn't much good either! It's also no fun to be in a place where everybody . . ."*

Suddenly someone knocked at the door. The poet's pupil grabbed his papers, opened the door, and left.

"Is Ordynin here?" said the voice of Aigolova, and he strode into the room, dressed up like a dandy.

"Greetings!"

"Where have you been?" exclaimed the overjoyed poet.

"I have a million things to do, Brother! I'm busy fifteen hours a week: preparing lessons, this and that, and then something else, so that I don't have a minute's free time!"

"Where have you been living?"

"I live with a friend, near where I'm employed as a tutor . . . So it looks like you're out of money again? Listen, would you like to try tutoring? Four hours a week for five rubles . . . You teach children proper Russian grammar."

"Who wouldn't?"

"Then get dressed right away, *en forme* . . . Put on a frock coat."

"But I don't have one, Brother. I sold everything."

"What's one to do with you! Selling your own clothing!"

"What was I to do? Even that wasn't enough: the innkeeper demanded his money. And after that, he tried to starve me to death!"

"Starve you to death! So you actually were dying!"

"I was practically on my deathbed: he wouldn't give me anything to eat, and where can you go in a bathrobe? I would have died if Petrushka had not fed me like a poor beggar—on the condition that I make him into a Russian writer."

"And you let them do that to you! And you still look like you're on your deathbed! Oh, what a scoundrel the man is!"

"I've had nothing to eat for two days."

"Oh, what a rogue! Come and stay with me!"

"He won't let me go until I pay him. He also wants to go to the police. Where am I going to get 150 rubles?"

"Oh, the swine! . . . Wait a minute, I'll settle with him! Get into the bed!"

"What for?"

"Get in bed, I tell you! We've got to get you out of here . . . Lie down and keep your eyes wide open while I get the innkeeper. Just lie there, Brother, if you don't want to bring more trouble on yourself."

And with these words Aigolova ran out of the room to find the innkeeper.

"Come this way!" he said in a voice that expressed mystery and alarm.

"What is it?" asked the innkeeper.

"What is it? You'll see what you have done!"

"But allow me to ask, what is it you want of me?"

"It's too late to ask, when what's needed is a priest."

"Lord! What is it?" repeated the frightened innkeeper as he followed Aigolova into the room and saw the poet stretched out on the bed with his eyes rolled back.

"What's happened to him?" the innkeeper asked.

"Exactly what you see, my esteemed sir! You have starved this innocent young man to death! You didn't want to wait a few days until he received the money; you forced him to sell everything, even his clothes. And that wasn't enough! You decided to use starvation to make him pay . . . Bloodsucker! Fortunately I came to see him, and he was able to tell me what happened . . . He's been asking for a priest . . . I'm going to the police! . . . You are a murderer! I'm going right now!"

"My dear sir, take what you want, only don't go to the police!" cried the innkeeper as he seized Aigolova by the arm. "I swear, I'm not guilty! Surely those swinish servants of mine neglected to bring him his meals . . . Please, sir, you can have whatever you wish, I'll have it sent up," continued the innkeeper as he went over to the poet who was still lying with his eyes rolled back.

"It's too late now; he has lost consciousness," said Aigolova.

"Don't ruin me!" cried the innkeeper, once more rushing over to Aigolova.

"What am I supposed to do! He was my friend! This is a terrible blow!"

"Don't ruin me!"

"Well, get a carriage as soon as possible. I'll take him home with me; maybe I can still do something for him . . . Quickly, quickly!"

"Whatever you wish, only don't go to the police!" And the innkeeper ran out and ordered his servants to get out one of the conveyances that he kept for transporting rich guests (passing them off as regular cabs, but charging three times the price).

"The carriage is ready," he whispered to Aigolova when he had returned. "I beg you sir, take this!"

"What's this for?"

"For treatment."

"I'll give you treatment! If I do show you any mercy, it won't be for money, my fine friend, but purely out of human compassion."

"I don't know how I can ever repay you!"

"Repay! To pay off everything with cash! You moneybags! Learn to be a man: if a person is in need, don't persecute him—that's how to repay! Well, get some of your people to carry him out to the carriage."

The innkeeper returned with some servants; Aigolova himself lifted the poet under the arms, and they carried him out to the carriage. They loaded in his things, and the carriage drove off in the direction Aigolova indicated. The innkeeper crossed himself, relieved to have gotten this burden off his shoulders.

This happened only yesterday. We don't know what will happen to the poet next. We only know that Moscow, now occupied with a European genius of music who has just arrived from the sticks, has already managed to forget the poetry genius.

It's Not a House, but a Plaything!

I

We humans are generally unaware, we do not see a great deal of what is happening around us; we are ignorant as to what exists in the world and what does not. This, of course, is human nature; in this, perhaps, is the essence of the problem: to see and at the same time not to see, to know and at the same time not to know. For example, everyone knows that Moscow perished in flames during the French invasion; but who knows what else perished besides the residents' homes and property? Moscow was rebuilt for display, for glory; it turned out more magnificent, but at the same time more sad, more boring than before—just as if its inner light, its joyful carefree spirit had come out into the open and left its heart in the darkness—and what could it do there? Remain alone and not let out a peep. How did this happen? It happened because, in addition to the buildings and the property, what also perished in the fire were Moscow's ancient house spirits.

No matter how strange it may seem today, in olden times it was the truth. The ancient grandfather-house spirit was not a phantom, not an apparition, not a scarecrow—but let me explain: once upon a time, as they say, when the original founder of a family line had become firmly established in his new home, then, with the coming of each new generation, he would

This story was completed in 1850 and published by the author himself as a separate pamphlet and printed in a small number of copies. The text published in the 1979 *Povesti i rasskazy* includes later corrections apparently made by the author himself to a copy preserved in the Manuscript Division of the Lenin Library in Moscow. The present translation is based on this latter text. The idea for the story was suggested by a dollhouse that once belonged to P. V. Nashchokin (1801–54), a close Moscow friend of Pushkin. Nashchokin, who was something of an eccentric, decided to order a dollhouse duplicating his Moscow residence. He ordered all the necessary furnishings in miniature from Moscow's best suppliers. As his fortune declined, he was forced to gradually pawn the house and its furnishings. Subsequently attempts were made to recover the lost items and those that have been found can be seen in the Pushkin Museum in St. Petersburg.

acquire the respectful titles of father, grandfather, great-grandfather, great-great-grandfather, continuing to abide and become rooted in that place. As the years passed he would grow smaller and smaller until finally he was back in the cradle. They would give him a spoonful of milk, and he would sleep peacefully; meanwhile the whole family went around on tiptoe in order not to disturb grandfather's grandfather. Having reached the size of a seven-month-old child, the grandfather, when he had awakened for the last time, would speak out clearly: "My children, it has become too cold for me on the hearth; put a white smock on me, wrap me up warmly, and then place me in the niche in the side of the stove. I will go to sleep while you go on with your lives; don't be concerned about me, but preserve my memory. I don't require food, only that when you hold a wake for me each year, bake me some pancakes and put out some holy water. I can no longer endure daylight, but there will be times when I will awaken during the night to see if your dreams are peaceful. When all is going well, I will remain at peace; but if I should begin to knock, beware, look around; remember that grandfather doesn't knock without a reason. There, now I have spoken: cherish my advice and my love."

Since they feared their grandfather-house spirit, everyone in the house from the youngest to the oldest carried out his last wishes. Through him, peace was maintained in the family: elders were obeyed, equals were respected, and the children were dealt with strictly but kindly. There was joy and harmony in the hearts of all. But as soon as discord arose, the grandfather would knock: everyone would immediately fall silent and look at one another—as if to say, "Grandfather doesn't knock for nothing! Be careful!"

So the old wooden house would stand—and endure forever; the walls had absorbed the human spirit, they had become like stone; the roof was entirely overgrown with moss, and rot could not take hold.

But those were the old days; now it's different: house spirits still exist, but they are within us; they still may find their voice at times—but only regarding minor matters. And therein lies the misfortune.

Before the French invasion, Moscow had many houses that retained their ancient house spirits, but after the French departed, at least as far as I know, only two remained—and these stood side by side.

Houses in the old days were somehow not like the ones they build now. The old houses were not nearly as elegant—here there is no comparison—but the old houses had such warm corners, such clever, cozy, well-worn places where, once you sat down, you wanted to stay. I don't even have to mention the stoves: they were like the hut of Baba Yaga with its three chicken legs, with hearths, little side niches, and sleeping shelves; on top of the stove, behind it, under it—there were all sorts of places to stretch out; and such warmth! There were all manner of abodes for the house spirit. That was in the old days, but now times have changed. In the old days everyone slept the sleep of the just; if it happened that someone's sleep was troubled, it was because his day had been sinful. Consumed with fear of the house spirit, he would promise to make amends: "I swear by all that's holy!" And now people also swear, but since nothing is holy to them, with the coming of dawn they revert once more to their sinful ways, and there is no one to fear: the old house spirits are gone, and the internal spirit has lost its voice.

One of these ancient houses we have been talking about that was still inhabited by a grandfather-house spirit belonged to a certain old woman. She was not simply an old woman, but something wonderful to behold: an old woman whose youth had been preserved. The grandfather-house spirit sweetened her dreams, went about on tiptoe, and, like the house spirit in Verstovsky's opera,[1] sang and played love songs on the *gusli*[2] instead of making frightening noises in the night. The house spirit was actually in love with the old woman, just like the one in the opera who loved Princess Zorya. And with good reason: when spiritual beauty does not fade, neither does that which is physical—at least in the memory. On the old woman's face there was always an angelic smile and a tender gaze. It was as if the wrinkles made her face more beautiful, and the missing teeth added a softness to her speech: after all, children lose their first teeth and this does not at all spoil their appearance. Ripe old age can also be childhood.

The old woman had a grandson named Porphyry. She so loved and cherished him that even inside the house he wore a little bonnet and had a kerchief tied around his neck to keep him from catching cold. Since according to the old custom a young person up until the age of twenty was considered a child, the old woman looked upon her grandson as a baby, even though he was already eighteen years old. He actually was a most lovable child and when in the summertime he sat at the open window of the upstairs room, wearing his little bonnet and grandmother's kerchief to protect his chest from the draft, the modern young men who happened to pass the house and glance up at the window thought they were looking upon a fair maiden in her bower. And just like the fair maiden, he modestly lowered his gaze when he met such bold glances.

The house next door was like a twin brother to the old woman's; it also had a small upper story, the side window of which faced its neighbor—but with time the glass had become as opaque as mother-of-pearl.

This neighboring house belonged to a sick old man—a man who had been made decrepit, suspicious, and willful by the ills and misfortunes he had suffered in his life. The one joy that remained to him was his granddaughter Sashenka—a child of rare sweetness. Sashenka had an old nanny and the old man himself had an old servant, Boris, more decrepit than his master, who used to chat with the house spirit when he was troubled by insomnia.

During the day the old man used to sit in a large armchair surrounded by pillows, breathing heavily from shortness of breath, and continually mumbling something to himself while he watched his granddaughter playing with rag dolls on the floor. Occasionally he would break his silence: if the nanny had made a new rag doll for Sashenka and she came running to show it to him, saying, "Grandfather! Look, a new doll!" The old man would say: "Ah! A rag doll? Good . . . just wait . . . I'll buy you a real doll."

"Yes, grandfather is always promising something," the nanny would answer for Sashenka.

"And so . . . when the weather turns fair . . . then we'll go into town . . ." Grandfather would say as he looked through the dust-covered double-paned windows. "But look how gloomy and overcast it is outside . . ."

"Yes, it's overcast all right," the nanny would say. "If that's overcast, then it'll be a long time before we'll see the sun again!"

"And there's a dampness in the air," the old man would say. "I can tell by the way it feels . . . it makes it hard to breathe."

At night the old man would keep tossing about in his bed and grumble, "There's no way of getting any sleep . . . surely it must be time for breakfast . . . Oh, is it time for morning prayers? Ohhh!"

"Oho!" the house spirit would answer as he rolled over in his resting place behind the stove.

"What's that? What's that noise? Where's it coming from? Ah?"

"Aha!" the house spirit would reply.

The old man would begin to listen, then he would call out to the sleeping Boris:

"Where's that noise coming from?"

"I don't hear anything."

"Wha-a-at?"

"No one is making any noise!" Boris would shout into the old man's ear.

"What do you mean? Is the noise inside my head, or what?"

And the old man would begin to listen again, trying to decide whether the noise was coming from inside or outside his head. Meanwhile Boris, as he left the room, would mumble to himself, "What noise! Why it's surely the house spirit, the Lord be praised! He's lying there, and the house spirit has been throttling him for his lies and bad temper."

II

And so the years passed. Sashenka grew bigger while the old man became more and more decrepit and, at the same time, more suspicious and more fearful about his granddaughter's fate. When he thought about his own days as a young rake, he realized that a fifteen-year-old girl is like dry kindling: one fiery glance and she would be set ablaze. Having no faith whatsoever in the old nanny, he began to forbid Sashenka even to go to church without his accompanying her. In vain the nanny tried to argue with him, saying that to miss church for such a reason was a great sin.

"So when do you think you might be going?" she would ask him.

"Well perhaps . . . when the weather is a little better . . . she can visit the churches . . . we will visit the churches . . . but for now she can pray at home . . . it's really all the same . . ."

"No! It's not all the same! It's a sin!"

"Well, well, well, you're a fool . . . According to you, it's not a sin to look over the suitors!"

"What are you saying? And how do you think it should be done? God grant that Alexandra Vasilyevna may find for herself a fine suitor," answered the nanny angrily.

The old man was horrified.

"Shut up, you fool! I'll have you run off!" he would shout. "Listen to what she is saying! And teaching the child to sit at the window in order to be seen! The windows facing the street are not to be opened for any reason! Do you understand? If not, I'll board them up, and I'll board you up!"

"Oh, Lord have mercy that I should have lived to hear such words!" the nanny would cry as she dissolved into tears.

The old man's apprehensions about his granddaughter increased with each day. This was all he thought about: how to protect his treasure from the spell of some enchanter.

"No matter how carefully you watch over a girl," he thought, "as soon as you look out into the street—trouble! Look at all those young jackals out there on the prowl, checking all the windows for possible prey."

And the old man's suspicious gaze was trained on any young man who happened to pass by. And, as if to spite the old man, most of them stopped to take a look at the two old houses, since they alone, after the events of the year 1812, stood out among the ruins and had enjoyed such an enviable fate that a passerby could not help but stop and exclaim: "Look at that, everything around them burned to the ground and yet those two old museum pieces stand there as if nothing had happened! By God, that's amazing!" But soon the surrounding neighborhood seemed to recover and prosper after the fire: in place of the wooden houses, they now put up mansions of stone so that the passerby, instead of sympathetically noting their honorable antiquity, was likely to say, "Look at how those two old museum pieces have ensconced themselves among these stone mansions! By God, that's amazing!"

These stoppings and curious glances of passersby at the old moss-grown buildings were seen by the suspicious old man in an entirely different light.

"Oh, they'll be the death of me," he grumbled to himself, "What they don't catch sight of, they seem to be able to smell out."

After long considering the problem of how to protect his granddaughter from temptation, the old man finally got an idea.

"All right, my fine young friends," he said, "I'll give you something to ogle at!"

And right then and there, ignoring both the suffering of his obedient granddaughter and the tears and protests of her nanny, he ordered them to cut short Sashenka's beautiful hair. Then he told Boris to open his trunk and bring him all the old clothing he found there. Boris carried in a large motley pile of garments and, groaning, laid it down on the floor in front of the old man. Looking at the layers of clothing, he seemed to be recalling the several generations of what had been a very large family. For both old men the sight of these clothes brought back vivid memories, but the master had something particular in mind.

"Kononushka's jacket should be here!" he said.

"What jacket do you mean?" answered Boris as he went through the pile of men's and women's clothes from the last century. "This isn't a jacket!"

"Show me that one! What kind of jacket is that? That's grandfather's waistcoat . . ."

"Oh my," said Boris with a sigh, "This one could still be worn! Why it's velvet! And here's one made of crinoline! I think it's Mother's, may the heavenly kingdom be hers."

"Let's see it. What kind of jacket is that?"

"Who said it was a jacket? Is this your caftan? Look at the stitching! Why Pelageya Vasilyevna must have sewn it with her own hands . . . Look at the cloth! You don't see anything like that today."

"That's not cloth, that's wool I tell you!"

"Wool? Well, you should have said . . . What do you mean wool? Here's your woolen uniform completely eaten up by moths . . ."

"What do you mean, eaten up? Show me!"

"It looks like a sieve."

"And have the moths swallowed up Kononushka's jacket?"

"God only knows; it's just not here . . . Perhaps it's in another trunk."

After a long search, the jacket was finally found. The old man was delighted; he called in Sashenka and ordered her to put it on and to tie a scarf around her neck.

"But what is this for, Grandfather?" she asked.

"What for? You are going to be my amazon . . .[3] Take a look in the mirror . . . What do you think, not bad? Yes, you will be my amazon . . ."

"But what's this? Sir, why have you dressed up the young lady in such a way?"

"Because I choose to. And you, foolish woman, keep quiet, since you know nothing. It is a little large . . . We can have a new one made, a better fit, for the holidays . . . So that's what you'll wear. You'll be my amazon—in amazon's clothing."

"Grandfather, you told me girls in amazon's clothing rode horses . . . Remember when those women rode by on horseback? Will you be teaching me how to ride a horse?"

"Ride a horse! Aren't you something! You'll have to wait a while . . . Well, let's say you grow a little bigger, maybe in about ten years . . . as for now that will do fine . . . and now if you sit by the window you won't catch cold. Sitting there with an open neck just won't do."

Having thus disposed of the problem, the old man calmed down; he was pleased with his stratagem. He would take his seat by the window and have his granddaughter sit down next to him so that he could silently mock the young men as they went by: "Yes, look this way! What do you think of my grandson? A fine lad, ah? Why don't you look? Because this is not a girl, but just another skirt chaser just like you? Well, so it is! No, you'll find nothing to ogle at here!"

III

Having thus been made invulnerable by her grandfather to all eyes seeking an object of love, Sashenka continued to live a carefree childhood, amused by her nanny's fairy tales, by the birds and flowers, and occasionally by a fluttering butterfly in the garden. But suddenly she began to experience a certain melancholy, as if something were lacking; the hours from morning to evening seemed to pass by too slowly: it was boring to sit there with her grandfather, and the nanny's fairy tales were becoming wearisome. All she felt like doing was to sit alone by the window and look out at the street in hopes of seeing something more amusing.

"Nanny, why am I always so bored?" she asked the old woman.

"Why should you be bored, Missy?" the nanny answered.

"I don't know myself."

"You're probably bored because you don't have any girlfriends."

"Girlfriends?" said Sashenka after thinking for a minute. "Where would I find a girlfriend?"

"Yes, where? Well, perhaps we could conjure one up."

"Conjure one up?" thought Sashenka after the nanny went out, and she began to sing in a mournful voice the conjuring refrain from the folktale about Alyonushka:

> Little friend, little playmate,
> Alone and lonesome here I sit;
> Come and chase away my woe.

Suddenly it seemed to her that her voice was echoing back to her from somewhere. She began to listen: yes, someone was singing in the house next door.

Sashenka opened the side window a crack, looked out, and blushed crimson—her heart had begun to knock so.

"Oh, how nice looking she is!" exclaimed Sashenka to herself. "That's the kind of girlfriend I'd like to have!"

And for a long time she looked through the partially opened window at Porphyry who, equally impressed, was staring fixedly at her and thinking: "Oh, what a nice-looking boy! Wouldn't it be nice if we could play together!"

"I think I'll wave at her," thought Sashenka. But at that moment her nanny came in, and, apparently fearing to reveal her newly discovered friend, Sashenka slammed the window shut.

When it began to get dark outside, the nanny sat down and took up her knitting. Thus the evening passed. They went to bed, but Sashenka couldn't sleep: she just couldn't wait for morning.

Morning came. She had to wash, say her prayers, greet her grandfather, have her tea with him, listen to his stories, and the whole time her heart was in a tremendous turmoil.

"I don't feel like any tea, Grandfather."

"Where are you off to? Sit down."

Oh, what longing! She started to get up again, but again Grandfather said, "But where are you off to?"

"I'll be right back, Grandfather."

Sashenka immediately went upstairs to her room, and there sat her nanny knitting a stocking.

Thus the morning went by; now it was dinnertime. Grandfather ate slowly, and after dinner, before he fell asleep, he said: "Sit there, now don't run off."

Lord, what an ordeal!

But finally Grandfather fell asleep. The nanny went out to sit by the gate with Boris. Sashenka was alone. She quietly opened her window and began to sing softly, "My little friend, my little playmate . . . ," but no echo came back to her; the window in the house next door was shut.

Oh, what longing!

Another day went by. Poor Sashenka was sitting with her nanny, lost in thought. Suddenly she heard the familiar refrain, and her heart leaped with joy.

"Listen," said the nanny, "There's someone out there singing—not bad, I must say."

"Nanny, I'm thirsty."

"Well, why don't you drink some of this kvass, Missy."

"No, I don't feel like kvass. I'd like some water."

"Lord! That means I'll have to go downstairs."

"Please!"

"Well, all right, I'll go."

As soon as the nanny left, Sashenka was at the window. She opened it, looked out, and was greeted.

"Hello!" said Porphyry.

"Hello!" answered Sashenka.

They looked at each other tenderly, but neither knew what to say.

Finally Porphyry said, "Come over to my house."

"No, you come over here; I'm not allowed to leave the house," answered Sashenka softly.

"What people!"

With this the conversation ended; the nanny's steps could be heard, and Sashenka slammed the window shut.

The following day Porphyry spent the whole morning singing his song under her window. As Sashenka kept listening, her impatient heart began to contract painfully, until finally her trembling hand furtively opened the window.

"Hello!"

"Hello!"

"Listen . . . Come out into the garden!"

"Into the garden? Well, all right."

"Quickly!"

"All right."

Sashenka closed the window and ran to the garden.

Boris, who was on the porch talking to the nanny, said hello to her as she went by.

"Hello, Boris," she responded.

"Where are you going, young lady?" the nanny asked.

"To the garden."

"Missy," Boris said, "take a look at the bench I made for you there under the linden tree; come, let me show you." And he proceeded to tag along after her.

Oh, what a nuisance!

"You see, Missy, here I . . . Would you like to try it?"

"Thank you, Boris."

"It's a pleasure to do anything for you, Missy; you are our treasure . . . May God grant you good health and a worthy suitor."

"Oh, that's enough, Boris," said Sashenka, blushing, "Just go about your business."

"But Missy, there's nothing wrong in wishing . . ."

At that moment the sound of Porphyry's singing came from the neighboring garden.

"Oh, what a pest this Boris is!" Sashenka thought to herself.

"But you see, Missy . . . There's no doubting your beauty . . . even your grandfather can't take his eyes off you . . . Of course he is a bit stingy . . . You shouldn't have to go around looking like that—you should be arrayed in silk and jewels—and he shouldn't keep you locked up all the time; how are the young men going to—"

"Enough, Boris, leave me."

"Oh, what people! What I really wanted to say was . . . Look, Missy, could you ask Grandfather for some money to get me a new pair of boots? If you will look at these, you'll see they're completely worn out."

"All right, all right, I'll ask."

"Look at this, my toes are sticking out."

"All right, all right; now leave me."

"You see, I bought them from a soldier, cost me three rubles . . . Soldier's boots, you know; people say they'll last longer."

Finally overcome by impatience and irritation, Sashenka jumped up from the bench and started to leave.

"But, Missy, don't you like my bench? I made it just for you."

And Boris began to smooth the seat with the palm of his hand.

Meanwhile, Sashenka was walking along near the fence.

"Hello!" was heard through an opening beyond the raspberry bushes.

"Hello," answered Sashenka softly, while looking around to see if Boris was watching her.

"How I love you!" said Porphyry.

"Oh, how I love you! If we only could be together always!"

"Missy! Missy! Where are you, Missy? It's time for tea," shouted Boris.

"Oh Lord, how boring!" said Sashenka.

"Come back later," whispered Porphyry.

"Later? All right."

And Sashenka ran toward the house.

After tea she was about to run out, but her grandfather sat her down beside him to sort some old letters.

"Oh Lord, will 'later' ever come?" said Sashenka to herself almost in tears.

The old man usually had an early supper; whether he felt like sleeping or not, he always went to bed at the same time. But now, as if on purpose, he sat there chatting to his heart's content with his granddaughter and her nanny, taking pleasure in the fact that he was putting them to sleep. He was telling them about the good old days when his grandfather was alive, about what a grand house he had, about the garden, the estate, the wealth, the magnificence, the life in the grand style. Boris had been summoned as the living bearer of testimony to the truth of Grandfather's story. He stood there, by the door, with his hands behind his back, and, whenever called upon, affirmed the truth of Grandfather's words.

"Do you remember that, Boris? Well?"

"But of course, sir; who could forget?"

"And on Grandmother Lizaveta Kirillovna's name day we used to stroll along the lake shore, and there was horn music . . . Yes I must tell you—"

"Begging your pardon, sir, it wasn't on her excellency's name day, but on her birthday."

"What do you mean on her birthday? You're talking total rot!"

"But sir, is it not true that the name day of her excellency, Lizaveta Kirillovna, may the kingdom of heaven be hers, was in October?"

"Why yes, in fact it was. What a memory!"

"Grandfather, I'm getting sleepy," said Sashenka getting up and yawning.

"You feel sleepy? How come I don't?"

"I don't know, Grandfather."

"You don't know, but I do. It's because Grandfather loves his granddaughter and likes to spend time with her."

"But look, sir, isn't it time to retire?" asked the old nanny, yawning.

"You old fool, you're always indulging the child! Go on, get to bed!"

Grandfather was angry. Sashenka and the nanny lowered their eyes and remained seated.

Grandfather remained silent, frowning severely. This angry silence usually lasted until everyone was totally worn out.

Sashenka started to cry, but she wiped away the tears: Grandfather didn't like tears.

"No, just go on to bed," he said finally in a softened voice; he was satisfied that he had taught them a lesson in patience.

Sashenka kissed him goodnight, ran up the stairs, threw herself on the bed, and burst into tears. For the first time in her life she felt a heaviness in her heart, for the first time her Grandfather's authority seemed intolerable. She felt like just throwing herself from the window so as at least to be able to die in freedom.

The nanny, who was trying to convince her that such feelings were sinful, helped her to get undressed and into bed. But the poor girl had no desire to sleep; her spirit was agitated, her heart was beating rapidly, and the room was stuffy; she so wanted to breathe some fresh air.

"What did she mean by 'later'?" Sashenka kept repeating. "When was I supposed to meet her? Oh, how my head aches! I'm going out into the garden . . ."

She put on her shoes, slipped into a robe, and, after making sure the nanny was asleep, carefully opened the door and left. The door to the entry passage was bolted. Sashenka slid back the bolt. It was only a few steps to the garden. The night was bright and clear. Just as she was approaching the linden tree where Boris had placed the bench for her, she heard something rustle.

Sashenka trembled with fear.

"Is it you?" whispered Porphyry as he jumped out from behind a bush and seized her by the hand.

For a long time Sashenka could not catch her breath.

"Why are you so frightened?"

"Well, for some reason it's terrifying," answered Sashenka.

"Terrifying? But why?"

"It just is."

"Well, I have been just waiting and waiting."

Holding each other by the hand, they sat down on the bench and remained there, motionless, silently looking into each other's eyes with some kind of joyful feeling.

"Oh, how nice it is to be with you!" said Porphyry.

"And how nice it is for me, too!" said Sashenka as she leaned her head against Porphyry's shoulder.

Freeing his arm from the old woman's coat he was wearing, he put it around Sashenka and pressed his lips against her hot cheek.

"Oh, if we could only spend every day together!"

"Grandfather never lets me out," said Sashenka with a sigh.

"What can you do! And my grandmother won't let me go anywhere without her."

"What can you do!"

"Yes, life surely is boring! Now if I could be with you, that would be fun!"

"For me, too!" said Sashenka softly.

Then they embraced.

"What's your name?"

"Sashenka.[4] And yours?"

"My name is Porphyry."

"How can that be? There's no such saint in Grandfather's calendar," said Sashenka, who, from looking at Grandfather's calendar, and from her nanny's instruction, knew by heart all the saints and all the holidays.

"What do you mean?" answered Porphyry. "There is too; in Grandmother's church calendar there is a Porphyry. My name day is 26 February, the day of St. Porphyry the Archbishop. And my grandfather was also called Porphyry."

"But that's a man's name!"

"Well, what else? Am I a girl or something? I am no girl."

"Oh, my God!" cried Sashenka, and, in a sudden impulse of fear, she took her head from Porphyry's shoulder.

"What's the matter? Why are you so frightened?" asked Porphyry as he looked around. "You really are skittish . . . don't be afraid."

"Let me go," said Sashenka.

"Where are you going, Sashenka? Please, don't go!"

"Let me go, I say!" said Sashenka, and freeing herself from Porphyry's arms, she quickly ran toward the house.

"Sashenka! My little friend! Listen!" Porphyry shouted after her.

But Sashenka was already in the house, frightened and thoroughly upset.

IV

The next day the nanny, surprised her young mistress had slept in, went into Sashenka's room. Sashenka, however, was not sound asleep but was just lying there in some sort of unhealthy trance; her face was flushed, and she was breathing heavily.

The nanny was alarmed; could it be some kind of fever? she thought. But as Sashenka turned toward her, the crimson glow on her face was suddenly replaced by an ashy paleness; her bright gaze became dull. It was as though she was earnestly seeking something but not finding it. Whenever the sound of the familiar song would come from the house next door, her face would flush like fire; thoroughly frightened, she would jump out of bed as if looking for a place to hide.

Thus the days went by. Not long after, the old woman, Porphyry's grandmother, was called to meet her maker. She used to let Porphyry out only when they went to church or to visit old friends, and then he was always bundled up tight. Now he was free, master of the house, but he did not know what to do with himself—his notions about life and the world were still childish ones.

His habit of unconditional obedience to his grandmother led to his being equally submissive to Semyon, the old servant, and to Darya, the housekeeper. This old woman still considered him a child, and she wanted to treat him that way, just as the grandmother had done. But Semyon had other ideas: "Aren't you ashamed, sir, going about dressed like a woman! Why your grandmother still had you in diapers while other lads your age were finding brides for themselves!"

Semyon's words had an immediate effect on Porphyry: he stood up straight, and he even looked taller. With the loss of his childish feelings, his eagerness to get to know the kid next door also disappeared. He no longer sang Sashenka's doleful song.

In order to carry out his grandmother's last wishes, he was supposed to visit a certain distant relative who had promised to find him a place in government service. So Porphyry made preparations for the journey. Semyon, who had just returned from summoning a cab, was helping his young master get dressed. As was his usual habit, Semyon was talking to himself: "It's such a pity—they don't know what to do, and there's no one to make the funeral arrangements."

"What funeral arrangements?" asked Porphyry.

"At our neighbor's—the old man has died. And who is left to do anything? Well, there's the young granddaughter, and then there's that old fool of a nanny and that useless old servant; why he's got one foot in the grave himself."

"Where do you mean? Which neighbor?"

"Why next door—on the other side of the fence. And that granddaughter, she is something, I tell you!"

"You mean right next door? The house with the small upper story? What granddaughter? That old man has a little grandson."

"Well now! I saw the young lady with my own eyes, and what a beauty she is . . . and crying, too!"

"Semyon, let's go and see," Porphyry interrupted. "Please, let's go over there."

"All right, let's go, why shouldn't we go and see them. After all they are neighbors; we should try to help out in some way. The girl is so young—and who has she to rely on?"

Porphyry grabbed his hat and ran out of the house. Semyon followed after him.

It was difficult to make one's way through the crowd of undertakers standing around the front door. In no other trade is there such fierce competition for business as in this one. Poor old Boris, while wiping away his tears, was quarreling with them.

"How much are they asking, Brother?" Semyon asked him.

"Five hundred rubles for a coffin! The scoundrels!"

"Not just for the coffin, sir, but for the cover, the carriage, and that's not everything."

"Shut up, you vulture! As soon as the master fell ill, why this redbeard was already coming around to offer his services. And he knew my name! 'I beg you, Boris Gavrilovich,' he said, 'Please keep us in mind; as soon as the master dies, we will furnish a first-class coffin, a cover, and all that's necessary . . .' Oh, you devil's maw! Get out of my sight!"

While Semyon was helping Boris make the arrangements concerning the *long box*, Porphyry went into the room where the deceased was lying. He noticed neither the corpse nor the crowd of intruders who seemed to be measuring the length of the deceased's body with their eyes; all his attention was concentrated on the girl in the black dress standing near the table, her head resting on the shoulder of an elderly woman. Tears were flowing from her eyes.

Porphyry's pulse quickened as if from fright. He could not believe his eyes: the face was so familiar, it had to be Sashenka . . . No, it must be his sister . . . Her face was more delicate than his, her eyes were darker, Porphyry thought. And he stared fixedly at her.

"The young lady isn't feeling well, she needs some water . . . Wait, I'll go and get it," said some stranger in an old-fashioned coat and with disheveled hair, as he made his way toward the next room.

"Where is he going?" cried the nanny, "Lord, there's no one to look after things! Please stay here, Missy . . ."

And she took off after the solicitous stranger.

The sudden departure of the nanny caused Sashenka to lose her balance, but Porphyry managed to stop her from falling. She looked at him and it seemed that all her feelings went numb, and her head came to rest on the young man's shoulder.

"Leave that alone! Please get out of here! If you don't leave, I'll call for help!" came the voice of the nanny from the other room.

"What's the matter? I was only trying to help . . . I was going to get her some water . . ." said the stranger, somewhat shaken, as he came back into the room.

"Sure! He was looking for water hanging from the ceiling! You just clear out of here!"

"But I . . . well, all right, I'm leaving . . . I just wanted . . . to pay my last respects to the deceased . . ."

"Yes, and we know your kind!" said the nanny. "Thank you, sir, for coming to the aid of my young mistress," she said as she turned to Porphyry.

"Please allow me to express my sympathy and offer you whatever assistance I can," said Porphyry to Sashenka when she had recovered, and the embarrassed girl turned away from him and looked toward her nanny.

"And who might you be, young man?" asked the nanny.

"I'm your neighbor. If you wish, my servant and I are at your disposal . . . You can rely on us."

"Well, we do need to send somebody to the cemetery to see about a grave."

"I'll go myself," said Porphyry, and placing his servant Semyon at their disposal, he left for the cemetery. When he arrived at the garden of the Lord, he walked around among the graves for a long time until he finally saw an old priest come out of a house.

"Father, can you tell me where I may find the gravediggers?" Porphyry asked him.

"What do you want? A grave?" asked the priest.

"Yes, Father, but I don't know whom to ask."

"A grave? Fine, fine, that's good. We would be very glad to . . . Come this way . . . You can either pick out a place or take one that's already been prepared."

"It really doesn't matter, I think."

"Well, it's up to you: we have some excellent graves! Dry ground, sandy soil . . . Hey, Ferapont! Where are you?"

"Here!" came the voice of a gravedigger from the depths of the hole he was digging.

"Has that one been ordered, or are you digging it just in case we need one?"

"This one's been ordered."

"Well, I want you to dig a grave for this gentleman."

"Yes, sir. You probably want it for an infant?"

"No, it's for an old man," answered Porphyry.

"Well, why didn't you say so? It's as good as done."

After ordering the grave, Porphyry returned to the house. Sashenka was asleep; she was worn out from the sleepless nights spent at her grandfather's bedside. But now she had someone she could rely on; Porphyry took care of everything, and when they carried out the coffin, he walked along beside her. When the coffin was lowered into the ground, it was onto his shoulder that the girl collapsed, almost unconscious.

"That must be the suitor," they were saying in the crowd that had gathered around the grave. "They make a nice couple."

And both Porphyry and Sashenka heard this.

Porphyry escorted her home and was about to say good-night.

"Where are you going?" she asked him.

Porphyry accompanied her into the house.

They sat down in silence, afraid even to look at each other.

After sitting there for a while, Porphyry got up.

"Where are you going?" repeated Sashenka.

"You must be tired, you need some rest."

"Will you be coming to see us again?"

"Only if you wish . . ." said the embarrassed Porphyry in confusion.

The very next day he appeared at the door to ask about her health.

This time she was a little more talkative, and Porphyry a little more at ease.

The word *hello* reminded both of them of the first mutual stirrings of their hearts, and now when they repeated it, they both blushed.

The nanny was extremely pleased with this modest young man.

"Now there's a fit match for her," she thought.

"Porphyry Alexandrovich, if you only could have seen how the old man used to dress my young lady. Why, you would've died laughing! Dressed her up just like a little boy!"

"No, he never saw anything like that!" thought both Porphyry and Sashenka at the same time, and, looking at each other, they couldn't help smiling.

"That was a riding outfit I was wearing, Nanny," said Sashenka, "and it looked better on me. I looked much worse in a bonnet."

Porphyry blushed crimson. Sashenka noticed this and realized that she shouldn't have said anything about a bonnet; she, too, then blushed, lowered her eyes, and fell silent.

"I actually did think you were a boy," said Porphyry when he found himself alone with Sashenka.

"And I thought you were a girl."

Porphyry told her how his grandmother, in order to keep him from catching cold, dressed him up in a scarf and bonnet.

"I wouldn't mind putting on the bonnet again," he added.

"My Lord! Why would you want to do that?"

"Well, you liked me that way."

"Oh, by no means! You look much better . . ." she hastened to say.

"But then you said to me . . ." Porphyry, out of open-hearted simplicity, was about to tell her, but then he remembered how frightened she had been, and he fell silent.

It appears, however, that Sashenka remembered everything, and she blushed and lowered her eyes.

But it seems there's a certain guile in the very nature of women.

"What is it that I said to you?"

"You said . . . 'If we could only be together always,'" answered Porphyry softly.

Sashenka once more blushed crimson and, trying to conceal her embarrassment, hid her face in her hands.

V

First love is timid, like a wild bird on the wing; it requires a very long time before it becomes "domesticated." Nature behaves with such extraordinary cleverness, order, and precision. Porphyry was free, and so was Sashenka; there was no watchful eye following them, no diligent ear eavesdropping on them, while their feelings drew them toward each other. Nevertheless, even if judged by the most strict and demanding code of conduct, no fault could be found in their behavior. It would seem that it would be dangerous for them to sit together on the bench under the linden tree; that the memory of that first kiss would stir up their emotions and lead to their being completely open with each other. But nothing of the kind occurred; in fact they began to show more restraint in their feelings toward each other. And it went on like this until their love had grown and matured in their hearts, so that suddenly one morning it burst out like a rose in full bloom. In their eyes, in their voices, a certain special tenderness appeared. Everything that was inside of each of them became clear to the other; they looked at each other and embraced.

"Remember, I told you how I loved you!" whispered Porphyry.

"I remember!"

"And you said: 'Oh, how I love you; if we could only be together!' Do you remember?"

"Yes I remember!"

It would seem that they would want to prolong such a blissful moment, to conceal their happiness from everyone, but again Sashenka cried out, "Let me go!" and, freeing herself from Porphyry's embrace, she ran out of the room.

"Where are you going? Why are you so frightened?" asked Porphyry. He thought Sashenka had once more become frightened, just as she had the first time in the garden.

But Sashenka had run off to share the happy news with her nanny.

Porphyry's heart had sunk; he was sitting there, plunged in thought, when suddenly he heard Sashenka saying: "Come with me, quickly!"

And dragging in her nanny by the hand, she exclaimed:

"Look, Nanny!" and she threw herself on Porphyry's neck.

"Lord save us, what are you children up to!" cried the nanny, shaking her head and wringing her hands.

Freeing herself once more from Porphyry's embrace, Sashenka threw herself on her nanny and began to smother her with kisses.

"Now, now, that's enough, you naughty child! Save your kisses for your sweetheart! But you'll have to wait a bit; the priest's got to marry you first and the stand-in for your father will have to present the whip to your husband."

The wedding preparations began.

Nature had done her part very well in fostering the young people's affection for each other. She had decreed that they should remain together in a state of mutual love; but it was no concern of hers where they should live.

It would seem that for them it wouldn't have mattered where they lived, as long as it was together. But it mattered very much: while the wedding plans were proceeding, a dispute arose between the two young people. Which house should they live in? Sashenka insisted on Porphyry's house, because it was Porphyry's house; Porphyry wanted to live in Sashenka's house, because it was Sashenka's house.

"I'll sell my house," said Porphyry. "We will live in your house."

"Oh, no, not for anything!" protested Sashenka. "We'll live in your house; we will sell mine."

"Oh, no, not for anything!" said Porphyry in turn. "I like yours much better."

"And I like yours."

And so a quarrel developed out of the desire to exhibit more tenderness than the other. Neither Sashenka nor Porphyry wished to yield on this point.

"You want to do everything your way," said Sashenka poutingly. "If you sell your house, I'll sell mine!"

"We'll see about that!" thought Porphyry angrily. He had been stung by her words.

Sashenka's agitation soon subsided. She went over to Porphyry, but he turned away.

The quarrel was on again; she turned away from him and sat down in a corner, covered her face in her hands, and began to cry.

"You don't love me!"

"Sashenka!" said Porphyry, and he rushed to her side.

"Leave me alone!" said Sashenka.

Hurt feelings were once more stirred up in him. His thoughts in some sort of fog, Porphyry took his hat and went home.

There, to make matters worse, he found a buyer for his house waiting for him. Earlier, when he was thinking about selling the place, he had asked Semyon to look for a buyer. Semyon had agreed that this was a good idea.

"Here you are, sir; take the money," said Semyon as he led in a certain citizen. "I have closed the deal."

The citizen counted out the money, placed it on the table in front of Porphyry, and presented him with a paper to sign.

"But, sir, are you going to sign that without first counting the money?" asked Semyon.

"That's exactly twelve hundred rubles. Agreed?"

"Agreed," said Porphyry as he idly fingered the notes.

The next morning this same citizen appeared at Sashenka's house next door.

"My lady," he said to her, "I have just bought the house next door, but I need more space. Would you be interested in selling me yours? I'll give you a good price for it."

"He's sold his house!" cried Sashenka.

"Well, why not, Missy," said the nanny. "It was a good idea. He asked me about it, and I agreed. Now there's no reason for us to sell: it's a well-worn nest, you're used to it—and so am I. May God grant that I live out my days in it . . ."

"He sold it!" repeated Sashenka.

"He sold it to me, my lady. A run-down wreck; I have to admit it, I got taken, gave him four thousand rubles for it, and now I'm stuck with it. Please, my lady, sell me yours! I'll give you five thousand."

"Five thousand! Missy, I want to talk to you for a minute," said the nanny quickly, and she led Sashenka into the next room. "Missy, take the five thousand!"

"Yes, I'm going to sell it, I'm going to sell it right now!" said Sashenka in a hurt voice.

"Sell it. Why your grandfather paid only two thousand for it when it was new! He's offering you five thousand! But wait, let me handle it; you stay here; I'll get him to pay six!"

"Go ahead and sell it! I don't want to live here any longer," said Sashenka with tears in her eyes.

"We'll hold on to the cash and find ourselves an apartment for around two hundred rubles; life will be much simpler that way."

And the nanny returned to talk to the citizen.

"Five thousand is not sufficient, my good man," she said. "My mistress would not dream of selling at that price . . . She will take six, if you're still interested."

"What do you mean, six? Well, since I am interested in the house, I'll add two hundred."

"You can't be serious!"

"Will you take fifty-five hundred? If not, well then you must excuse me," said the citizen, and he turned toward the door.

"Wait a minute, I'll have to ask my mistress."

The price was agreed on, the house was sold, and the deposit was in hand when Porphyry walked in.

"Hello," he said quietly, and looking as though he were guilty of something, he went up to Sashenka.

"Hello," she answered without raising her eyes.

"You're angry with me, Sashenka," said Porphyry after a prolonged silence.

"Yes, I'm angry with you," answered Sashenka.

"For what?"

"I asked you not to do it, but you wouldn't listen; you went and sold your house."

"Well, it really was quite old; Semyon said it would take at least a thousand rubles to fix it up . . . ," began Porphyry, trying to justify himself. "I also talked to my nanny, and she advised me to sell and move in with you."

"But I have followed my nanny's advice and sold mine!" said Sashenka.

"You sold it!"

"Yes, I sold it."

"Well, if that's so . . ." Porphyry started to say.

"Where are you going?"

"I'll have to look for an apartment," he answered as he rushed out.

Sashenka was about to cry out his name as he left, but her voice failed her.

VI

The man who had bought the two houses had a better idea about what to do with them than Porphyry and Sashenka: he had them connected by a gallery, which, in effect, put everything under one roof so that, in less than a month, he had a new, very decent-looking house. It was covered with new siding, painted gray with green shutters and there was a sign on the gate saying that the house belonged to Citizen so-and-so, that it was exempt from being assigned to the military for billeting, and that it was available for sale or rent.

A certain low-ranking government clerk, who happened to have married a young and rich wife, immediately bought the house in her name and the couple settled in to their new home. But they got more than they bargained for.

While the two houses were separate, all was quiet and peaceful: nothing stirred in the attic or ceiling or behind the stoves or in the cellar; the walls didn't creak, the furniture didn't crack, and the scurrying of mice was not heard. But as soon as the houses became one and the clerk and his wife had moved in, and after proudly surveying their new home and complimenting each other on the purchase of a completely renovated home for such a cheap price—twenty-five thousand rubles—the couple retired for the night. At the stroke of midnight they were suddenly awakened by a terrible uproar: there was a rumbling, cracking, groaning noise. Now it seemed to come from under the house, now from above the ceiling—as though a thundercloud were passing—now it was on one side of the house, now on the other.

The terrified couple awakened the servants.

"Well, I always go to bed early, and I never hear anything," said the cook who always slept soundly all night and only dozed during the daytime.

But when the old porter had heard their story, he lowered his head and decided it was a bad sign; apparently the house spirit was not pleased with his guests.

"Oh, you're acting like an old woman!" said the cook.

"I am not staying here another minute!" cried the terrified young mistress of the house. "Not for anything in the world!"

The very next day her husband put up a sign on the gate saying that the house was for rent, and then they immediately found themselves a new apartment and moved out.

Soon a young gentleman passing by happened to notice the sign, which read: "House for sale or rent: inquire within." He looked the place over and decided to rent it.

He sought out the porter, and while placing money in his hand, said: "Go to your master and find out what his latest price is. I'll be back this evening."

"Yes, sir!" answered the porter.

"Well, what are you waiting for?"

"Well, you see, sir . . ." began the porter, who was already tasting the vodka he would buy with the money and therefore could keep nothing hidden in his soul, "I must tell you, sir . . . It is a nice house . . . Of course there's no denying that . . . but . . ."

"But what?"

"Well, I'd have to say that if a person was of the timid sort, he wouldn't want to live here."

"Why not?"

"Why not? Well, I don't want to lie to you . . . there are house spirits about."

"What are you saying?"

"By God it's true sir! They'll give you no peace at night."

"And in the daytime?" asked Pavel Voinovich.[5]

"Well, of course in the daytime it's quiet enough; it's only at night you have to worry."

"Then everything's fine," said the gentleman. "I don't sleep at night, but in the afternoons, so I won't be disturbing the house spirits and they won't be disturbing me."

"What? Really? Oh, yes, that's the way it is with you gentlemen . . . Well, if that suits you, it's up to you . . . There's really nothing else wrong with the house . . . You can ask the master yourself and he'll say the same thing."

Thus it happened that, in spite of the porter's warnings, the gentleman rented the house and moved in. On the very first day of his occupancy, he invited five or six of his closest friends to dinner. Awaiting their arrival in a dressing gown and slippers and smoking his pipe, he walked about the house, supervising the servants who were setting the table, checking supplies in the larder, making sure the champagne was chilled and the La Fitte was not, and making sure that in general everything was ready. The company assembled. The dinner was delicious. The wine was excellent.

A poet happened to be among the guests. He raised his glass and proclaimed:

I love an evening feast
Where gaiety presides
And liberty, my idol,
Rules over the proceedings;
Where til the morning light,
"Drink up!" drowns out the singing,
Where wide is the circle of friends,
While the bottles are in tight rows.[6]

"But you'll have to excuse me, my friends," said the host. "We won't be able to drink on until morning—it's just not possible."

"But why? What's the matter?"

"Well, it's because I rented this house from Grandfather House Spirit himself with the condition that I spend the night wherever I please, but not in this house. And since it is almost midnight, I am heading for the English Club.[7] You see, gentlemen, that my reasons are valid. You will have to excuse me."

Pushkin laughed out loud as was his habit, and everyone else laughed with him. But the host was speaking seriously; he insisted that he wasn't joking, and to show them that he meant it, he shouted: "Hurry up! Bring our coats!"

No servant appeared in response to this order. It seemed there was not a soul in the foyer nor in the waiting room. The servants, having assured themselves that the gentlemen were totally engaged, decided to celebrate their own housewarming.

"Well, there's nothing for it, I'll have to get my own coat," said Pavel Voinovich, "but who can I leave in charge here?"

"The house spirit of course!" shouted Pushkin.

> Hey, Grandpa, no more dozing!
> Treat the thief as you see fit,
> Guard this house with watchful eye
> And keep all valuables safe and sound![8]

And the poet gave a hearty laugh.

"Oho!" came back the reply from all corners of the house.

"There, you see, he has given his answer!" said the poet. "And now we can depart without a worry. Did you hear him, gentlemen?"

"We heard him! We heard him!"

"Well, if you heard him, then we can leave," said the host.

And so everyone left.

As soon as the gentlemen had gone, the serving people came back from their revelry and assumed their usual positions as if nothing had happened. They sat there in the foyer, dozing, thinking that the masters were still inside enjoying themselves.

"What do you think? They'll be at it till morning no doubt."

"Oh, how I'd like to get some sleep . . ."

"Go ahead, masters, drink up!"

"You know, that's not the way to drink . . . Now when I—"

"Shh! What the devil was that? It sounded like groaning!"

"What do you mean? I didn't hear anything."

As soon as this discussion in the foyer had been replaced by the sound of snoring and nasal whistling, suddenly a loud knocking and cracking rang out.

"Vasya! Did you hear that?"

"What?"

"What can it be? Are the masters in there having a brawl, or what?"

"What did you say?"

"The masters . . . Don't you hear all that commotion?"

"Well, that's none of our business."

"I guess you're right."

And Vasya and Petya dozed off.

Meanwhile, it sounded as though a house wrecking were in progress.

Believe it or not, this is what happened: we have already said that a house spirit dwelled in each of the two old houses. They peacefully lay behind their stoves, content that all was in order in their domains, occasionally turning over from one side to the other. When Porphyry and Sashenka sold their houses and construction was begun to unite the two buildings under one roof, the house spirits were alarmed by the noise; they soon calmed down, however, deciding that it was only repairs being made to the roof and the eaves, and they were actually in favor of this. As soon as the work was finished and the government clerk who had bought the newly renovated house moved in, the house spirit who inhabited Sashenka's house—now the left half of the building—got up at midnight to see if everything was in order.

"Hmm, what is that strange smell?" he thought as he entered the hall that connected the two houses.

At about the same time the house spirit from the right side was also beginning his nightly rounds.

"Aha! There's something amiss here!" he thought as he paused to listen. "What can it be?"

Just as he entered the hall, he felt something tap him on the head.

"Who's there?" he growled.

"Who's there?" came a voice from right above his ear.

"What?"

"What?"

"Who's there?"

"The master of the house."

"What! How can that be? I'm the master of the house."

"No, I am."

"What's that? You're the master?"

"That's right, I'm the master."

"No! I am the master! Clear out!"

"Clear out? No! You clear out!"

Shouting louder and louder they began to struggle, raising such a tumult of rumbling and roaring that the clerk, and especially his wife, could not help but be frightened out of their wits and forced to flee the house the very next morning.

VII

After that, the house spirits continued to raise a terrible ruckus every night, each trying to overcome the other. But the struggle continued to be a draw. And so it was on the night that the young gentleman who had just rented the house left with his guests for the club.

It was just growing light as he was returning home. He was feeling out of sorts, as though some illness was coming on. He had not slept all night, and he felt he would not be able to sleep during the day. He sent for Fyodor Danilovich.

"What's the trouble?"

"I don't feel well."

"Oh? Well, I understand."

And Fyodor Danilovich prescribed a sedative.

"Is this a powder?"

"Yes; take it every two hours."

"Just what I need! I would much rather be taking money."

"Yes, of course, that would be better," said Fyodor Danilovich as he left on his way to see his other patients.

The gentleman spent a dull evening; as night approached, failing to abide by his agreement with the house spirit,[9] he went to bed, and contrary to his usual habit, fell asleep.

In the right side of the house, the half that had been the home of Porphyry's grandmother, the gentleman had set up his study and adjoining bedroom. In this same room was the stove which was the house spirit's abode. As soon as the clock struck midnight, he began to stir, and like a newly awakened rooster, he was already spoiling to renew the fight with his opponent. Suddenly he heard the sound of snoring.

"What's that?" the house spirit said and cautiously approached the sleeper and placed his ear close to his mouth.

"Oho, there's a brave fellow for you!" he said as he stepped back from the bed.

"I'll bet the whole pot!" shouted the gentleman in his sleep; the house spirit shuddered and then tiptoed out of the room.

"Aha! So you're still here!" growled the house spirit from the left side of the house as they collided in the doorway.

"So you haven't cleared out yet?" said the house spirit from the right side as he ground his teeth and began to grapple with his foe.

As they struggled and struggled, they raised a huge cloud of dust, each trying to dislodge the other, until they both had become exhausted.

"Look, just get yourself out of here while the getting's good!"

"You get out—any way you wish, it doesn't matter to me."

"Look, there are plenty of houses."

"So there are, go and find one."

"You find one; I'm older than you."

"How do you figure that? I myself have lost count of the years."

"We don't count by years but measure by beards."

"Well, mine got badly singed in 1812."

"Look, let's stop the fighting."

"If you want to stop—we can stop; but I must have a house that's richly furnished and has all the conveniences, one that is warm and dry and not inhabited by a single human soul. The house must be for me alone, for me, a grandfather house spirit: I don't want to be bothered by anyone! Let the house be a plaything and not a real house."

"Is that what you want? But look at what you're asking for: a house just for you alone—and who's going to build a house like that?"

"That's not my problem."

"We could play a trick on the youngsters."

"Well, that's up to you."

"Wait, let me think a bit."

"Go ahead, think about it."

"I'll think about it," the house spirit from the right side repeated to himself, "I'll try to think of some way this can be managed."

He went back to lie down behind the stove and began to think. Too agitated to just lie there, he began to walk about the room and repeat out loud: "Hmm . . . A plaything, not a house! A plaything, not a house!"

"What's that?" said the gentleman in his sleep.

"Build a house that will be a plaything and not a house!" repeated the house spirit, occupied with his own thoughts and still pacing about the room.

"A plaything and not a house," repeated the gentleman in his sleep, "a plaything and not a house!"

The night passed. The house spirit was unable to think of anything, while the gentleman arose, lit his pipe, ordered tea, and began, like the house spirit, to pace about the room in deep thought, repeating to himself: "A plaything and not a house! Where could such a bizarre idea have come from? I just can't seem to get it out of my head. To actually build a plaything that's not a house? Well, why not? I'll build it!"

As he continued to pace about the room, smoking his pipe and considering the problem of building not an ordinary house but a plaything, the gentleman's train of thought was interrupted by his servant's announcement that some tradesmen had come to present their bills.

"Oh, the rascals! I told them to come yesterday!" shouted the gentleman. "Nothing but scoundrels! Always worried about their money! I'll have to place some additional orders with them . . . Who are they?"

"Well, there's the man who builds pianos, the furniture maker, the man from the crystal shop, and people from some of the other stores."

"Bring in the piano maker."

In came a German.

"Are you here for money?"

The German nodded.

"Why weren't you here yesterday? Well?" demanded the gentleman.

"Well, it's all the same," answered the German.

"No, it is not all the same! Yesterday was one day, today is another . . . But look here, this is what I require: can you make a small piano, one-seventh the normal size?"

"Do you mean a toy piano? I am not a toy maker," answered the German.

"No, not a toy but a real piano, only one-seventh as large."

"What do you mean?"

"You see there is this tiny virtuoso . . . a dwarf . . . so that he can play . . . is that possible?"

"Hmm . . . Yes, it can be done . . . Why not, anything is possible if the price is right."

"Then please, get started on it . . . at one-seventh size . . ."

"At one-seventh size? All right, only it's going to cost just as much as a real piano."

"Right now I'm not talking about the price," said the gentleman. "You just get it done, and then we'll settle up."

"Hmm," said the German to himself as he began to think about the problem. He was thinking about what an achievement it would be to create a tiny piano. *Das ist ein kurioses Werk!* he thought as he went out. He had completely forgotten about the money.

After him came the furniture maker, and then the clerk from the crystal shop. From the former the gentleman ordered luxurious furniture in the rococo style, one-seventh the normal size, and from the latter, also one-seventh the normal size, a complete set of tableware: a china service, goblets of all sizes, and monogrammed carafes for the serving of every kind of wine.

Thus began the construction and acquisition of the furnishings for this plaything which was not a house. An artist friend offered to provide a collection in miniature of the paintings of the most well-known artists. The silverware was ordered from the cutlery factory, linen from the cloth merchant, kitchenware from the iron monger—in a word, artisans, tradesmen, and merchants of every kind received orders from the gentleman for the supplying and furnishing of a rich nobleman's house that was to be one-seventh the normal size.

For the gentleman money was no object.

And now the plaything which was not a house was completed. It cost a little more than an actual house; all that remained was to insure it and take out a mortgage on it.[10]

The gentleman actually considered this.

"Isn't it strange," he thought. "Prince Vasily had a 'plaything' built for himself that was much more ridiculous than this—a house no one could live in—and yet he was able to mortgage it, while I'm sure any application by me would be rejected. Nevertheless a house really needs to be mortgaged: in the old days it was *laid down*[11] before construction, whereas now it's considered both prudent and economical to *lay it down* after it's finished. One must follow the fashion."

VIII

The whole time the plaything that was not a house was being built and furnished, the grandfather house spirit from the right side was beside himself with joy; every night he would walk around it, rubbing his hands in anticipation.

Look at it, he thought, *Look at how the world can manage things . . . This gentleman must be a sorcerer: as soon as I showed myself, he recognized me; as soon as I began to think about how to solve the problem, he figured out a way to oblige me!*

"Well, you will be getting a house that will suit you," said the grandfather house spirit from the right side to his rival.

"We'll see," he responded.

"You definitely will."

"Well, all right, show me."

"You'll have to wait a bit, it's not quite ready."

"You're lying!"

"I swear it's the truth!"

"Well, we'll see."

As the time passed, the building and furnishing of the miniature house approached completion. The grandfather continued to watch its progress impatiently and marvel at the ingenuity of people.

"It really is a plaything, and not a house! I have really put one over on him!"

Finally the house was complete in all respects. It was about fifty inches high and had a magnificent salon as well as a dining room—the dining room was also a billiard room. The salon had a parquet floor, silk wallpaper, luxurious furniture, chandeliers, lamps, candelabra, mirrors, pictures, a grand piano—in a word, everything.

"Well, it's time!" said the house spirit from the right side to the house spirit from the left, and he led him into the study. The master, as usual, was not at home. It was a bright night; the moonlight came through the window and was reflected on the miniature house's polished parquet, bronzes, and furniture: it was as bright as day.

"Well, where are we going?"

"Just follow me."

"What's this, a table?"

"Just crawl in . . . Well, what do you see?"

"Just a minute, I've caught my beard on something . . . Oh my!" exclaimed the house spirit from the left side as he passed through the carved, gilded doors of the salon.

"Well, what do you think?"

"Yes! What an amazing thing! It's not your usual stove!" And the house spirit tried out an armchair, then a couch, and then lay back against a pillow stitched with chenille on a background of muslin.

"Well, I must thank you. What's this, a *gusli?* Oh, this is wonderful! This is the place for me . . . What luxury! It certainly beats lying behind the stove!"

The house spirit from the right side thought to himself, "Yes, in fact it really is luxurious; it's a pity to let him have it . . ."

"Remarkable! Thank you again!" continued the spirit from the left side, remaining stretched out on the couch. "You can have the whole house, live behind any stove you like, and I'll just move in here."

"Hey, wait a minute; have you noticed that they haven't put the stoves in yet?"

"You're right, there are no stoves; how could they have forgotten to put in stoves?"

"You can't get along without stoves . . . Winter is coming, you'll freeze."

"That's right, that's right; will they be putting them in soon?"

After convincing his rival that the stoves would definitely be installed by winter, the sly house spirit conveyed him to the door and then he himself lay down on the couch to stretch out and relax his bones.

"No, my friend, sorry, you will never see the inside of this house, just as you can't see your own ears; I'm the one who is going to live here . . . How could I have not thought of it before? What peace, what comfort! It's just as if I ordered it . . . and look at those mirrors . . . and everything . . . Damn! Those people outdid themselves! But what's this in these sealed-up bottles? Let's see . . ."

And the house spirit rummaged through the kitchen utensils until he found a corkscrew and opened the bottle of champagne.

"Oh! . . . It's like some sort of mead. Oh, the things that people come up with!"

And glug glug glug, he drank the whole bottle, and blinking his eyes, he lay down on the couch and fell asleep.

Meanwhile the master, who had ordered the building of this plaything that was not a house, following the custom of our modern builders, had promptly mortgaged it. The following morning some men came and carried it off to the moneylender's.

At midnight the house spirit awakened. What was that noise? Why all the commotion? Where was all that light coming from? The house spirit looked out—and was paralyzed with fear.

There was a great crowd of people, music was blaring, some sort of figures in motley costumes were swaying and gyrating about in contorted poses while mumbling and shouting in some unknown language—in a word it was pure bedlam! The bright light made the house spirit feel dizzy, so he buried his head in the pillow, curled himself into a knot, and lay there, barely able to breathe.

This went on for several days. The house spirit was exhausted—no peace day or night. The lights seemed never to go out, until finally there came an interval of darkness. The house spirit strained his ears: there was no one there. He crawled out of his house and wandered through all the rooms . . . looking for a stove. He looked and looked, but there wasn't a stove in the entire house.

"Oh ho! Where can I have gotten to?" he thought.

Suddenly he thought he detected the smell of smoke; there was heat coming from somewhere. He looked and found a pipe.

"What can this be? Usually chimneys lead outside the house, but this one leads the other way."

He crawled into the pipe, crawled and crawled until he found himself in a huge stove in the damp basement of the building.

What was to be done? He sat there for a while lamenting the situation, and then he thought: "You shouldn't set traps for other people, because you may fall in yourself," and he sadly found a niche for himself in the side of a new-fangled Amosov furnace.

IX

Meanwhile, you will recall that Porphyry, after getting angry at Sashenka, had found an apartment and moved in.

He sulked for three days, not wishing to face her. Finally he could resist no longer, and he went back to her house. When he got there he was horrified to see that both houses had their roofs removed, and that they both were surrounded by a common fence.

He climbed over some lumber piled in the courtyard and asked the carpenters: "Do you know, my lads, where the young lady went who used to live in this house?"

"The young lady? How should I know?" answered one of the carpenters as he sharpened his axe on a stone.

"Well, who would know?"

"Who would know? Well, it beats me."

"We don't know anything about her; maybe you could ask the neighbors," said the others.

Porphyry's pulse was racing. For a long time he walked about the neighborhood, trying to find someone who knew where Sashenka had gone. No one knew. He continued down the street, asking at the gate of each house: had not such and such a young lady moved in here? No, she had not. He covered all the side streets, but there was no trace of her.

Porphyry was in despair. A day went by, and then another—he kept looking, but there was no trace of her. He covered all Moscow, chasing down the speculations of one doorkeeper after another.

"A lady? Very young? Oh, yes. Was there a maid with her? Yes, she was here, but she didn't like the apartment, so yesterday she moved out, found a place in the Razgulyay district . . . just opposite the public bathhouse."

Porphyry hurried to the Razgulyay district.

"A young lady? Yesterday? She just moved in."

"Can you show me where she lives?"

"Just follow me."

And the accommodating doorkeeper led Porphyry up a flight of stairs and knocked on a door.

"Who's there?" said a voice.

Porphyry started forward in anticipation.

"There's someone here to see you," shouted the doorkeeper.

The door opened, a girl appeared and looked at Porphyry with a welcoming smile.

"Please come right in!"

Porphyry, thinking he had found Sashenka, rushed into the room.

"Is Alexandra Vasilyevna here?" he blushingly inquired of a woman who came out of the next room.

"Alexandra Vasilyevna? Perhaps she did live here, but now we're here . . . Why don't you sit down so we can get acquainted."

"Excuse me," said Porphyry, "I must be going . . ."

And he ran out of the room, his hopes completely shattered.

"Where shall I go now? Where can she be?" he thought to himself as he unconsciously headed for his former house, his head hanging down in utter despair.

Looking at the new structure that now occupied the space of the two old houses, Porphyry shuddered and leaned against the fence on the opposite side of the street as if he were drunk.

"Perhaps Sashenka will come to take a look at her former hearth," he thought.

But it was already getting dark, and there was no sign of her.

"Oh, Master, Master, what has happened to you?" said Semyon shaking his head.

"Please find her, Semyon," said Porphyry, and he took up his search once more. He checked the lists at the precinct stations, but there was no record of Sashenka.

He searched on and on and once more came back to the house. Surely Sashenka would eventually come back to see what had happened to her house!

One day when Porphyry was standing there, leaning against the fence, his hands covering his face as if in mourning, a loud voice rang out quite near him:

"Porphyry! Porphyry!"

He looked around and Sashenka threw herself into his arms.

"Oh, what happiness!" exclaimed Porphyry as he embraced her. "From now on I'm not going to let you out of my sight!"

"But it's too late!" said Sashenka sobbing.

"What's that? What do you mean?"

"It's too late. I'm married!"

Porphyry turned white.

"I thought that you had left me, forgotten about me, so I got married."

Sashenka broke down in tears.

Porphyry stood motionless, staring at the ground.

"Mistress, Mistress Alexandra Vasilyevna my dear, come away or there will be trouble!" came the frightened voice of Sashenka's nanny who had come up and recognized Porphyry.

"Porphyry!" repeated Sashenka, embracing him.

"Mistress! Some people are coming!" exclaimed the nanny, and she seized Sashenka by the hand.

"Porphyry! Porphyry!" cried Sashenka.

The nanny dragged her away. Porphyry remained rooted to the spot.

X

Several months later we find our friend, the gentleman who had rented the house that had formerly been two, sitting, as was his custom, by the window with his pipe and glass of tea.

At the moment his thoughts were turned inward, although his eyes were focused on the street. It looked as if he were examining the architecture of the fence and house on the other side of the street.

The gentleman happened to be nearsighted, and therefore the people passing by looked like moving spots. But for several days in a row a constant spot by the fence that seemed to remain motionless had attracted his attention. It began to irritate him. *There can't be anything over there, I must have gotten something in my eye,* he thought.

At about this time Fyodor Danilovich stopped by.

"Fyodor Danilovich! Take a look, have I got something in my eye?"

"What are you talking about?"

"Look, there's nothing in the room, but when I look toward the light—toward that white background—I suddenly see a huge dark spot."

"There's nothing in your eye, nothing at all."

"I don't understand it! There it is again when I look at that fence."

Fyodor Danilovich looked out the window.

"Oh! Now I understand! So that's the spot you are seeing! That's some spot!"

"What are you talking about?"

"Remarkable! Give me your lorgnette . . . Amazing!"

"What?"

"Charming!"

"What are you saying?" demanded the gentleman, and he grabbed the lorgnette out of Fyodor Danilovich's hands and looked out into the street. "Aha! Well, what do you know! A young lady!"

"And she can't take her eyes off your window! Bravo! I congratulate you . . . Oh ho, we must have spooked her, she's leaving!"

"I must say, I know nothing about it," said the gentleman. "Yes, she's gone."

"Well, surely she'll be back . . . Good-bye and good luck."

"Where are you off to?"

"I have to be going. But what happened to the doll house?" Fyodor Danilovich suddenly asked as he stopped in the hall.

"I pawned it."

"There's one for you!"

"And there's going to be two, three, four, and so on, as long as there is something to pawn."

Fyodor Danilovich left. The gentleman sat down by the window, picked up his lorgnette, and began to scan the white fence like an astronomer scans the sky in expectation of the passage of a new star.

"There she is!" he exclaimed as he jumped up from his chair. "Hey Vaska! Petya! Get me my clothes!"

He got dressed, went out into the street, and headed straight for the fence where the mysterious young lady was standing.

"Yes, she's still there," thought the gentleman, squinting as he walked toward the fence. "But what's that I'm seeing?" he asked himself as he took another look through his lorgnette.

He went a little closer and saw before him a young man and a young woman in a black dress standing as if they were chained together in an embrace; it seemed as if their joyful kiss upon finding each other had sealed their lips together.

"Aha!" said the gentleman when he had come up to them.

They started and looked at the gentleman with fright.

"It's all right, don't be afraid," he said, "I was just trying to find out if I was seeing spots or what."

"Porphyry, let's go," said the young woman as she took the young man, who seemed to be in a trance, by the hand. "Come on, Porphyry, let's go!"

And they quickly left.

"Aha!" said the gentleman. "That's really nice."

Notes

INTRODUCTION

1. V. I. Kalugin, introduction to Aleksandr Vel'tman, *Romany* (Moscow, 1985), p. 16.

2. V. F. Pereverzev, "Predtecha Dostoevskogo," in *U istokov russkogo realizma* (Moscow, 1989), p. 152.

3. V. S. Kiselev-Seregin, in *Poety 1820–1830-kh godov* (Leningrad, 1972), vol. 2, p. 205, gives the following assessment of the results of Veltman's research: "Superficial dilettantism and naive, fantastic hypotheses brought the writer's 'scholarly' works close to his artistic [i.e., literary] prose."

4. Throughout his career V. G. Belinsky (1811–48) continued to comment on the works of Veltman, from enthusiastically welcoming the appearance of such an original talent in 1834 to deploring the misuse of that same talent in 1847.

5. Dostoevsky's younger brother, Andrei, recalls that the future author was "in rapture" over Veltman's novel *Serdtse i dumka* (A. M. Dostoevskii, *Vospominaniia* [Leningrad, 1930], p. 69). There is also a favorable response to another of Veltman's novels, *Novyi Emelia ili prevrashcheniia,* in a letter from F. M. Dostoevsky to his brother, Michael, dated May 4, 1845 (*Polnoe sobranie sochinenii v 30-ti tomakh* [Leningrad, 1972–90], vol. 18, kn. 1, p. 110).

6. In Maksim Gorky's reminiscences of Tolstoy: A. M. Gor'kii, *Sobranie sochinenii,* 30 vols. (Moscow, 1949–55), vol. 14, p. 292.

7. The source usually cited for this claim is the memoirs of Tatiana Passek, who was personally acquainted with Veltman; according to her, "Veltman's ancestors were Swedes. His grandfather owned a small island in the Baltic Sea, but his father emigrated to Russia, acquired Russian citizenship, and married a Russian" (T. P. Passek, *Iz dal'nikh let* [St. Petersburg, 1889], vol. 3, p. 278. However, I have found no mention of Swedes or Swe-

den in any of Veltman's personal papers or anywhere in Veltman's writings, published or unpublished.

8. An extensive collection of Veltman's papers (Fond 47) is held by the Manuscript Division of the Lenin Library in Moscow. The service records of F. F. Veltman are cataloged as Fond 47/II/11/2.

9. For a Russian's description of life in Reval, for him "still a German city" at that time, see Ia. I. DeSanglen, "Zapiski," *Russkaia starina* 36 (1882): 444–45.

10. The letters of F. F. Veltman to his mother are cataloged as Fond 47/II/8/4.

11. See, for example, the speech of Vralman, the German tutor, in Fonvizin's comedy *Nedorosl'*.

12. Fond 47/II/11/2.

13. *Raznochinets* (literally, "of various classes") is basically a term that refers to a member of the intelligentsia. In the story presented here about the pot of geraniums, Veltman's narrator (who sounds a lot like Veltman himself) refers to himself as a *raznochinets*.

14. Vel'tman, "Povest' o sebe," Fond 47/I/28/16.

15. In his "Povest' o sebe," Veltman says he was accepted as an "orthodox *armer kind* [poor child]."

16. The most complete description of this school, the *Korpus kolonnovozhatykh*, can be found in an article by N. V. Putiata entitled "Nikolai Nikolaevich Murav'ev," in *Sovremennik* 33 (1852): Sec. 2, pp. 1–26.

17. A. F. Vel'dman [*sic*], *Nachal'nye osnovaniia arifmetiki* (Moscow, 1817).

18. A. F. Vel'tman, *Nachertanie drevnej istorii Bessarabii s prisovokupleniem istoricheskikh vypisok i karty* (Moscow, 1828).

19. Fond 47/I/27/4.

20. A. F. Vel'tman, "Vospominaniia o Bessarabii," in *A. S. Pushkin v vospominaniiakh sovremennikov* (Moscow, 1974), vol. 1, p. 275.

21. Ibid.

22. I. P. Liprandi, "Iz dnevnika i vospominanii," *Russkii arkhiv* 4 (1866), column 1250.

23. Vel'tman, "Vospominaniia," p. 284.

24. Letter to E. M. Khitrovo, dated May 8, 1831, A. S. Pushkin, *Polnoe sobranie sochinenii v 10 tomakh* (Moscow, 1966), vol. 10, p. 348.

25. Pushkin, *Polnoe sobranie sochinenii*, vol. 10, p. 351.

26. A. S. Pushkin, "Pikovaia dama," *Polnoe sobranie sochinenii*, 3d ed. (Moscow, 1962), vol. 6, p. 331.

27. The most complete record of Veltman's service is in the Central State Archive of Literature and Art (TsGALI) and is dated October 24, 1868 (Fond 96/1/3).

28. V. G. Belinskii, *Polnoe sobranie sochinenii* (Moscow, 1953–59), vol. 2, p. 115.

29. Official memorandum from Prince P. M. Volkonskii to Prince A. M. Urusov, president of the Moscow Office of the Imperial Court, Fond 47/II/10/1.

30. "Priemysh," Fond 47/I/32/1.

31. Quoted in the introduction to A. F. Vel'tman, *Serdtse i dumka* (Moscow, 1986), pp. 14–15.

32. *Delo Petrashevtsev* (Moscow-Leningrad, 1937–51), vol. 3, p. 289.

33. The most complete account of Veltman's life during these years can be found in N. V. Berg, "Posmertnye zapiski," *Russkaia starina* 65 (1890): 293–319; 69 (1891): 229–79.

34. *Russkaia stikhotvornaia parodiia* (Leningrad, 1960), p. 765.

"EROTIDA"

1. Here Veltman is comparing the form and contents of this after-dinner conversation to the format of a typical Russian "thick journal" of the nineteenth century.

2. Many Russian writers of the nineteenth century have commented on, both humorously and seriously, the fabulous lifestyle of the rich nobles of the time of Catherine II. See, for example, A. S. Griboedov's comedy *Gore ot uma*, act 2, scene 2.

3. Among the rich holdings of the Counts Sheremetev were the Moscow estates of Ostankino and Kuskovo, both of which can still be seen today.

4. These lines may recall the beginning of Pushkin's *Ruslan and Liudmila:* "Deeds of long bygone days, / Legends of remote antiquity."

5. This was an elaborate headdress called a *caliche* or a *calash,* which was a sort of cage made of wire or whalebone covered with tulle or black taffeta and used to support a huge coiffure. See R. Turner Wilcox, *The Mode in Hats and Headdress* (New York, 1948).

6. This item is illustrated in R. Turner Wilcox, *The Mode in Costume* (New York, 1944).

7. I was unable to identify this item, other than that it can mean "staff" in Spanish.

8. Giv is one of the heroes in Firdousi's Persian epic *Shah-Namen.* I was unable to find the passage specifically referred to here; Veltman is reported to have been working on his own Russian translation of Firdousi's epic.

9. It may be worth pointing out that the Russian word here, *amazonka,* means "horsewoman" and not "female warrior" or "statuesque woman."

10. Now located in the Czech Republic and referred to as Karlovy vary.

11. Also a cardplaying term.

12. In Pushkin's *Pikovaia dama,* which first appeared in the March 1834 issue of *Biblioteka dlia chteniia,* the queen is also the losing card. V. M. Fridkin, in his *Propavshii dnevnik Pushkina* (Moscow, 1987), has found an interesting connection between Pushkin's story and Carlsbad. It seems that the French composer Fromental Halévy staged an opera in three acts entitled *La Dame de Pique* in Paris in 1850 with a libretto by Eugene Scribe that was loosely based on Pushkin's tale. In the third act, which takes place in Carlsbad, a character similar to Pushkin's Herman stakes everything on the queen of spades and loses.

13. Here Veltman is apparently intentionally mistranslating the French (which I have reproduced exactly from the Russian edition), perhaps to show that this young rake is not as cultured as he thinks he is.

"ROLAND THE FURIOUS"

1. *Zhidki* in the original.

2. *Zhidenok* in the original.

3. A character in Griboedov's comedy *Gore ot uma.*

4. The Russian Orthodox Church calendar does indeed indicate that September 10 is the day of the holy martyrs Minodora, Mitrodora, and Nymphodora.

5. *Veuve Cliquot Pontchartrain,* a champagne also mentioned by Pushkin in *Evgenii Onegin* (ch. 5, stanza 45).

6. A confection made from fruit, sugar, and egg whites.

7. *Zavtrak na vilkakh:* here, for humorous purposes, Veltman has the postmaster using a literal translation of the French expression *déjeuner à la fourchette.*

8. August von Kotzebue (1761–1819), a prolific German dramatist, was well known in Russia for his sentimental plays. A political conservative and possibly a tsarist agent, he was despised by the more radical elements in Russian society, and his assassination by the German student Karl Zand was lauded by Pushkin in his poem "Kinzhal" (1821). Veltman here may be obliquely referring to these events; in any case, Senkovsky omitted all reference to Kotzebue when he published the story in his journal. Kotzebue's *Erinnerungen aus Paris* appeared in 1804.

9. In a footnote here, Veltman "explains" that this is the Russian translation of the French *tous les genres sont bons, excepté les genres ennuyeux.*

10. On the basis of Veltman's description I have tentatively identified this town as Mogilev, now located in the republic of Belarus.

11. The planet Venus, when it appears above the horizon before sunrise, is sometimes referred to as Lucifer or the bringer of light.

12. A three-sided prism *(zertsalo)* with Peter the Great's three decrees on justice inscribed on it; it was prominently displayed in the courtrooms of tsarist Russia.

13. Zaretsky is declaiming passages from Fiesco's soliloquy in Schiller's tragedy *Die Verschwörung des Fiesko in Genua* (act 3, scene 2). According to Iu. M. Akutin (in his edition of Veltman's *Strannik* [Moscow, "Nauka," 1977], p. 251), one of Veltman's early unpublished attempts at poetry was a translation of one of Fiesco's monologues.

14. From *Fiesco,* act 5, scene 12. Zaretsky's further rantings in this chapter are all taken from this scene.

15. The play referred to here is *Les Franc-juges, ou les temps de barbarie* by Jean Henri Ferdinand La Martelière. A Russian production of this play was presented in Moscow in 1831. The other play that the Impresario's troupe put on (besides *Roland the Furious*) was F. Matveev's *Dobrodetel'naia prestupnitsa, ili prestupnik ot liubvi* (Moscow, 1792).

16. In Ariosto's *Orlando Furioso,* Sacripant is one of Angelica's lovers, not her father.

17. In Schiller's play, Fiesco mistakenly kills his wife Leonora; Rosa and Arabella are her maids.

"TRAVEL IMPRESSIONS AND, AMONG OTHER THINGS, A POT OF GERANIUMS"

1. Maria Taglioni (1804–84) was a famous Parisian ballerina; she appeared in St. Petersburg in 1840.

2. *Meshok* is Russian for a simple cloth sack.

3. See introduction, note 13.

4. Here Veltman is indulging in some word play based on the fact that the Russian word *bumaga* can mean either "paper" or "cotton."

5. The name of a street in Moscow that in the nineteenth century was known for its fashionable French shops. In Griboedov's comedy *Woe from Wit,* Famusov complains that these Frenchmen are the destroyers of hearts and of pocketbooks (*Gubiteli karmanov i serdets,* act 1, scene 1).

6. Homeopathy was a widely applied theory of medicine in the last century and Veltman often refers to it (usually metaphorically). In Turgenev's *Fathers and Sons,* for example, Nikolai Kirsanov is an amateur practitioner of homeopathy.

7. In Alexander Radishchev's famous *Journey from Petersburg to Moscow,* the village of Valdai (in the chapter of the same name) is described as being notorious for its loose women and the scandalous goings-on in its bathhouses.

8. Like Veltman's traveler, Pushkin's Eugene Onegin was prevailed upon by the Valdai maidens to buy some rolls: "Before him lay Valdai,

Torzhok, and Tver' / Here from persistent maidens / He takes . . . rolls" ("Onegin's Journey," unpublished draft, stanza 7).

9. David Teniers (1610–90), Flemish painter.

10. A pun based on the word *polushtof,* which usually means a bottle size for vodka (half a *shtof*), while *shtof* can also refer to material used for upholstery.

11. This painting by K. P. Briullov (1799–1852) created a sensation when it was first exhibited in the Hermitage in 1834. Gogol's enthusiasm for the picture led him to compare it to the works of Michelangelo and Raphael.

12. Here Veltman is punning on the Russian word *dusha* (soul) and such related words and expressions as *odushevlenny* (animate) and *bez dushi* (in a state of rapture; literally, without a soul).

13. That is, become inanimate (see note 8, above).

14. The railroad line from Petersburg to Pavlovsk was completed in 1838, and it was Russia's first. At that time it seems to have been not so much a practical means of transportation as an object of curiosity and a source of trepidation. In her memoirs T. P. Passek quotes from a letter from her husband, Vadim, about his trip to Petersburg in 1840: "I took a ride on the railroad to Tsarskoe Selo and Pavlovsk. At first it was strange, but then, toward evening, I dozed off. Many conveniences. Now keep calm, I won't ride it again so as not to worry you" (T. P. Passek, *Iz dal'nykh let* [Moscow, 1963], vol. 2, p. 283). Incidentally Veltman's brother-in-law, D. P. Veidel, was hurt in an accident on this same railroad at about this time (see Veltman's letter of September 1840 to F. A. Koni in *Russkii arkhiv* 49, no. 12 [1911]: 542).

15. The name of the steam engine—author's note.

16. The public gardens at Pavlovsk were patterned after the Vauxhall Gardens in London. Since the Pavlovsk "Vauxhall" was next to the Pavlovsk railroad station, the name *vokzal* was extended to the station and thus became the standard Russian word for "railroad station."

17. A segmented worm of the polychaete family.

"A TRAVELER FROM THE PROVINCES; OR, A COMMOTION IN THE CAPITAL"

1. *Tilemikhida* or *Telemikhida* (1766) was a verse translation by V. K. Trediakovskii of François Fénelon's *Les Aventures de Télémaque* (1699). In Russia the work was widely recommended as edifying reading for a young man. The epigraph to Radishchev's famous *Journey from Petersburg to Moscow* was taken from Trediakovskii's translation.

2. Veltman's title here is an inversion of the title of a comedy by G. F. Kvitka, *A Traveler from the Capital; or, A Commotion in a Provincial Town,* written in 1827 and published in 1840.

3. This may be directed at Veltman's critics, since this was the most frequently repeated criticism of his works—that they lacked a central, unifying idea.

4. Veltman may be alluding to the comedy *Svoia sem'ia* (1818) by A. S. Griboedov, A. A. Shakhovskoi, and N. I. Khmel'nitskii.

5. The word used here is *rozvalni;* according to Belinsky this is just one more example of Veltman's predilection for using strange words (*Polnoe sobranie sochinenii,* vol. 7, p. 635). According to him, Veltman has chosen here to refer to a Voltaire armchair by using the peasant's term for a broken-down sleigh.

6. A French newspaper—author's note.

7. Don Carlos, brother of the Spanish king Ferdinand VII, attempted to seize the throne after the latter's death; the attempt failed, and he fled to France in 1839.

8. A slightly inaccurate quotation from G. R. Derzhavin's poem "Khrapovitskomu" (1797). Derzhavin was lamenting the sad plight of the poet in Russia, where he was reduced to being a slave to monarchs.

9. Veltman probably has in mind the French expression *bête à manger du foin,* or "a complete idiot."

10. Yar's was a restaurant on the Kuznetsky Bridge frequented by the literati. Pushkin often dined there; in his poem "Dorozhnye zhaloby" (1829), he jokingly holds a wake for Yar's truffles by eating cold veal. The restaurant took its name from its owner, a Frenchman identified in Russian spelling as Trankl' Yar who opened the place in 1826.

11. The name could be translated as "Oh, my head!"

12. Overcoat (French).

13. *The Library for Reading* was a popular "thick" journal founded by O. I. Senkovsky in 1834. Veltman was an occasional contributor.

14. In his review of this story Belinsky was especially impressed with this description of a Moscow merchant, finding it truly copied "from nature" (*Polnoe sobranie sochinenii,* vol. 7, p. 634).

15. A hot drink made from honey and spices.

16. According to Ginzburg in Benediktov, *Stikhotvoreniia,* p. 311, this poem on Napoleon is something of a parody of Benediktov's "Vaterloo" (1838).

17. The actual title of the poem by E. A. Baratynsky quoted here is not "Disillusion" *(razocharovanie)* but "Dissuasion" *(razuverenie).*

18. Veltman has also changed the first line of the poem which in the original reads "Don't tempt me" *(Ne iskushai menya),* by substituting "Don't console me" *(Ne uteshai menya).*

19. In 1839 a military expedition under general V. A. Perovsky set out from Orenburg with the intention of conquering the Khanate of Khiva. The

operation was a total failure and the survivors made their way back to Orenburg in June 1840.

20. I have been unable to identify this name. The syntax suggests that it is an establishment referred to by a person's name. For some reason Veltman italicizes "Yar's," but does not italicize "Liuke's."

21. "Klyuch," written by G. R. Derzhavin in 1779.

22. This line does not occur in Benediktov's "Vaterloo," although Napoleon is referred to there as a giant *(gigant).* According to the editors of *Poety 1820–1830-kh godov* [Leningrad, 1972], vol. 2, p. 709), other possible targets of Veltman's parody were poems on Napoleon by M. A. Dmitriev and A. V. Timofeev.

"IT'S NOT A HOUSE, BUT A PLAYTHING!"

1. *Churova dolina, ili Son naiavu,* an opera by A. N. Verstovsky (1844).

2. Old Russian stringed instrument played by plucking.

3. See "Erotida," note 9.

4. Veltman probably chose this name because it can refer to either a male (Alexander) or a female (Alexandra).

5. In the text as originally published, this gentleman is not identified by name; in the 1979 text, following the corrections referred to in the unnumbered note on page 149, he is identified as Pavel Voinovich, i.e., P. V. Nashchokin. In the same way, the poet who comes to visit is now identified as Pushkin.

6. This is the complete text of Pushkin's "Veselyi pir" (Joyful feast), first published in 1824.

7. The Moscow English Club, a building of classical architecture on the Tverskaya and now the Museum of the Revolution, opened in 1831 at that location. According to A. I. Gessen in *Vse volnovalo nezhnyi um* ([Moscow, 1965], p. 380), on his visits to Moscow Pushkin would often stay at Nashchokin's and would remain at home while Nashchokin visited the English Club, which was not one of Pushkin's favorite places.

8. A reworking by Veltman of some lines from Pushkin's "Domovomu" (To the house spirit) (1824).

9. When the editors of the 1979 text were adding the author's corrections, they may have misread his handwriting. A close reading of the microfilm of the corrected copy of Veltman's story held by the Manuscript Division of the Lenin Library in Moscow suggests that Veltman intended to insert the word *neispolnyaya* (not fulfilling or, as I have translated it, "failing to abide by") rather than the word *ispolnyaya* (fulfilling) which appears in the 1979 text (p. 360). This makes much better sense in terms of the logic of the story.

10. Here Veltman mentions the *Opekunsky sovet* or "trusteeship council," an institution that was established by the tsarist government to fund and administer orphanages; it also lent money to landowners against the value of their estates, and it is in this function that it is most often mentioned in nineteenth-century Russian literature.

11. Here Veltman is punning on two meanings of the verb *zalozhit*: "to lay a foundation" and "to pawn."